# STOLEN FROM THE HITMAN

## ALEXIS ABBOTT

PATHFORGERS PUBLISHING

Get an EXCLUSIVE book, **FREE** just as a thank you for signing up for my newsletter! Plus you'll never miss a new release, cover reveal, or promotion!

http://alexisabbott.com/newsletter

*I* step out of the black sedan and into the midnight rain that's drenching all of Paris tonight. The raindrops roll down my black leather jacket, trailing down my gloved hands to trickle in thin drops onto the dark cobblestone of the streets beneath my feet.

It's past midnight, and most people are already either sleeping or shuffling out of the bars to get ready for the next day's drudgery in the city of lights.

The apartment building in front of me is an upscale kind of place, not unusual for some of the city's wealthier residents. The stone on the outside might have been white once, but it is now faded, the lion statues near the entrance having lost their bite long ago. As I step towards the door and swipe the cardkey, the glass doors open for me, and I make my way in swiftly, my weapon low at my side.

I pull my collar up and keep my gaze down as I make my way to the stairs leading below ground level. I have one stop to make before seeing to the main event for tonight. A short flight of stairs brings me to a door, and I can hear a television playing behind it. Raising a fist, I pound on the door.

"What?" comes the superintendent's surly French voice from within the room. I wait a moment before pounding on the door again, a little more demanding this time. I hear an angry groan from the other side before footsteps approach the door. "If the internet is out again, it can wait for the morning," he says as he opens the door, but his eyes widen at the sight of me for only an instant before I'm upon him with a cloth to his mouth and nose, his whole body seizing up as he draws a sharp breath before slipping into unconsciousness.

Closing the door behind me, I carry the limp body back to the chair he'd been sitting in. There are reruns of old football matches playing on the television, giving me a backdrop while I shuffle through the man's belongings, knowing I only have a small window of time to find what I'm after.

In another few seconds, I discover the apartment master key sitting under a soiled napkin, and I take it, leaving the room as swiftly and silently as a phantom.

My footsteps make little noise as I ascend the staircase, key clenched in my hand. The stairs go in a spiral up the side of the building, and a glass pane window gives me a full view of the world outside as I move.

As I near the top floor, my gaze glances out over the cityscape to my right, and the soft glow of the remaining city lights hover over the Parisian skyline like a corona. I slow my steps for just a moment, my cold gaze pausing to appreciate the tarnished jewel of Europe before I pick up my pace again.

The soft glow of the city lights have only an instant to shine on a glint of metal on the silenced-pistol I'm drawing from my jacket pocket.

I soften my steps to near-silence as I reach the top floor, a wide and polished foyer leading to a single ornate door with a large man posted outside it, his arms folded as he thumbs through a dirty magazine.

He has time only to raise his head while I raise my pistol. When he crumples to the ground a second later, I wonder if he even had time for fear to swell up in his heart. His is the only life I might have had a shred of remorse for taking tonight, if I hadn't hardened my heart to such business long, long ago.

I walk over to the man's body, and the roaring laughter and music coming from inside the door tells me that not a soul heard my approach. I bend down to check the bullet hole in the guard's head before pressing an ear to the door.

The voices within are mostly older men, some slurred, some merry, but all speaking in Russian, my mother tongue. But I hear some of them speaking to women.

"Boris, tell that bitch of yours to bring another beer and take a seat on me."

"She doesn't speak Russian yet —the only language these French girls understand is cock, don't you know?"

"Well shit, she'd better start giving me some poetry then, unless she wants to be given to the help outside!"

There's a sound of a terrified, quiet voice in French I can't quite make out, but it's followed by laughter from the men. "Hey, maybe she should meet her date for tonight, go get the guard and have him come strip her for us, I'm bored with poker for tonight."

As they've been speaking, I've been sliding the master key into the lock and turning it quietly, slowly. My muscles tense as I hear heavy footsteps approaching the door, and I see that my chance is coming faster than I expected.

Just before the footsteps reach the door, I throw it open, cracking the corner against the face of whomever was being sent to fetch the dead guard, and he crumples to the ground as I move in and bring my heel down on his throat and hold up my pistol.

The room is a haze of cigar smoke in the palpably tense instants I enter the penthouse. It's a luxurious suite, with marble floors and mahogany furniture giving the place the look of an upscale antique store. There's some art hanging on the walls, all rather high-quality forgeries. At least ten men turn their eyes to me, many of them in recognition. Some are old, some are young. Three are sitting around a table, playing poker. Another few men are sitting around on couches and armchairs, apparently having been talking before I came in. There are two women in the room, one of them on a man's lap in an armchair, the other holding a tray of cocktails.

"You bastard," one of the men playing poker has time to growl at me before three rounds of my weapon strike true on all three men at the poker table, my aim moving with deadly precision before one of the women screams, and I duck behind the half-wall that leads into the room as chaos breaks loose.

The remaining men stand up, some of them reaching for their guns as they dive for cover, and shouts in Russian fill the room. I hear footsteps and movement the moment I'm out of sight, and I make a note to watch for those who've left the room. Bullets hit the wall behind me as I duck, but I can tell from the number of shots fired that not all the men have weapons at the ready. Meaning I have only a matter of moments to end this before this becomes a full firefight.

I hear a cry from one of the men and the sound of glass breaking on the ground, and I seize my opportunity, popping out of hiding.

One of the enslaved women had struck one of the armed men with her tray, and before he can get his bearings and retaliate, I put a bullet between his eyes and charge into the room.

Having been distracted by the scene, one of the armed men starts to turn to me, but I reach him first, grabbing his wrist and shoving his arm up as he fires, blasting a hole in the ceiling above before he cries out as I break his wrist and bring my pistol to his heart and pull the trigger.

*Five rounds.*

The gunfire had ceased, and I turn in time to feel a sting on my right arm as one of the older men brings a kitchen knife across it, and there's blood on his blade as he finishes. I recognize the man, the one they'd called Boris, and his steely eyes lock with mine.

"You think this game of yours will go unnoticed?" he snarls. "You think the Bratva will just roll over and play along with your wishes, you fucking upstart?"

I have no words to waste my breath on, and even as he brings his knife in for another strike, my fist is faster, and I catch him in the stomach, doubling him over. I wrench the knife from his hand and ram it into his belly faster than he can react, and as blood runs down the man's front while he gasps, collapsing into the hot fireplace, I turn my attention to two younger men who are barreling for me.

Grimacing, I hurl the knife at the wall, not far from the first woman, who jumps back, her eyes wide as she looks at it while I brace myself to deal with the two men.

One dives for me, and I easily use his weight against him, hurling him to the ground as I swing to catch the second man with a blow to the chin, sending him staggering. He comes back around to tackle me to the ground, but a swift kick to the knee cripples him with a pained shout, and he falls to the ground with his partner.

While they gather their bearings, I reach down to one of the bodies of the armed men, picking up a pistol and putting a bullet into each of the men who dove for me. Their bodies thud to the ground unceremoniously.

With the room cleared, I move to the wall near the entrance to the hallway. My heart jumps to my throat as a man I'd missed stands up from behind the couch, pistol in hand, but before I can turn my weapon to him, I hear him grunt as the first woman sinks the kitchen knife into his back from behind, and she stands back as he falls to the ground, her hands shaking as the weapon falls from her grip.

My eyes watch her for a moment as she looks up at me, fearful. "Flee. You saw nothing tonight," I inform her in French, and she simply nods before dashing for the door, her footsteps echoing down the stairs.

Returning my attention to the hallway, I brace myself before blind-firing two rounds with the pistol I'd picked up, and I hear two men shout and shuffle for cover as I turn around the corner. One of my shots catches the hip of a man diving into the bathroom, and swiftly, I follow him in before he can regain his bearings.

I point my pistol to his head as I press myself against the wall, and he holds his hands up in surrender, terrified. I nod to the hallway and mouth 'how many?' He glances to the doorway and holds up one finger. I nod and fire my pistol, catching him between the eyes before whipping around into the hallway and aiming for the far bedroom doorway.

A bullet from the man standing there catches me in the shoulder before my shot hits him in the throat, and he slumps to the floor as I clutch my wound, moving forward with no time to waste. One bullet remaining in the gun I came into the room with, I kick the door open and instinctively aim it at the bed.

My target is there, sitting on the lavish silken

sheets and holding a pistol to the head of the second woman I'd seen him sitting with when I first burst into the room. His eyes are the coldest of any of the other men I saw on my way in. His room is lavish, gold vases and a few pieces of real art hanging on the walls, a large amount of cocaine on a table near the bed and a closet hanging open, full of expensive, tailored suits. He's every bit the man of hedonistic pleasures I always knew him to be.

"Move, and she dies," he says, calm and collected. The woman in his grip looks at me with wide, petrified eyes, and I know the one question on her mind is whether or not I value her life enough, even as I have my barrel trained on her captor. He isn't the oldest man in the room, but of all the mobsters I've killed tonight, he's the highest ranking by far. "A lot of the men in this room might have called you a friend before tonight, you know," he says coldly. "Maybe even more. Others might have had you killed before you got ambitious. I must admit, my one regret is speaking on your behalf all those times."

We stare each other in the eyes for several seconds. There's so much I want to snap back at him, so much I want to tell him of how much hatred I have for him and all that he represents.

But I will not play his games.

The woman shrieks as I fire my pistol, blood spattering on the rich pillows behind the mob boss as he drops his gun and falls back on his bed, lifeless. The woman recoils from the sight, some of the blood in her hair as she screams.

I lower my pistol, my eyes moving to her momentarily before I walk over to look at the man's lifeless eyes before turning to her. She quiets, looking up at me in terror, the unspoken question of what is to become of her written all over her expression.

"Go," I say simply, and it's a moment before she nods hastily and darts out of the room. I give her a few minutes head start to move around the house and ensure that everyone was dead. This job could afford nothing less than perfection.

Bodies are strewn across the entire apartment. Smoke still hangs overhead as the dull Russian music drones from a stereo by the television. Blood is spattered across the unfinished game of poker, and there are bullet holes in forged paintings that must be worth hundreds of thousands.

I survey my work with neither a smile nor frown, but I feel a certain sense of peace as I stride out the door, dropping the superintendent's keys by the guard's body. I have no intention of cleaning the place or even doing so much as closing the door.

Tonight, I mean to send a message.

LIV

"Smile, honey!" my mom calls out, grinning widely from behind a big black camera. I struggle to balance both my clunky valedictorian plaque and the enormous bouquet of roses my father presented to me. My face just barely peeks out from behind the flowers and my dad pulls me close in a tight hug just as my mom snaps the photo. I blink rapidly, the flash burning behind my eyes. It's probably the hundredth picture taken of me today at my high school graduation ceremony. The sun is beginning to make its slow descent down the horizon, casting a dreamy pinkish glow across the football field.

"Oh, that's a great one!" exclaims my mother, who rushes over to show Dad the photo, kissing the top of my head along the way. Both of my parents are taller than me and very athletic; my mom is an avid runner and my dad used to compete in body-building competitions. As a result of their shared passion, I have been raised with the expectations of attaining and maintaining physical perfection. But while I lack my parents' height and overt athletic appearance, I am certainly a contender in my own right.

Ever since the day I was born a couple months premature, I have been tiny. I've always been a little smaller than all my friends and fellow students. So it was a struggle for my sports-obsessed parents, trying to situate me in an athletic track that I could feasibly do. I mean, it's not like a five-foot-one girl is going to make it big as a basketball star or anything. And since I was also lucky enough to be born with asthma, I have never been the runner my mom hoped I would be (not for lacking of trying, I might add). But after years of bouncing back and forth between different sports programs, we finally settled on the one sport that's become my ticket to success, my passion, the thing that drives my every thought and heartbeat.

Gymnastics.

I may not be able to sprint a mile in record time without hyperventilating, and I may not be able to even reach most of the exercise bars at the gym. But I can bend and twist and flip my body in ways nobody ever expected from me. I'm a pretty damn good gymnast, if I do say so myself, and getting to this point has meant years and years of hardcore dedication and training. There's something so freeing and fulfilling about teaching my body to fly through the air, every muscle straining to the brink. Every time I run and leap, spin and stretch, I feel my heart soaring in my chest. And there is nothing in this world so satisfying as landing a difficult move, my feet grounding me gracefully to the earth once more. It makes me feel like a superhero. It makes me feel like I can fly.

And nothing — nothing at all — can get in my way.

Even the fact that I happen to live in a tiny, rural town in upper North Carolina. Nobody here does much of anything beyond the humble grind of hard work and gentle play. People here are quiet and modest, content to live simple lives away from the bustle of cities like Raleigh and Charlotte.

I have to admit that I, too, love living here. I mean, sure, sometimes it does get pretty boring. But the lack of things to do has proved to be beneficial to my gymnastics training. There are so few distractions that I've been easily able to throw myself wholeheartedly into the sport. I do have friends, but most of them are planning on going off to college and then returning to live here for the rest of their lives. There's nothing wrong with that at all, but it's not the plan I foresee for myself.

Don't get me wrong, it *is* nice to live somewhere

so safe and comfortable. People here don't even really lock their doors or anything — everyone knows everybody else and we all collectively look after each other. So I can totally understand why bigger-city people like my parents, who hail from Chapel Hill, decide to settle down here. It's also why people who are born here in Toast, North Carolina, are likely to stick around here. This place is picturesque and quiet, the people kind and humble.

And yes, the town really is called Toast.

"Oh, sweetheart. I can't get over how beautiful your speech was," Mom coos, stroking my cinnamon-brown hair back out of my face and beaming at me. "Even nearly made your Daddy cry!"

"Hogwash," Dad retorts good-naturedly. "I've never cried once in my whole life!"

All three of us laugh at the inside joke: my dad is actually a notorious crier. He's the sentimentalist of the family, always poring over old photographs and tearing up over cute videos of baby animals. It's especially funny, too, considering the fact that he's a huge, muscular guy. A bodybuilder who happy-cries at the drop of a hat — that's my dad. He's the gentle giant and my mom is the energetic go-getter. Both of them have big personalities, and I am often just the quiet, soft-spoken daughter trailing after them.

Not that they see it that way at all. My parents are almost embarrassingly proud of me and my accomplishments, probably prouder than I am.

"Are you ready for dinner with the team tonight after your last performance?" Dad asks, nudging my shoulder excitedly. We've been looking forward to the annual celebratory get-together with all the girls from my gymnastics studio and our coaches for months. It's one of the biggest events of our year, which isn't saying much, really.

But tonight will be different. The stakes are much higher. It's not just a low-key dinner with friends and colleagues tonight — it's the first time I'll be in the same room as athletic recruiters from all over, including Europe! As far as I know, nobody this fancy has ever even looked at Toast on a map, much less come into town, but we earned a lot of attention when some videos got a lot of hits online recently.

"More nervous than excited," I answer, biting my lip. My parents, my ever-present cheerleaders, rush to reassure me.

"No, no! Don't be nervous! You've got everything going for you, Livvy," Mom says, leading me away from the crowds of hugging graduates and families.

"They're gonna love you. I bet they'll even have offers for you," Dad comments, waggling his eyebrows. I giggle at how silly he looks.

"And if they don't, well, there's always next year!" my mom concedes.

* * *

THE PERFORMANCE WENT off without a hitch, and while the last competition of the year is generally a light-hearted affair that none of us take too seriously, this one is different. We know we have special eyes upon us, and each of us wants to put on our best performance. Or at least, that's how I feel.

When we finish our routine to thunderous applause, I run to my parents with a smile and they usher me on out. We have to go back home and get changed quick before the celebratory get-together.

When we get home to our little red brick house, I run to my room and head to my closet to pick out something nice to wear.

Living in such a small, empty town has always meant that fashion is at least a few years behind the rest of the world. In fact, when I was much younger, I was content to just wear whatever my mom could sew and knit for me. But of course, as I got older, I outgrew that. So now most of my clothes have been collected from various weekend trips to Greensboro for shopping.

Poring through my clothes, most of which are more suitable for a day at the gymnastics studio than a nice dinner, I finally decide on a knee-length emerald green dress, brown wedge heels, and a white knit cardigan. I look at myself in the mirror, sizing up my petite frame and fresh-faced look. I'm eighteen years old, but I often get confused for a younger girl because of my size and innocent appearance. People tend to treat me like I'm fragile, like I could shatter into teeny tiny pieces at any moment. I do look pretty delicate. But looks can be deceiving, and in my case that's certainly true.

I sit down at my little wooden vanity (handmade by my dad) to put on a quick coat of mascara and a dab of red lip gloss. I smile into the mirror, hoping I look mature and talented enough to catch the eye of some elite recruiter tonight. As much as I love my little hometown and all its pastoral comforts, part of me has always wanted to venture out into the big, blue world and discover new places and experiences.

"Honey, are you ready to go?" my dad calls from across the house. I can hear his heavy footsteps creaking over the old wooden floors. This house has been standing here for decades and decades, and it shows. I love living in a home steeped in history like this. But I wonder what kind of history and art and culture I could discover living abroad!

"Yeah! Coming!" I shout out, slinging my purse over my shoulder and hurrying downstairs to meet my parents.

"You look beautiful," Mom remarks. My dad sniffles a little at the sight of me and I grin. He's such a sap.

We all pile into the car and drive to one of the few non-fast food restaurants in the area to meet up with about ten other girls from the gymnastics studio and the team of coaches, parents, and trustees involved with the program. As soon as the station wagon parks behind the restaurant, a couple of my friends catch sight of me and come running.

Holly Hixon and Ashley Wilson, my best friends, hug me tightly when I get out of the car, their faces flushed with excitement. "You'll never believe who all is here!" Ashley gushes.

"There are people from New York, Los Angeles, and Chicago!" Holly gasps, taking my hand and pulling me toward the entrance to the restaurant. We've rented out the back dining room for the occasion and when we walk in, we go straight back, my parents following behind hand-in-hand.

There's a long table in a decorated room, a white banner hanging on the wall that says *GOOD WORK!* It's all a little cheesy, but it's still sweet of them to put this together for us. The table is populated mostly by familiar faces, colleagues I train alongside every week, but there are several exceptions. The high-class men and women from big cities stand out like sore thumbs in this crowd. Even dressed in our modest best, we native residents look like country bumpkins next to the sleek black suits and designer makeup jobs of the talent scouts and recruiters. For a moment, I feel slightly embarrassed. I have a feeling these big-time folks look down on us just a little bit. After all, they've probably never been to a town with a population this small, in a place this far off the beaten path.

I take a seat between Holly and Ashley at the table, my parents sitting closer to the far end with the other parents and the coaches. After we all place our orders, I sip my homemade sweet tea and glance idly up and down the table at the unfamiliar people. Right across from me is a rather severe-looking, yet handsome man with olive skin and sleek dark hair. His eyes are a striking grayish-green, standing out in his serious, dark features. He looks to be at least five to ten years older than me, but he's considerably younger than the other out-of-towners. He also looks less like a gymnast himself and more like... well, like a secret agent type. It's the only way I can think to describe him. He has a grave, calculating expression, like he's deep in thought the entire time, despite all the lighthearted banter surrounding him. I wonder what's on his mind.

Then, just as I'm blatantly studying his face, those expressive jade-colored eyes turn toward me, locking gaze with mine. I instantly feel my cheeks burn, as I've been caught staring. I quickly look away, smiling at some silly remark Ashley is making to her coach. I try to play it off like I wasn't just openly gawking at the attractive older man in front of me.

*Smooth move, Olivia,* I think to myself.

Our food arrives and the conversation quiets down a little as we all eat, but I can't shake the sensation of being watched. I can feel those intense eyes burning a hole in my head from across the table, even if I don't dare to look up and check. I focus on my chicken parmigiana and green beans instead, occasionally laughing at a joke someone makes.

And when the meal is over and we're all transitioning into the schmooze and mingle part of the banquet, my parents sidle over to me to whisper in my ear what kind of intel they've gathered about the talent scouts and agents in the room.

"That woman down there used to train with former Olympic gymnasts," Mom says softly, pointing to a butch-looking woman in a pantsuit.

"That guy over there is a talent agent from an elite studio out in California," Dad tells me, nudging me toward a snively-looking man with a mustache.

"Wh-what about him?" I work up the courage to ask, gesturing subtly toward the green-eyed man who sat across from me at the table earlier. My mom shrugs.

"No idea. Never seen him before and nobody else seems to know him," Dad comments, shaking his head. "But he looks European, doesn't he?"

Mom nods and whispers, "Maybe he's just a spy for the Russian gymnastics team. They're always neck and neck with the Americans at the Olympics."

My parents both chuckle to themselves and I roll my eyes, sighing. Their laughter halts abruptly as the subject of our conversation turns to look toward us from across the room, his smoky gaze startling all three of us.

Then, the tall, severe-looking man comes sauntering over to us, looking like a lion stalking up to his prey.

My heart races, wondering if maybe he has supersonic hearing or something and he's miffed that we've been talking about him. He stops just in front of me, and now that we're standing so close together, I'm overwhelmed by our size difference. I'm barely over five feet, and he's well over six. While my frame is petite and slender, everything about him is imposing and powerful.

I gulp, and I can feel my parents bristling uncomfortably behind me.

"You're Olivia Greenwood," the man says, and I realize now that it's the first time I've heard his voice all night. In fact, a lot of other people have stopped their conversations to glance over at the surprising sound. His voice is deep and somber, with just a lick of an accent I can't quite place. Every word from his lips seems to vibrate in the air.

"Y-yes, that's me," I reply awkwardly.

He nods. "I have seen videos of your training and competitions and read your stats. You have a few achievements under your belt," he explains. Coming from anyone else, it might have sounded like a compliment, but in his grave tone it sounds almost like a put-down. Or a threat.

"Thank you," I murmur, blushing.

"May I speak to you in private for a moment?" he asks, glancing briefly at each of my parents behind me. All three of us nod in response and the man gestures for me to follow him to the little outside patio. I'm half-afraid that my father is going to demand to come along, but to my relief, he doesn't. I need to be able to handle whatever this guy has to say. On my own.

So I follow Mr. Mystery outside, where the air is slightly chilled. Goosebumps prickle along my arms and bared legs, but I suspect that may be less due to the weather and more about the fact that an intimidating stranger has cornered me alone.

"My name is Maksim Pavlenko, but my colleagues often call me Max. I have come on behalf of an elite gymnastics company with a close affiliation to the Sorbonne in Paris. After reviewing your progress as an athlete and sending me out to review your last performance live, the company has chosen to offer you a place in their highly competitive program. You would study at the Université de Paris and train under the tutelage of world-renowned instructors, such as myself," he explains, his expression never lightening up for even a second.

I am stunned and overwhelmed by this barrage of information, and apparently it shows, because he then gives me an even colder, impatient look.

"This is an opportunity to die for, and it is not

offered lightly. If you wish to accept, it is imperative that you tell me now," he commands. My mind is racing, my heart pounding. How am I even supposed to respond to something like this? I had no expectation of anything so serious happening tonight — especially not to *me*!

But I quickly stammer, "Yes, I-I would love to. I just —"

"Very well," he interrupts, guiding me back into the restaurant and toward my waiting parents, who both looked utterly bewildered. Without another word to me, Pavlenko describes the details of the arrangement to my parents, leaving me standing stock-still and silent the whole time. Holly and Ashley shoot me concerned, questioning looks, but all I can do is give them a strained smile and shrug. I know they'll be happy for me, but it also means that I've bested them. We're all friends, but we're competitors, too. Besides, if I go away to Paris — which still seems like an impossible pipe dream — who knows if I'll even ever see them again?

Still, I tell myself as Pavlenko arranges my travel and schooling plans with my parents, he is right. This is an opportunity I cannot pass up. On the ride home from the banquet, I don't say a word even as my parents chatter excitedly about Pavlenko's offer. It's all happening so fast, but it's definitely for the better, isn't it? Gymnastics is my passion, and I will never fulfill my ambitions if I just languish away here in Toast.

Paris is the place to be. Even if it means leaving behind everything I've ever known or loved.

Right?

But then I remember what happened the last time I flew anywhere...

I've only been on a plane once in my life, when I was ten and we flew to Orlando for a family vacation at Disney World. I was so scared that my parents had to give me a special medicine from the doctor to chill me out and calm me down for the flight. Every slight turbulence felt like instant death to me. I just knew we were going to drop out of the sky and plummet to our doom at any moment. My mom spent the entire flight stroking my hair and reminding me that it's more likely to get in a car accident than a plane crash.

Which only had the effect of also making me terrified to get in the taxi waiting for us when we landed in Orlando.

I'd like to think that I've matured a little bit since then. Mellowed out, even. But when the day of the flight arrives, I'm trembling yet again. It looks like my old phobia is still going strong, unfortunately. And this is a scarier flight than just hopping on a plane to Florida: this time I'm flying over the Atlantic Ocean.

And I'm doing it all by myself.

"You'll be just fine, sweetheart," my mother assures me, her voice wavering. Both of my parents have been excessively hovering over me for the past few weeks, fussing over every little thing and wanting to spend all their time with me. I understand why. This will be the first time I've ever lived away from home, and Paris is a long, long way away from North Carolina. I'm an only child and my parents have always been like my best friends, so this is going to be very difficult on all of us. I can't imagine what it will be like not seeing them every day. Don't get me wrong, in some ways I am looking forward to the freedom and independence of my new life.

But I'm also scared.

What if I get there and I can't make any friends? I don't even speak French! What if I get lost? Or mugged? I know frightening things can happen in big cities, and I've spent my whole life living in a place where nobody even thinks to lock their doors.

"It's not just the flight, Mom," I admit, sitting on a bench in Raleigh-Durham International Airport. My dad puts an arm around my shoulder and squeezes me tight.

"Don't let the city intimidate you," he says. "Livvy, you're a tough cookie and I know you can handle whatever comes your way."

"It's just that… well, what if nobody likes me?" I ask meekly, my voice very small. Both of my parents rush to reassure me.

"Honey, I don't think you've ever met a person who didn't like you," Mom says.

"What's not to like?" Adds my father.

I can't help but think of Pavlenko, remembering the way he regarded me as though I were just some small annoyance, a gnat buzzing in his face. He delivered the Paris offer almost begrudgingly, like he didn't agree with the company's assessment of my talent.

Like he didn't think I was good enough, but he didn't want to say anything.

But that's not a problem I want to worry my parents with. So I keep it to myself. Then a woman's voice comes over the intercom and announces that my flight, Raleigh to Charles de Gaulle Airport in Paris, is boarding in thirty minutes. My parents exchange heartbroken, desperate looks. I know they're going to miss me. I hope they don't fall apart without me around to keep them busy. They're both so involved in my life that I wonder how they'll manage living their own lives now that I'm leaving.

My father is already in tears, wrapping his arms around me and rocking me back and forth. Mom joins in the group hug, petting my hair and kissing the top of my head.

"Oh, we're going to miss you so much," Mom sniffles.

"Promise you'll call every day, no matter how much it costs," Dad blubbers, his tears staining my sweatshirt. "We love you, Liv. Please be careful."

"Text us the second your plane lands, okay!" Mom adds.

As they finally release me from their combined embrace, I assure them that I will keep in contact and that I will love and miss them more than anything. And it's true. While I've always had casual friendships here, no relationship has ever even come close to the tight-knit dynamic of my little family unit.

They walk me as far as security will allow, and then I'm on my own. Waving tearfully to my weepy mother and outright sobbing father, I pass through the security checkpoint and proceed nervously on to the terminal. When I board the plane, I feel that old fear settling in again. The plane is so cramped and warm inside, and I feel slightly claustrophobic. And this time I don't have my mom to reassure me the whole way.

But I can do this. I have to.

My seat neighbor is a rather attractive guy who looks to be in his twenties, and when he notices me fidgeting, he asks if I'm a nervous flier. I sheepishly confess that I am, and he pats my hand, giving me a wink.

"Don't worry, I'll keep you safe," he tells me, smiling. I blush, not accustomed to a lot of male attention. Every guy I interacted with in my hometown I've known since I was a little kid. When the population is that low, you kind of get to know everybody more intimately than you'd like. So no matter how objectively cute a guy in my graduating class might be, I would always remember him as the kid who picked his nose in first grade. Besides, gymnastics has always superseded any interest in romantic entanglements, for me.

So I am about as experienced as a nun.

The guy introduces himself as Will and says that he's also going to Paris to study at the same school as me! Of course, he's going as a graduate student, whereas I will be a lowly undergrad. Still, he flirts with me in a non-threatening, easy going way, and we spend the whole flight chatting about how excited we are. Will explains that he's been to Paris many times before, and he offers to help show me around and get used to the place. I can't believe my luck!

When the flight attendant comes down the aisle, Will purchases a miniature bottle of champagne and sneaks me a sip. It's the first time I've ever had champagne — or alcohol, period. It burns in my mouth a little bit, but I actually enjoy the taste once I get past the bubbles.

"You've really never had a drink?" Will asks in an undertone, his eyebrows raised.

I shake my head and shrug. "No. For a long time my hometown was in a dry county so people still don't really drink a whole lot. Plus, you know, I'm underage."

He laughs. "Yeah, that never stopped me."

As we share the champagne, I start to feel a little giddy — definitely more upbeat and optimistic about my Parisian experience than I was when I boarded the plane. I mean, I've been excited all along, but until now my anxieties have kept my elation to a minimum. But now I just want to jump up and down and turn backflips!

The rest of the flight passes by much more quickly than I expected, probably thanks to the booze and Will's pleasant company. It's exciting to have a cute boy so interested in me, and when we finally land in Paris, he suggests that we share a taxi together. I agree happily as it's nice having an older guy to guide me through the massive airport, and the two of us collect our luggage and walk out into the French sunshine.

"We did it!" I exclaim, breathing in deeply as the sounds of the big city whirr around me.

"You're in Paris!" Will says, nudging my shoulder. "How does it feel?"

"Like a dream," I breathe, my heart soaring. I cannot believe I've made it all the way here — little Liv Greenwood, all the way from the middle of nowhere to the almost mythical city of Paris! It almost feels like I'm watching a movie starring myself, and at any second the end credits will pop up and transport me back to Toast, where I'm a nobody once again.

Will and I take a taxi to the University, where we get out and walk around on campus for a while. It's mind-blowing to be somewhere so deeply entrenched in history beyond my own nation, the white walls of the old school nearly vibrating with centuries of memory. Then we simply stroll along the streets, dragging our luggage along behind us. I feel so small in this massive, beautiful, vibrant city — like an ant crawling on the face of a gigantic marble statue. Every building tells a story, every corner we turn reveals another architectural masterpiece I've only ever seen in the pages of an art history textbook.

This is a fantasy, a wild daydream — but it's also my life now!

Around noon, I check my phone and realize I forgot to text my parents, I have been so distracted. I finally reply to their barrage of concerned texts, assuring them that the plane landed and I'm perfectly fine. I'm more than fine, though, I'm floating on cloud nine.

"Oh, I believe I've got to head back to the campus to meet with my gymnastics coordinator," I tell Will, a little sadly. I am excited to meet the trainers and my fellow gymnasts, but I'm also reluctant to leave Will. It's so nice to have found a friend already, especially one who seems to genuinely care about making me feel welcome.

Suddenly, Will catches me in his arms and dives in to kiss me.

I'm so shocked that I actually yelp in surprise, barely managing to dodge out of the way before his lips collide with mine. His kiss lands awkwardly on my cheek instead, and when he releases me, he looks a little miffed. "Did I misread something?" he asks, ruffling his hand through his blond curls.

"Oh, uhh, I just — um — I need to get going," I tell him quickly, backing away to hail a cab. On the one hand, I am flattered that such a cute boy has deemed me worth trying to kiss, but at the same time I am taken aback by how forward he is. After all, we barely know each other! Does everyone move this quickly in France?

Thankfully, a taxi pulls up and I start to hastily climb inside. Will rushes forward to ask through the window, "Wait! When will I see you again? How will I contact you?"

I shrug and say, "Oh, um, I'm sure we'll see each other around campus!"

And with that, the taxi peels off down the

winding Parisian streets toward the school. I slump in the back seat, my heart pounding after such a strange, sudden encounter. I've only been in the city for a few hours, but it's already been a much different experience than anything I ever had in North Carolina. If this is how quickly things can happen in just one morning... what all will happen in a year or two?

LIV

hen my taxi pulls up to the curb and lets me out in front of my stop on campus, I'm still trying to shake off my encounter with Will. The last and only other time a boy tried to kiss me was in second grade at my birthday pool party. His name was Michael, and I pushed him into the pool and ran away. And this time, I merely jumped in a cab and ran away. I'm starting to wonder if this is how I will always react to male attention — immediately jump into extreme evasive maneuvers. It's becoming my trademark move.

It's about one in the afternoon now and the exhaustion of flying and then dragging my luggage around the city all morning is getting to me. But it's my first day in France — the first time I've ever left America! — and I am not going to let jet lag nor a weird sexual advance get me down! The instructions

I have pulled up on my phone in an email from Pavlenko inform me that I'm supposed to be meeting my roommate in a courtyard on campus at half past one. So I'm just barely going to make it on time. I hurry down the beautiful, historical, arched hallways and rush out into the lazy afternoon sunshine to meet the girl I'm going to share a place with. I'm incredibly nervous and a little bit self-conscious, afraid that something will go wrong.

What if she doesn't like me? What if we don't get along?

I wonder if she'll be from a small town like me or if she'll already be acquainted with city life. I can't decide which would be better. If she's also a small-town girl, then maybe she'll understand me. But if she's used to taking public transportation, dodging in and out of traffic, following the hustle and bustle of the city... well, then maybe she can help me adjust.

I cross the courtyard, pulling my wheeled suit-case behind me, looking around for someone who looks like they're waiting for me. Most of the people I see here look distinctly French — sleek black cloth-ing, effortless style. Then I see her.

There's a girl who looks to be about my age, standing in the center of the courtyard. She's glancing around nervously, her hands fidgeting in front of her. She is much taller than me, and maybe even slimmer. This girl looks to be the very epitome of the gymnast image. Her straight auburn hair is pulled back into a neat ponytail and she's wearing jeans and a pink tank top with a green cardigan over it. She stands out in the sea of dark, probably designer duds. She has to be the one, for sure.

I hurry toward her and she finally looks my way, her hazel eyes going wide and round.

"Are you —?" she begins, her voice sweet but a little shrill.

"Olivia Greenwood," I greet, holding out my hand to shake hers. "I'm assuming you're waiting for a roommate? For the gymnastics program?"

She nods, somehow looking both relieved and anxious at the same time. "Yes, hi. My name is Margaret-Ann Mason, but I go by Maggie, please."

"You can call me Liv," I add, giving her a smile to try and ease her anxiety. She seems a little stiff, like she's still uncertain of me. I hope it's not something I've done wrong.

"Have you been by the flat yet?" she asks, then takes notice of my luggage and blushes. "Oh, I guess probably not since you're still pulling a suitcase around. Duh."

I relaxed a little, realizing that her aloofness probably has less to do with judging me and more to do with her own insecurity. She seems sweet, but I can already pick up on the fact that she's a little too hard on herself. A lot of gymnasts are. We're forced to compete within such strict guidelines that some of us develop complexes about it. Just like my short stature marks me as an outsider, I can imagine that Maggie's height and awkwardness set her apart, too.

"Yeah, I just kind of spent the morning, uh, looking around."

"Well, I can take you to the apartment, if you like," Maggie offers, brightening up. "My parents sent me here a week early to get accustomed to the city, and I've visited Paris a bunch of times before, so I know my way around pretty well!" She immediately blushed, probably feeling like she's rambled too much. But I like people who talk a lot. My parents were always chattering back and forth while I just listened contentedly. It was comforting to me.

"That would be awesome," I assure her. "I'm totally new here."

"Okay," she says, biting her lip. She still looks nervous, but there's a sparkle in her eye. Maggie leads me across the large campus and out to the street. Instead of hailing a cab — which is how I always assumed everyone in big cities got around — she just started walking, with me trailing slightly behind.

"Is the apartment close to here?" I pipe up, my shorter legs struggling to keep up with this Amazonian new acquaintance.

"Oh, yes! It's within walking distance of the university. The training studio isn't far from here, either," she explains. We walk for a while longer down the wide, busy streets, and then we turn a corner and Maggie points upward at a gorgeous old building with black, wrought-iron balconies jutting out from its stony face. "Home sweet home!" she exclaims, beaming.

"Wow," I breathe, tilting my head back to gaze up at the many stories. I had no idea we would be staying in such a gorgeous place. This looks like a movie set, like a postcard. I'm expecting a Juliet to appear on a balcony and call out for her Romeo at any moment.

"I'm sure you're tired of lugging that thing around," Maggie comments, gesturing toward my suitcase. "Wanna go inside? I'll show you our flat!"

She leads me through a giant set of carved wooden doors and we climb several flights of shining marble stairs, my suitcase clunking along behind us. I'm nearly out of breath by the time we reach the sixth floor.

"Yeah, the walk-up is a bit of a hike. But just wait until you see the inside!" Maggie remarks. We walk down a long hallway to room 608, where she takes out a key and opens the door to a spacious, airy apartment. My jaw drops instantly.

Everything is decorated in stark, clean whites and pale powder blues, with quaint little fixtures and floral designs on the molding. The ceilings are surprisingly high, and as I walk into the main living area, I am stunned nearly to tears by the sight of a massive, wall-to-wall set of windows. I rush over and look down to see that our apartment overlooks the street below, as well as a blooming green park across from us. Thin, gauzy white curtains are draped at either side of the wall of windows, pulled back to let in the lovely sunshine. I spin around and gawk at Maggie, who is also beaming excitedly.

"Isn't it wonderful?" she says, clasping her hands in front of her.

I nod vigorously, still at a loss for words. There's a soft white sofa and two straight-backed blue armchairs with carved wooden legs. I can see the tiny kitchen area back toward the entrance, a line of gleaming white counters and minimalist appliances recessed in a smartly-lit alcove.

"Where's the bedroom?" I ask, and Maggie guides me to a little room off to the right. It's a bit tight, with two twin beds pushed against opposing walls, but it's very cute. Just like the rest of the flat, the walls are a milky white and the floors a deep, natural hardwood. We both have white bedspreads with blue quilts folded on them — and here I realize that I'm rooming with a girl who actually makes her own bed every morning instead of leaving it a mass of tangled sheets like I do.

The bathroom is connected to our room through a door with a crystal-blue novelty doorknob. It's fairly standard, with a pedestal sink and a shower stall. The floors are bright white marble, however, and so highly polished that I can nearly see my reflection.

"This is amazing," I gasp, turning back to Maggie. She toys with the end of her flouncy ponytail, looking nervous once again.

"I —I've never had a roommate before. In fact, I've never really had a lot of friends," she admits, her eyes riveted to the floor bashfully. "Oh, that makes me sound pathetic, doesn't it?"

"No, no," I assure her. She's blushing furiously, her cheeks patchy with rosy splotches.

"It's not that I don't like other people or anything. I've just always been so busy with gymnastics, of course, and then there's the homeschooling thing…"

Ah, there it is. That explains everything.

"I understand," I tell her, walking over to pat her on the arm. "I've only had a few close friends, my whole life, and they were gymnasts, too. It's hard to get out and meet people when you're so focused on the future."

"Exactly," she says, looking a little relieved. She seems to soften instantly, her stiff edges melting away.

"If it makes you feel any better, I've never had a roommate either. I've only ever lived at home with my parents. This is totally new for me," I go on, walking over to my bed and sitting down. Maggie follows suit, perching on the edge of her bed.

"Me, too. I have to confess that my parents are a

little, um, overbearing," she describes, twirling the tip of her ponytail. "I love them and I know they have my best interests at heart, but they've never really let me do my own thing. This is the first time they haven't been right behind me telling me what to do every minute of the day."

"How does it feel? Having all this sudden freedom?" I ask, pulling my legs up to sit cross-legged on the bed.

Maggie chews her lips thoughtfully for a moment, then replies, "It's a little scary. I mean, I've been to Paris before, but never on my own. My parents only just left yesterday to go back to Chicago. I thought they'd never leave..." she trails off.

I laugh, "Yeah, mine aren't that bad, but it's still kind of liberating to be able to do whatever I want, whenever I want. Or at least I assume it will be."

"I've only had less than twenty-four hours of freedom but I haven't done much with it yet," Maggie sighs. "I spent the whole morning being too afraid to leave the apartment alone until I finally worked up the courage to go to campus and meet up with you."

Suddenly, my cell phone chirps, alerting me to a new email. It's a message from Pavlenko, informing me that my training will start first thing tomorrow. My heart sinks momentarily. I was hoping to get a little more time to settle in and see the city before jumping right back into the wham-bam schedule of training, studying, and more training. I have no illusions about what this career will mean for me: constant exertion, single-minded focus, and no time or energy for much else. And I've accepted that, since I have to.

But damn, I was hoping to at least see the Eiffel Tower first.

"What's that?" Maggie asks.

I sigh and slump back onto my bed. "Looks like my training picks up tomorrow."

"Oh, yeah, they don't give you a lot of time."

"Yea... Are you with Monsieur Pavlenko as well?"

She nods her head, and I see the corner of her mouth twitch.

"He's... a hard man, isn't he?" I say, testing the waters and avoiding what I really want to say.

"Yea, I heard he was like... raised really strict or something. But that's what gets results, right?"

"I guess. It's just... when I first met him..." I trail off, not even sure how to finish that sentence. Do I tell her how sexy I thought he was, and then how disappointed I was when I realized how cold and professional he treated me? But then, isn't that just how teachers have to treat their students at this level? Just thinking about his gorgeous eyes, though, sends a flush through my body. He's totally different from every other man I've known, and thinking about the childish and brutish attempt at seduction that Will tried on me, I know that Monsieur Pavlenko would be far more suave.

"When you first met him...?" Maggie prods, and I realize I've drifted off in thought, and I shake my head, embarrassed. There's no way I can tell her any of that.

"I just got here," I murmur, trying to change the subject. "I just wish I had a chance to experience Paris and settle in before I get shoved into a gymnastics studio twenty-four-seven." Even if that does mean long hours trying to please my new instructor.

There's a long pause. Then Maggie bounds over and jumps onto my bed beside me, surprising me with her sudden display of enthusiasm. She struck me as the kind of girl who was always prim and proper, keeping a polite distance between herself and everyone else. But maybe, just maybe, that's only due to her parents' overprotection. Maybe the real Maggie is going to break free now that she's got an ounce of freedom.

I kind of hope so. It'll be interesting to see someone so straight-laced spread her wings a little bit. She nudges my shoulder excitedly.

"Hey, we still have the rest of the afternoon and the evening!" she exclaims. "We could totally explore the city and still be back in time for you to get a good night's sleep to be ready for tomorrow. Don't you think?"

I sit up and give her a quizzical expression. I

know I've only just met her, but nothing about her so far has indicated a streak of spontaneity. Still, I have to admit that the offer is tempting, even if I am pretty exhausted.

"You know what? Hell yeah. Let's do this. I'm in Paris, damn it! I can sleep when I'm dead!" I say, jumping up and starting to unzip my suitcase. If I'm going to see this beautiful city, I am sure as hell not doing it in my jeans and a sweatshirt!

Maybe I show up tomorrow for practice exhausted. Big deal. What can go wrong?

LIV

"Okay, open your eyes!" giggles Maggie, who has led me by the arm for the past few minutes of walking, after a short cab ride. "Open and look up!"

My eyes have been shut tightly, as per her instructions, ever since we got into the cab off the Champs-Élysées. But now I slowly open them and tilt my head upward, my stomach immediately twisting into excited knots. I'm staring up at the powerful, criss-crossing metal beams of the Eiffel Tower! My mouth falls open to admit a long, awestruck exhale.

"Isn't it beautiful?" Maggie says, nudging my shoulder.

I nod, feeling like I've been abducted by aliens and set back down gently in some kind of fever

47

dreamscape. How in the world did I manage to end up here, standing underneath this magnificent structure, surrounded by the sights and smells of such a legendary city?

"It's... so much bigger than I expected," I breathe, my chest swelling with emotion. When I was in middle school, the desktop background on my old hand-me-down laptop was a black and white photo of the Eiffel Tower. I used to close out of my homework assignments sometimes just to gaze at the picture, pretending that I was there.

And now... here I am. I swallow back the lump forming in my throat. This has to be a dream that I'm going to wake up from. Any second now my alarm clock will go off and I'll open my eyes to see my old bedroom back in North Carolina.

"Wanna go up?" Maggie asks enthusiastically, in a way that suggests there is only one correct answer: yes, yes, yes!

"Obviously!" I laugh, leaning into her as we both grin and run for the entrance. She pays for our way in, since she's already got her dollars converted into euro. Maggie's been paying for me left and right today, and at first I balked, too proud to let her just buy me things. But once she explained, in a surprisingly matter-of-fact manner, that her parents are very wealthy and they're giving her a hefty monthly stipend — I backed down. In fact, the very first stop on our miniature tour of Paris a couple hours ago was the Triangle d'Or, a fancy boutique spot. I was fully prepared to simply window shop, but Maggie marched straight in and out of Dior, Givenchy, and Chanel like she belonged there. And once I saw her drop several hundred euro on a soft black hat at Hermès on a whim, I realized that she truly *did* belong there. She wasn't homeschooled for some religious reason or because her parents were suspicious of the educational system. It was because they spent so much time traveling the world that they required a tutor who could travel with them.

I've landed myself a rich, generous roommate with a bottomless pocketbook and a newfound taste for freedom. But for all her (as the French might say) bourgeois privileges, I have to give it to her; Maggie has none of the snobby condescension I've come to expect from what kids back home pejoratively dubbed "city slickers." So far, she's been incredibly open and kind to me, treating me like an equal rather than a charity case. Granted, I've only known her for a few hours now, but I can already tell she and I are going to become fast friends. It's a huge relief, knowing that I've found at least one friend in the city. Things are definitely looking up for Liv Greenwood.

Especially now that we're about to ascend the 704 steps of the Eiffel Tower! Wait… are we really going to walk up 704 steps right now? I know we're both athletes, but…

"Where are you going, silly?" Maggie laughs, waving me over away from the entrance to the stairway. "We're taking the lift!"

"Oh, thank god," I gasp in relief. "I was about to say, you must be in way better shape than I am to wanna take the stairs!"

"No, no, training doesn't start till tomorrow, remember? Today we're lazy," she giggles, pulling me into the lift alongside a group of elderly tourists arguing in Portuguese. I've never been around so many different languages and accents, the foreign words colliding with my own English train of thought like a calamitous wreck. But I love it. I love having my entire worldview shaken and crumbled to the ground. I can feel the pieces of my old, sheltered self falling by the wayside, stepping out of the way to make room for a new, worldly Liv. Maggie and I wriggle through the little crowd, muttering *excusez-moi* as we go.

Staring down breathlessly at the earth pulling away beneath our feet, I almost feel like I've left an old part of myself down there on the ground, the fresh, new version of myself ascending into the Parisian evening sky. When we reach the top, Maggie takes my hand and pulls me out onto the landing. We lean into the railing and gawk open-mouthed at the panoramic view of Paris below us, the old buildings mingling alongside the new, twinkling lights dotting the darkening air all around us in every direction.

"I can't believe I'm really here right now," I murmur, finally permitting the sting of elated tears in my eyes. "This is like a dream."

"Yeah, no matter how many times I've been here, it always feels the same. Magical," Maggie agrees, yanking her hair out of its ponytail, shaking it out, and pulling on her new designer hat. I turn to look at her and she smiles. I can tell she's not used to having friends with her on these adventures. I love my parents, and I'm sure Maggie loves hers, but there's just something so much more exciting about seeing the world without a guide. Without limits.

And that's how it feels tonight — like there are no limits.

"What do you wanna do next?" she asks.

"Well, first I definitely wanna take a photo just to prove that I'm really here! Nobody back home will believe me, otherwise!" I say, whipping out my phone and pulling Maggie in beside me as I turn the camera toward us. We both flash our most genuinely blissful, goofy grins and I snap the photo. Paris sparkles in the background, like the city herself is smiling, too. Always ready for a photo op.

"Have you ever had a crepe with Nutella?"

Maggie asks suddenly, grabbing my arm as though it's the most important question in the world.

"What's Nutella?" I ask, furrowing my brow. Maggie throws her hands up and squeals.

"Girl, you're gonna find out *en ce moment!*" she replies, the French phrase rolling delicately and expertly off her tongue. For the first time, I feel the slightest dash of envy toward her. It's not her money or her privilege that unsettles me — it's the fact that she can speak the local language with such ease. While my high school only offered either Latin or Spanish as a half-hearted foreign language option, Maggie explained off-hand that during her lifelong travels with her parents she's picked up French and Italian pretty fluently, and enough Spanish, German, and Russian to get by if need be.

So not only is my roommate rich, but she's also a language savant.

Still, just like her money and familiarity with Paris are a benefit to both of us, her ability to easily communicate with the locals and read street signs are an enormous advantage. As long as I'm with her, I'll never really be lost here.

And I'm realizing, as we race back to the lift, that I am not simply a leech in this blossoming friendship — I have something else to offer. Maggie is coming out of her shell, possibly for the first time in her life, now that she has someone to adventure with. In the few short hours we've spent together, she has unfolded like a morning glory under the dawn of a bright sun. When we first met on campus, she was stiff and almost cold, her words and gestures awkward. Everything about her screamed 'fish out of water.' But with me encouraging and reassuring her, she's really begun to express herself.

For even though she may have felt at home waltzing in and out of designer boutiques, she was still reluctant to address a man selling pretty scarves on a street corner. She couldn't meet the eye of the taxi driver. She apologized profusely any time she had to cross a street, even when we had the right-of-way.

But now, the two of us are skipping and laughing down the Champ de Mars, the green grass tickling our bare ankles. At my insistence, before we left the flat to embark on our citywide tour, I managed to get her into a little black dress from my own suit-case. For although Maggie has many items of designer clothing, they all fall on the hyper-conserv-ative side. She wears the kinds of clothes one would expect of a Sunday school teacher, not a world-trav-eler with a perfected French accent. So with much coaching, she put on my black dress, and I slipped into a white, lacy frock. The pair of us look like we belong in a hipster photo shoot, but I think we pull it off swimmingly.

We find a crepe vendor on the edge of the green, and Maggie buys us both banana-Nutella crepes and a giant bottle of water. Then we settle down on the grass, staring up at the starry sky. The crepe is spectacular! Chocolatey, nutty, and just oh so light and delicious! And the evening? It's amazing to me that we can still see the stars, faintly illuminated beyond the fuzzy glow of city lights. Back home, everyone always says that city people never get to see the stars. But sitting here now, I realize how very wrong they are. I'm catching onto the fact that they may be wrong about a lot of things about the world. I know there must be danger lurking somewhere in the shadows of the city, but right now all I can see is the shining light.

"This is gonna be so awesome," Maggie gushes, wiping the chocolatey smudge from her lips with a pink napkin. "I was so nervous about coming here and being without my parents. I've never really done anything on my own before and I was so scared that I'd get a roommate who hated me. You always hear horror stories about college roommates, you know. But you and I... we're gonna have so much fun, I think."

"We are," I agree, smiling at her.

"So, what's next?" she chirps happily, leaning back and starting to idly braid her hair over one shoulder. I shrug and take another bite of my delicious crepe, thinking hard. I don't really know what all there is to do in Paris. I mean, I'm sure there's a lot — but I wouldn't have the slightest idea where to begin.

"Well, it's your city, Maggie! What do *you* wanna do next?" I shoot back, winking. She looks positively intimidated to have been given the reins yet again. She's clearly not accustomed to being in control. I get the sense that, just like I've spent most of my life trailing after my parents who are in their own little world, Maggie has been her parents' silent shadow for a long time.

"Hmm," she begins thoughtfully, chewing her lip. "Well, we are both eighteen now... so we could do something *bad*."

I have to snort at the way she says "bad." She sounds like a little kid suggesting that we raid her mother's cookie jar or something.

"Uh, like what?" I press her. She blushes.

"We could go to a bar or something," she suggests, so quietly I have to strain to comprehend her words.

"Don't we have to be twenty-one to drink?" I ask, confused.

She shakes her head, blinking at me in shock. "No, Liv. The drinking age in France is eighteen. We're both old enough to buy alcohol."

"What?" I gasp in full disbelief. I can't believe how much of an idiot I am for not knowing this. I feel like such a stereotypical dumb American, assuming the laws are the same as they are back home. Except back in Toast, drinking at any age is severely frowned upon. That's one of the many downsides to living in a formerly dry county. A lot of the stigma remains.

"I've only had a few sips of wine with my parents, though. Ever," Maggie admits, looking ashamed of herself.

"I've never had alcohol except for… well, this boy on the flight over here gave me a little bit of his champagne," I tell her, the whole awkward scene with Will jumping back into my mind.

"Ooh! Was he cute?" she asks, wiggling closer and resting her chin on her hands.

"Uh, yeah. He was alright," I say, downplaying how cute he really was. Sure, he's cute, but he crossed a line when he tried to kiss me. Didn't he? Now that I'm sitting in the shadow of the Eiffel Tower, sucking the intoxicatingly mystical air of a Parisian evening into my lungs… I wonder if maybe I overreacted. Perhaps I was the one who got it wrong. Maybe that's just the way things happen here — all of a sudden, with no warning and no real reason or rhyme beyond the fact that it feels good at the time. Back home, most of my friends hardly even held hands until the third or fourth date. But maybe here in Paris, it wasn't unusual to kiss an almost-stranger.

Maybe Will deserved a second chance.

But, I realize with a sinking heart, I never gave

him my number, nor did I get his. I simply ran away before I could really take full stock of the situation. Maybe he was really a nice guy who simply liked me and wanted to show it with a sweet gesture, and I just slammed the door in his face. Suddenly, I feel incredibly rude and cruel. And foolish.

Just then, as though summoned by some spirit of kismet, my phone screen lights up to indicate a new email. It's a weird time of evening to get a school message, but I open my email just the same... and see that it's not a message from the university address, nor from Pavlenko.

It reads:

*Bonjour Olivia!*

*Found your email address in a student registrar online, since I didn't catch your number in time before you left this morning. Hope I didn't freak you out too badly. Sorry if I was being too forward. I just got swept up in the moment, I guess. Anyway, if you're feeling up to it, there's a big party happening tonight in the 11th arrondissement. We're meeting up at Zero-Zero on Rue Amelot in an hour if you want to join. I want to make it up to you for overstepping boundaries today. Please let me show you a good time. I promise not to kiss you... unless you want me to.*

*À bientôt!*

*- Will*

"Oh my god, speak of the devil," I murmur, staring in shock at my phone screen.

"Who is it?" Maggie asks, peering over my arm. I look up at her, biting my lip.

"It's the guy from the plane," I say flatly. "And he wants me to go to a party tonight."

"Ahh! Liv, you have to go! Can I come with you? Please, please, please!" she gasps, wiggling up and down excitedly. Gone is the nervous, fidgety girl of this afternoon. I raise an eyebrow at her.

"I don't know, Maggie. They're meeting up at a bar… I've never really been a part of that scene, you know," I wheedled, my stomach turning anxiously. The logical, sensible part of my brain is urging me to ignore the email and just go home since I have to be up early tomorrow for my first day of training.

But another voice in my head reminds me that I'm in Paris — if I don't take this chance now, then I'm still just the same old boring girl who had no social life in Toast, North Carolina. Everything about Paris has been like a dream, and I might as well see how much farther this crazy ride will take me. Within reason, of course.

"Okay, fine," I sigh. Maggie lets out a giddy squeak. "But we have to get back in time for me to get some sleep tonight? And we have to stick together, alright?"

Maggie nods vigorously and jumps up, tugging my hand to pull me to my feet.

"Come on, come on! Let's go! The night is young! Let's do this!" she exclaims.

I can't help but laugh at how enthusiastic she is and the oddness of the situation, this guy tracking me down like that... but deep inside I'm beginning to wonder what the hell I'm getting myself into. Call it intuition, but I feel like I'm making the biggest mistake of my life.

LIV

The cab rattles along down Boulevard Saint-Germain, taking us away from the Eiffel Tower and toward the eleventh arrondissement, with the sun only barely peeking out above the horizon behind us. I glance back over my shoulder through the rear window of the taxi, an ominous pit settling in my stomach. The sun is going to sleep while we ricochet through the darkening city in the opposite direction, like we're trying to outrun the rise of the moon. I fold my hands in my lap and stare anxiously out at Paris passing by, watching the street lights dance on the glossy shop windows. Next to me in the backseat, Maggie is positively vibrating with nervous excitement.

"I've never been to a party at a bar before," she mutters, fidgeting with the hem of her black dress.

I'm pleased that it fits her so well, considering that it's my dress, and Maggie is at least four or five inches taller than me. It falls to just about mid-thigh for her, and I suspect that this look is the most scandalous one she's ever attempted.

I look over at her to see that she's now looking slightly downcast and she continues sadly, "Actually, I've never really been to a party before without… without my parents around. They took me to a lot of charity galas and society balls, but I was pretty much just another accessory for them, I think. My dad with his cuff links, my mom with her pearls, and then me."

"You got to travel the world, though," I remind her, trying to brighten her spirit.

She shrugs. "I know, and I'm grateful for that. But it would have been nice to have a friend my own age, you know?"

I nod and bump her shoulder with mine. "Yeah, I know what you mean. So, this is kind of your one chance to break free, huh?"

Maggie smiles weakly at me. "Mhmm. Sorry for pushing you into this, it's just that — well, I don't know if I'll ever be in this position again. As soon as the gymnastics program ends, I'm sure my mom and dad will ship me off to some other training seminar for whatever new hobby they've picked for me. You know, I always wanted to be a veterinarian but my parents wanted me to do something flashier, more fun to tell their friends about at parties."

"But it's your life, not theirs," I rebut, frowning. Maggie sighs heavily.

"Try telling them that," she replies softly. The cab turns a corner and we drive across a long bridge over dark, glimmering water down below. A sign indicates that we're now on Boulevard Henri IV, approaching the Place de la Bastille, where the famous prison once stood. Traffic here is a little tight, and I can't stop gritting my teeth together, my hands clutching at the seat to hold myself in place as though we might collide with another car at any moment.

"Well, if this is the one chance you'll get, then we better make the most of it," I tell Maggie, who responds with a wide grin.

"Thank you for understanding and not judging me," she says. "Usually as soon as people find out what my life is like, they treat me like the weird homeschooled kid."

I instantly feel a twinge of guilt, recalling the fact that I did think that of her upon our first encounter, taking in her conservative clothing and high-strung personality. I inwardly pledge to make up for this harsh first impression by giving her a really good night. Despite her wealth and privilege, I still feel a little bad for her, having to trudge around in her parents' shadow all the time. Besides, she's a sweet girl, and it *is* nice to have a friend who forces me to open up and expand my horizons a little bit.

"Well, if you don't judge me for being a sheltered small-town girl, I won't judge you for being a jet-setting cosmopolitan," I tell her with a wink, some of France seeping into my words more and more all the time. She giggles.

"Deal," she agrees. The cab lurches forward suddenly and we both instinctively reach over to hold onto each other, our faces wearing identical expressions of panic. Once we look at each other we immediately burst into laughter at how jumpy we are.

"*Je suis désolé*," comments the cab driver, glancing at us apologetically in the rear view mirror as the taxi slides into another lane.

"*Pas de quoi*," answers Maggie with a wave of her hand.

The driver takes us down Boulevard Beaumarchais and then Maggie taps his shoulder to tell him to let us out at the next cross-street, which reads Rue Saint-Sebastien. He obliges, pulling to the sidewalk. I slide out of the backseat onto the pavement and look around, blinking in the fuzzy glow of the street lamps.

"*Merci beaucoup, bonne nuit*," Maggie quips to the driver as she pays him, smiling. He nods and waves at us as he drives away, leaving the two of us standing alone on the street, far across town from our apartment and the relative familiarity of the most touristy area around the Eiffel Tower. I get the sense that we've now moved much closer to the heart of where native Parisians hang out, where the French go to evade the gawking stares of loud-mouthed, confused tourists and sightseers.

It's dark and the air is getting cooler by the second. I shiver ever so slightly, suddenly feeling very small and out of place in this enormous hodge-podge of an ancient city. Maggie takes my arm and looks around for a long moment, surveying the area. Then she seems to get her bearings and starts leading me down the street.

"If I remember correctly from the map I looked at this morning, Rue Amelot should be right around this corner," she says, thinking aloud. "Aha! I was right."

We find ourselves across the street from a tiny bar with heavy graffiti coloring the shop front with indiscernible lettering and symbols. The words ZERO ZERO appear in weathered letters above the narrow doorway, and there doesn't seem to be any light emanating from the place. However, we can certainly hear loud music sending thrills of bass through the ground to tickle our feet as we stand on the street corner. Maggie squeezes my arm.

"Ready to go in?" she asks cheerily.

I'm still surprised at how enthusiastic and brave she is for wanting to do this — at first glance she certainly doesn't seem like the partying type. But I suppose all it takes is a miniature dose of courage and suddenly the reluctant wallflower can bloom into a vibrant rose.

I still feel more like I'm wilting rather than blooming, though.

Something instinctual in the back of my mind warns me not to step through the door. There's a small, gloomy voice telling me that I've fallen too far off the beaten path, that I'm only two steps away from stumbling down the rabbit hole. And I don't know if Wonderland is what awaits me at the bottom, or perhaps something much, much darker.

But maybe I'm just being overly cautious. After all, it's just a bar. It's a public place, and it's not like I'm totally alone here. I'm with Maggie, who has both money and the ability to speak French. No matter what happens, the two of us will make it out okay. I assure myself that everything is fine and there's no need to overreact. With a nod to Maggie, we walk up and open the door, stepping over the threshold into a dimly-lit bar scene.

There are neon signs on the walls, no chairs or tables whatsoever, and there's graffiti absolutely everywhere. People are hanging over the bar counter, sipping cocktails and beers, while others are swaying and toe-tapping on the dance floor area. The whole bar could easily fit inside our little apartment, it's so small. But what it lacks in size, it clearly makes up for in character. The crowd here is a little more edgy and hipster than what we've seen elsewhere, with jagged haircuts, tattoos, and piercings galore. Still, I don't get a particularly bad vibe from the place, to my relief. It actually feels somewhat cozy, in a way.

"This is awesome," Maggie murmurs under her breath. "Let's get drinks!"

"I have no idea what to order," I say worriedly. I wouldn't even know where to begin.

"I'm sure we'll figure something out," she replies, dragging me up to the counter to order. The bartender is a tall, skinny guy with heavily-lidded eyes and a shock of dark hair. He looks cool and detached despite the noise and chaos happening all around him.

Maggie leans in and hands him our driver's licenses, tucking her hair back behind her ear and saying, *"Bonjour, que recommandez-vous?"*

Before the bartender can even respond, a guy comes up and all but smashes into us, his hard body pressing up against me at the bar. I turn to look at him with a glare, only to fall back in surprise at the sight of Will's smiling face. He looks back and forth between Maggie and me with a look of mingled glee and confusion on his handsome features.

"No wonder you left in such a hurry this morning," he says to me. "I had no idea you already had a beautiful French date to meet up with."

Maggie's face goes bright pink and she stammers, "Oh n-no, we're not together or anything, and I-I'm not French."

"Oh, you're not...?" he presses, a twinkle in his eye suggesting to me that he never suspected that in the first place at all. But Maggie has fallen for it hook, line, and sinker.

"We're not — uh, we aren't..." she trails off, looking very perplexed.

"This is my roommate Maggie," I interject, eager to dissipate the awkward tension.

"*Je m'appelle Will, ça va?*" he says, holding out a hand for her to shake. She takes it gingerly, looking like she might actually melt into a puddle and drip through the floorboards at any second. She's definitely not used to any kind of attention from cute boys, I can tell. Not that I'm particularly accustomed to it, either. But I still feel a pinch of wariness in regard to Will, after his forwardness earlier today. I hope he doesn't hold it against me or try it again anytime soon. Although, I have to admit that he does look absolutely fantastic tonight. His flaxen-blond hair is brushed back, with a few pieces hanging artfully around his temples and forehead. His California-esque tan and bright blue eyes almost glow in the surreal neon lighting, and every time he brushes up against me I can feel his sculpted musculature.

At his insistence, he buys us both cocktails with a name I cannot pronounce nor remember for the life of me. Whatever it is, it tastes like strawberries and sweet liqueur, with a slight fizz that tickles my nose when I take a sip. It's delicious, and because I'm so nervous, I drink it much more quickly than I probably should.

Maggie does the same, downing hers in record time before ordering a second one. Will leads us over to a group of beautiful girls and handsome men all dressed in the same hip, slightly ragged style of the crowd here at Zero Zero. Everyone is very accommodating and kind, enthusiastically inviting us into their circle without question. They mostly speak French to each other, with the occasional phrase of what sounds like possibly Russian being tossed around. At first it seems slightly off to hear Russian, but then I simply chalk it up to the fact that Paris is such a metropolitan, worldly place. There are people here from all over, mingling together. It's no big deal. So I force myself to relax a little.

Before long, Maggie is substantially liquored up and bantering loudly with a few guys in lilting French. I don't know what she's saying, but the way she's leaning on them and twirling her hair suggests that they're flirting. For a while, I manage to sneak her away from them by asking her to dance with me.

The heady mix of unfamiliar territory, alcohol, and seductive music creates an intoxicating concoction, urging me a little further down the rabbit hole one drink and one dance at a time. Maggie holds her plastic cup above her head and spins slowly in front of me, her other hand grasping mine as we both giggle and sway to the music. I can feel myself getting slightly carried away, but Maggie is another story. She's long gone, stumbling and laughing and blowing kisses to every guy who walks by.

"What the hell did we drink?" she murmurs, giggling as she leans in close to me.

"I don't know, I don't speak French," I reply, shrugging. Maggie tilts her head back and wraps her arms around me, starting to lose her balance. However, she's much taller than me and I am nowhere near equipped to hold her up, so we both start to fall backward. Just in time, Will slides in behind me and braces us both, pinning me between them in the process. In front of me is my new friend, her dark hair falling around her rosy cheeks and her eyes cloudy with intoxication. Behind me is the handsome, charming man who tried to kiss me today, his strong arms holding me in place. His hands slip down to grasp at my hips and roll me back against him.

I realize, through the fog of alcohol muddying my thoughts, that I can feel his dick hard against my lower back, just above my ass. Will smoothly swipes my hair back over one shoulder, then bends down to gently brush his lips against my exposed neck. I shiver and close my eyes, not sure if I want to recoil or just embrace the moment.

"We're heading to the flat now," says a male voice somewhere to our left. I open my eyes to see one of Will's friends taking Maggie by the hand and letting her slump against him. She's still conscious and grinning, but her expression is dazed. Somewhere in the back of my mind, I see a warning sign flashing dimly in the darkness.

"*D'accord,*" Will replies. "We're coming, too. Aren't we, Olivia?"

I manage to fight my way through the numbing sensation to push off of him slightly and reply, "Oh, I think we'd better get back to our apartment, actually. I have training early in the morning, and it looks like Maggie's about done for the night, anyway."

"Nonsense," my sloshed roommate slurs, waving her hand dismissively. "I'm good!"

"*Oui,* you are, baby," murmurs the guy holding her up. He leans down to kiss her and to my shock she simply accepts it, kissing him back.

"Yeah, we'd better get going," I interrupt, reaching for Maggie's arm. But the guy pulls her away, the two of them all but limping out the door and onto the street. I try to follow after, but I keep stumbling, suddenly realizing just how deeply fucked-up I am.

"Whoa, there. Wait for me," Will remarks with a chuckle as he comes up behind me and pins me to his side with a strong arm around my shoulders. We walk out of the bar and I see a black car pulled up to the pavement. Will's friend is pouring Maggie into the backseat and climbing in after her, beckoning for us to follow.

My head is swimming, alarm bells ringing. "No, no. I'm not going. I've gotta get back home. Right now," I balk, planting my feet firmly on the sidewalk even as I sway slightly. Will nudges my back, pushing me toward the open door of the black vehicle.

"Without your friend?" Will reasons. "How're you gonna leave without her?"

"I don't know," I murmur, fumbling in my pockets, unable to find my phone. I have no idea where it's gone, so I can't call anyone to come get me. I haven't exchanged any of my money for euro yet, so I can't buy a taxi ride back to the apartment. And I'm realizing just how far away I am — I'll never be able to walk all the way back home. I'm stuck.

"Don't worry," Will says, his breath hot at my ear as he steers me toward the car. "If you don't wanna go to the party, it's fine. We'll just drop you off at your apartment on the way, alright? I won't let you go home all by yourself in the middle of the night. It's not safe out there."

Without any other alternative, and with the pounding clouds of oblivion gathering in my drunken brain, I allow him to push me toward the open door, feeling like I'm stepping through a dark portal to a world from which I may never return again.

*I* step out of the black sedan and into the morning sunlight that's lighting up the whole city as it wakes. The university will soon be bustling with activity as always, the streets around and within the campus teeming with fresh-faced or dreary-eyed students, as well as faculty, like myself.

But I arrive on campus a few hours before most of the activity really gets started. I always do. Before the rest of the faculty arrives, and long before the students begin to show up, I make my rounds about the facilities I've been put in charge of.

I stride into the gymnasium proper, breathing in the air of the training facility and enjoying the moment of peace before the hustle of the day that will be starting before much longer. There's something about the inside of a gym even more peaceful than the world outside, something unique to this place in particular.

I know what it is, though I dare not dwell on it long. This place has become something of a refuge for me. A shrine where I can distance myself from the past and maybe earn some absolution for the things I still remember, the things that still keep me up some nights.

"*Bonjour*, Max," greets Marcel, one of the custodians who is finishing cleaning the floors for the morning. "Still don't trust old Marcel to make sure everything is up to snuff, eh?"

He laughs, and I shake my head with a half-smile. "Your work is impeccable, my friend. I'm just here to keep you on your toes. Can't have the best custodian at the university resting on his laurels."

"No, I don't blame you," he says as he starts to put up his cleaning equipment. "I've seen this round of girls checking out the gym this past weekend, and I swear, some of them could trip on a flat surface, they're so starry-eyed. You've got your hands full with this lot, Max."

"Don't discount them so early," I say with a wag of my finger, bending down to stretch my legs out idly while I wait for the first arrivals. "All these girls worked hard to get here. Can't be more than three or four of them just here on their parents' dime — most of them are first-rate athletes, where they come from."

"There you go with that 'hard work' speech again," Marcel says, shaking his head. "I tell you, I'll be impressed if half of them last past their starry-eyed welcome to this city. Happens to all the Americans."

"We'll see," I say firmly, "but there's real potential in this bunch, and maybe you'd see that if you'd take a day off once in a while."

Marcel laughs as he heads out the door, but only waves to me as he goes. "You should take your own advice. Good training, my friend!"

I give him a nod as he goes, then get back to warming up for the day. Marcel is a jaded old man, but he was one of my first friends coming to the university. My Russian accent still shows, whether I'm speaking French or English, but the custodians here are one of the few groups of people who don't hold that against me.

Before long, the athletes start filing in, and I must once again stop being Max and become the distant instructor, Monsieur Pavlenko. The role suits me more, I believe. Or at least hope.

Within about ten minutes of each other, just about everyone has arrived. I try not to smile at the thought of how long that habit will last. Today is only the first day of the semester, and my experience tells me that the majority of these students will be bright and eager for the first month or so, but only a few will maintain such punctuality the whole way through. Most of them still speak little or no French, too, so they have each other to rely upon as social outlets.

But I intend to extend that punctuality as long as possible, or weed out the weak ones trying.

"Welcome to training, everyone," I announce after enough of the class is assembled, clapping my hands to get everyone's attention. "Glad to see nobody's booked a flight home yet. We have a long day ahead of us, so I expect all of you at your best." It doesn't take long to herd everyone together. I don't patronize them with the routine of having everyone line up or stand at attention like trained dogs; I know better than to treat skilled athletes like soldiers. My skill and my voice are enough to command the respect I give them in due part.

"My name is Maksim Pavlenko. To you, I am Monsieur Pavlenko, as our gracious French hosts insist. Let me be clear on one thing alone," I say, pausing dramatically, to look each of them in the eye for an instant. "You are here because you have potential, not because you have any edge over your peers. I will not tolerate anything but exceptional teamwork going forward. I will not hesitate to cut you from this program if you fall short of my expectations, and I have seen some of the finest gymnasts in Paris come through these doors. While you are here, you must give this training your all — I say this for your benefit as well as your peers'. Do I make myself clear?"

"Yes, Monsieur!" comes the general reply from the group, many of them nodding hastily.

"Good," I say, granting them neither smile nor shift in expression. "Now let's get to work."

Drills begin immediately, and as I send the athletes through the routines that their muscles will know as intimately as walking by the time I'm finished with them, I monitor their progress with hawk-like attention.

"Williams! Run that routine again, you know not to hold your back like that."

"O'Connell, you and Anderson help each other with your posture, I want to see both of you with your shoulders level without thinking about it before lunch today."

"You didn't eat breakfast, did you, Jurkowski? You need to take care of yourself, no skipping meals while you're on my watch."

I have to drill the athletes harshly. Gymnastics is already an incredibly demanding sport, but in Paris, the expectations surrounding the gymnasts is tripled, easily. Many of these girls have been used to being the best of the best in their respective hometowns, and it is even true that many of them have earned that respect from their childhood classmates and peers. But the feeling of superiority they've enjoyed for part of their lives must be stripped from them if they are to advance any further.

As I bark orders at all of the trainees, I see some of them appear to be chafing under my commands, many of them never having been pushed this hard, this fast in a very long time, if ever. But this is by design.

No part of me feels guilty for pushing the athletes so, not even as they're fresh off the plane in a foreign land, probably feeling more vulnerable than they ever have before. This must be part of the process.

This breaking period serves another purpose, too. As an instructor, it is essential for me to establish a clear hierarchy in the class as well as maintain my distance as a mentor rather than a fellow athlete.

Every time I send one of the gymnasts through a routine, whether on a bar or beam or flat-footed, I personally demonstrate the technique they must use as a baseline for their development.

"That," I say after sticking a back layout with a half-twist while some of the students look on, "is not a technique I demand that you mimic to perfection. If I were here to teach you how to pantomime, I'd send you out on the streets to emulate the silent performers." There's a bit of laughter, and I afford them a half-smile. "I want you to look at the examples of me and the other trainers you'll meet and develop your own, personal style from that template. Nobody can perfect your technique but you. It's easy to forget that in a place like this — as a fellow foreigner, I can attest to that," I say, and my words seem to encourage most of the gymnasts.

"Now back to it, come on!" I shout, and in a moment, they're off to training again.

I admit, I have more of a teacher in me than I thought I would before starting here. It feels good to give the encouragement to these young women I never received when I was growing up, particularly not so in Russia.

Memories of an old, weathered, dreary orphanage flit through my memories, me and my one friend in that cold and wretched place sticking together to steal food from the administrators and teaming up to defend one another from the other boys.

I shake my head, snapping myself out of the memories. At least that place served to let me be cold and distant when I needed to be.

As I monitor the progress of the gymnasts, I don't fail to notice that some of their eyes rove to me when they think I'm not paying attention. I am a tall man, easily towering over all of them at six and a half feet, and my workout clothes shows off muscles far larger and harder than most gymnasts, both in my rippling arms and cut calves. My tight shirt leaves little to the imagination in my pecs and abdomen, as well as my stony back muscles that flex and stretch with each technique.

These women are very young, and all of them are out of their element. It would be the easiest thing in the world to become unprofessional with them, and at least once a year, every faculty member has a story about a student who's tried just such a thing. And there are more stories yet of those professors who *have* taken advantage of the women's vulnerability.

That is, in part, why I distance myself so harshly, so early, often before the women even arrive in Paris. There was one student in particular with whom I was especially harsh...and I haven't failed to notice her absence today. As well as one other young woman's. I know some of the students are prone to dropping out mysteriously, but such a thing is a rarity before the first day starts.

"Martins," I call one of the women over, and she looks up from her training. "Where are Greenwood and Mason?"

She looks confused for a moment, then blinks in comprehension. "Oh! You mean Liv and Maggie? Uh, I don't know. Heard they're roommates, but haven't heard much from them."

"Does anyone else here know them?"

"Don't think so," she says with a frown. "Everything okay?"

"Nothing for you to worry about," I say with a

frown, taking out my cellphone and waving her off. "But thank you."

I make my way across the gym to somewhere a little quieter, scrolling through my contacts to find their numbers — I made sure to have everyone's contact information as they came over. These foreigners were all in my care, after all, and this was not the kind of program to be taken lightly.

Not that I would suspect Liv to be the type to blow off training, which is why I felt a touch of concern as I listen to the droning ring go on and on. I furrow my brow and try Maggie's number, but only to the same result.

I can't shake a strange feeling about their silence. In my years of running this program, some students had indeed blown off the classes to go enjoy Paris, but to do so on the first day?

Liv was the most puzzling of the two. She'd been so submissive and meek when we'd met, obediently falling into step. When I first caught her staring at me, I thought she'd melt into the floor of embarrassment.

That's not the type of girl who wanted to ruffle feathers, especially not with her dedication.

I can't explain it, but I feel a certain connection to her, as I have since I first met her to invite her to the program. My professionalism required that I be harsh with her, perhaps more so than the other students. I'm not the type of trainer who'd succumb to my baser desires, but I wanted to establish early than I was off-limits, and much too hard and cold for her.

But my impression was such that I had truly high hopes for her at the time we met, and my instincts are rarely so far off.

I peer at the students for a moment more before making another call — this time, to one of my colleagues.

"Max? How's the new batch of students?"

"Excellent, but I've got to go track a couple of them down. Can you cover for me? I'll owe you a drink later."

"Ehhh, fine, no problem, I'm around the corner."

"Thanks, I'll leave my chart by the door — I've got to run."

"Good luck, Max."

I hang up the phone and head out of the building, leaving the athletes to handle themselves for the time being. By now, most all of them are self-sufficient enough to handle themselves for five minutes.

For some reason, with every passing heartbeat, I feel a growing sense of urgency regarding the two students. My mind keeps recalling my first meeting with Liv, occasionally wondering if I was too harsh with her despite all the potential I saw, and perhaps that's what rouses my sense of responsibility even more strongly than usual. Maggie strikes me as more inclined to cut loose, but both are still extremely talented, and the fact that they share an apartment and both haven't shown concerns me all the more.

I care deeply for my students. In all my time as a teacher, I've given more than a few rides home in pouring rain, helped them pay for their equipment and travel costs, and even given little lessons on how to cook cost-effectively. I have a personal stake in such things. So when a young woman fails to appear for the first day of training, I become concerned.

Especially in the case of a talented young woman like Olivia.

LIV

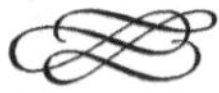

Something smells like death.

I struggle to open first one eye, then the other, feeling like my eyelids weigh a thousand pounds apiece. My body is numb and heavy, and I can't seem to orient myself. I have no idea where I am, only that I feel a damp, dank coldness sinking into my clammy skin. Even opening my eyes doesn't help very much, as it's almost pitch-black wherever I am right now. I might as well be blindfolded, for all the good my eyesight does me here. I blink impotently in the darkness, willing my arms to move, to feel, to do anything at all. But everything is so stiff and immobile, like I've been paralyzed. My muscles simply won't answer to my brain's instructions.

Am I dying? Am I dead?

My throat feels coarse and thick but I need to

make some kind of sound. What if I'm not alone in here? Where are my parents? Am I in the hospital?

Then it dawns on me that I'm not in North Carolina anymore; I'm in France. My sluggish brain trudges through the train of memories. I came to Paris to study and train under world-renowned gymnastics coaches. I came here alone. This is my first night in Paris, and…

*Maggie!* Where is she?

I was with her earlier tonight — I know that much, even though the rest of the night is still so foggy. I try to open my mouth to speak, but it appears that some kind of restraint is wrapped around my head, cloth fabric pressing in on my lips to keep me from forming words. Summoning all my strength and focusing every sleepy nerve of consciousness, I manage to push a moaning sound out of my vocal chords. Somewhere to my right I can hear a similar groan, more akin to a whimper, high-pitched and fearful. Maggie.

My heart starts to race as the full gravity of our predicament settles in around me. We're being held somewhere dark and dank, we cannot move or speak, and we have no idea where we are. At least, I have no idea. I wonder if maybe Maggie knows something — not that I can ask her, since neither of us can talk at the moment. I decide that's got to be the most important thing, the first order of business. I've got to get this thing off of my mouth.

But how can I do that when my arms don't work?

I grunt and strain, willing my arm muscles to respond to me, all in vain. I feel so detached from my own limbs, like they don't belong to me. I can't even figure out if they're restrained or if I'm simply paralyzed. Closing my eyes, I decide to start small, with just my fingers. I try to recall the sensation of wiggling my fingers, and slowly but surely my fingers start to twitch. I let out a gasp of relief, realizing that I must not be totally paralyzed. I wonder if I may have been drugged, and now the effects are beginning to wear off. That must be it.

Who would have drugged me, though? Where did this happen? How did we get here?

A handsome, smirking face framed with sunshiny golden hair swims lazily to the forefront of my mind and I remember with a jolt: Will met us at a pub. He bought us drinks. We danced and I felt him rubbing up against me from behind, his hands grabbing at my hips as I feebly resisted. I remember being led into the backseat of a big, black car…

And from there, the sensation of something sickeningly sweet and icy cold being pressed into my face, that frigid sweetness swarming into my nose and making me feel weak. I suddenly recall watching some crime drama on television years ago in which a girl was knocked out with a rag to her face — chloroform, it was called? Did that really happen to me? How could this be happening? I have training in the morning. I haven't spoken to my parents in hours and hours. Surely somebody will notice that I'm missing, that something is terribly wrong.

I work on bending my wrists next, and from there the rest of my arms. To my shallow elation, I find that my arms are not bound with anything, only my face. So as soon as I manage to regain control of my arms I reach up, fumbling blindly in the dark to find the binding around my head and tear it off. It's only a piece of ripped fabric knotted at the back of my head. It's secured too tightly to pull away without severely hurting my face, so I have to figure out how to untie it. My fingers are still clumsy, and it takes me a long time to undo the knot. Finally it comes loose and I throw it aside, opening and closing my jaw to try and work it back into normal condition.

"Agghhhh," I groan, my lips struggling to form coherent words. There's another moan of response from the area to my right, which I can tell now for certain is Maggie.

I feel around beneath me. I'm lying down on my back, with a hard, freezing cold concrete floor under my spine. I brace my hands on either side of me to push myself up into a sitting position, every nerve in my body protesting the effort. It feels like trying to walk on a leg that's fallen asleep — everything is tingling with pinpricks of pain, urging me to be still and compliant, not to try and save myself. Every part of my frame longs to just lie back down and wait for whatever grim fate is coming for me. But I can't give in so easily. I'm an athlete; I'm used to pushing myself through obstacles and disregarding the pain and discomfort warnings my body gives me.

"M-Maggie?" I manage to croak, my throat still scratchy and my vocal chords weak.

"Mmm!" she whimpers, and I can hear the rustling sounds of her own body trying desperately to move. She must have been dosed with the same stuff they gave me. I have to figure out how to reach her, reassure her that everything's okay... even though I don't know if things *are* going to be okay. Things definitely don't seem great right now.

I grit my teeth as I struggle to scoot closer to her. I can feel that I'm still wearing my white dress, same as before. So at least I know they didn't undress me or anything. I shudder at the thought. Some timid voice in the back of my head suggests that maybe this is just a misunderstanding. Maybe it's just a really, really bad hangover. I've never had one before — maybe it's always like this. Maybe you always feel this scared and lost.

But I know that's not the case. As much as I want to believe that any second now the lights will flick on and we'll find out that we were panicking for no reason... it's not going to happen. This is a grave situation. And Will and his friends put us here. I kick myself for ever trusting him in the first place. I should have known from the very second he offered me a drink of his champagne on the flight here that he was bad news. Cute boys like that don't talk to me just because they like me. Of course he saw me as easy prey — small town girl with no real world experience, no solid footing, desperate for a friendly face. And Maggie was easy, too. All it took was one charming smile and she was hooked. I wanted to cry in frustration at how stupid we were, going to that bar. How could I have been so irresponsible? So trusting?

Finally I scoot across the floor and feel my knee brush against something vaguely warm and trembling. Maggie yelps and starts wriggling around in fear.

"Shh, it's me. It's Liv," I mumble, my lips finally remembering how to shape real words.

"Mm! Mmm!" she whines. I fumble around until I find her hand. I give it a squeeze and feel her instantly relax a little bit while I start untying the fabric strip binding her mouth. Once it's pulled off, she starts to sniffle and cry.

"Wh —what happened? Where are we?" she murmurs, her words slightly garbled.

"I don't know," I tell her honestly. I can feel her heaving with quiet sobs as I help her to sit up. She falls into me, shaking and weeping. I let her fold into my arms, her frame crumpling into the fetal position as I hold her.

"Those guys… they must have taken us," she chokes out between sobs.

"Yeah. I think you're right," I concede sadly, forcing myself not to cry, too. At least one of us has to hold it together, and it might as well be me. I have the feeling that if we were to both fall apart there would be no hope at all. I have to be strong, for both our sakes.

"Do you hear that?" Maggie gasps suddenly, clutching at my arms. We sit stock-still and silent, listening intently. There's a faint rustling, scraping, squeaking sound. Rats.

"Oh, gross," I breathe, shaking my head. Maggie, however, is inconsolable.

"I hate rats. Oh god, oh god. What if they crawl on us? Or bite us? They carry rabies and other diseases, you know. And oh my god, if there are rats there are probably cockroaches, too," she rambles, trembling as her voice gets higher and higher.

"It's okay, it's okay. They won't mess with us, I'm sure," I tell her quickly. But I pull my legs in close just in case, trying to minimize the space I take up. I just wish we could see something, anything at all. But it's so dark.

Even with my eyes trying to adjust to the lack of light, I still can't even make out shapes in the darkness. As cold and smelly as it is here, my mind starts going crazy trying to figure out where we could be. Maybe we're underground? The atmosphere and total lack of light seems impossible for a house or building above ground. We've got to be subterranean.

"What is this place?" Maggie whimpers. I can feel her tears dampening my arms.

"I —I think we might be underground or something," I answer. She shivers, her shoulders shaking with sobs. "Listen, we're gonna figure this out, okay? I promise everything is gonna be alright. Do you have your phone or anything, or did they take it? I think they took mine."

She shakes her head. "No, no, they have everything. I've just been lying here in the dark. I didn't even know you were down here until you made a sound. I thought I was alone."

"Well, let's be grateful they didn't separate us."

"Yet," she adds ominously.

"Hey, don't talk like that. Let's see, what do you remember about how we got here? About last night?" I press, trying to take a more proactive stance.

I can feel Maggie shrug. "Not much. I remember… being in the cab and getting to that bar in the eleventh arrondissement. With the graffiti."

"Zero Zero, yeah," I agree, the memories trickling back to us both.

"Oh god, Liv. This is all my fault. I'm the one who made us go there. You just wanted to go back to the flat like a good girl and I — I got us into this mess.

I'm so stupid," she cries, sitting up by herself. I can feel her withdrawing into a tight ball, rocking back and forth slightly.

"No, I could have stopped us. I wanted to go, too," I lie, trying to assuage her guilt. It's true that I didn't really want to go to the bar. I'd had my suspicions before we even arrived on Rue Amelot last night, but I ignored the warning bells in my head and went along anyway. And besides, I'm the one who was gullible enough to get involved with a guy like Will. So the guilt is equally shared between Maggie and me. We're both to blame.

"I'm so sorry, Liv," she weeps. "What if they kill us?"

"Stop! Don't say things like that. You don't know what they're doing or what they're planning, but you can't just keep assuming the worst. You'll fall apart if you give in to that kind of thinking, Maggie," I protest, reaching out to pat her shoulder. She flinches at my touch.

"My parents were right. I can't handle the real world on my own. My first time striking out by myself and *this* happens," she whimpers, clearly too distraught to heed my advice.

"Well, what about me? My parents trusted me enough to let me go off to another country on my own and I allow something awful to happen! But it's not our fault, okay? These guys… they clearly know what they're doing. I don't think this is their first rodeo. In fact," I continue, realizing the truth of my words with a painful jolt as they come out of my mouth, "I bet that Will started hunting me the second I walked onto that plane. How was I to know he was a bad guy? And how were you to know a get-together at a public bar would end up this way?"

"My parents always told me there were bad people in the world," Maggie goes on, heedless of my words. "They always warned me to stay within the lines and follow the rules. Don't do anything stupid. And here I am! God, if I ever get out of this, I'll never disobey my parents again."

I want to reassure her, remind her that even though we might have screwed up this time, her parents aren't totally faultless, either. I know that if they hadn't kept such a tight, restrictive leash on Maggie her whole life, she probably wouldn't have felt the need to rebel in the first place. I saw it all the time with sheltered kids: the more closed-off and limited their upbringing was, the more outrageous their rebellion was. It was like pulling back a sling-shot. The farther you try to reel it back, the farther the stone will fly once it's released.

I know I'm a victim, too. It wasn't until arriving in France that I realized just how bored and starved for new experiences I was after a lifetime in rural North Carolina. As soon as I set foot on that plane, I was itching for an adventure. And by god, I got it.

"Maggie, listen to me. We're gonna get out of this,

somehow —" I start, but my sentence is interrupted by the sudden deep, low creak of door hinges somewhere out in the darkness. Maggie squeals and falls into me again, grasping for my hands in terror.

We both blink uncomfortably in the dim pillar of light widening before us as a door swings slowly open to reveal the massive, hulking silhouette of a man.

I pull up to the student living quarters and head up the stairs. There are a few residents hovering around, and I get a few peculiar looks as I make my way towards the room Liv and Maggie were assigned.

I have to admit, the student housing is pretty nice, as far as student housing can go. The area is somewhat secluded by Parisian standards, mostly in hopes of giving the students and athletes the chance to lead a somewhat adult lifestyle rather than tossing them to the wolves, so to speak. The gardens of the park nearby are well-maintained, and the sidewalks leading around the buildings are spotless. More interestingly, there's nothing around indicative of a wild party last night.

The girls have a place on the sixth floor, and I march up the staircase, my eyes flitting out to the city skyline, the sun lighting the whole sea of buildings up like a glittering sea of color. I try to put myself into the perspective of a foreigner experiencing this place for the first time, but I've been here far too long to relive such things.

Reaching the door, I raise a fist and pound on it several times. I say nothing as to not reveal myself on the off-chance they truly are dodging class, but as I turn my head to listen, I hear nothing — no shuffling, no hushed whispers, and no groggy moans of a hangover. Strange.

My fist pounds on the door again, but the whole floor is silent. All of this particular building's residents are back at the class I left in the care of my associate. I realize it's possible the two of them could be out enjoying the city in the morning, but to alienate themselves from everyone else in their class so early?

Something sits very ill with me, and I run a hand through my short, dark hair and down to my stubble-ridden face as I check the stairs to make sure nobody is coming. What's running through my mind could get me fired easily. But I have a gut feeling, and it isn't a pleasant one I can easily ignore.

I feel around in my pocket, and my fingers brush against a large paperclip I kept from some papers I'd been working on earlier this morning. Drawing it out and keeping it low, I use my fingers to subtly pry it open into a shape I can work with. I quickly draw my jingling keys out of my other pocket to make it look like I have a legitimate means of accessing the door before stepping forward and moving both to the lock, slipping the paperclip into the keyhole and carefully twisting it and turning it before I hear the lock click in short order, and I pop the door open, slipping inside before swiftly shutting it behind me.

A quick survey of the room tells me that my suspicions were correct — the apartment is empty. Americans are notorious for finding European living quarters cramped, the walls thin, and someone inside would have been stirred by my knocking and entry.

But it strikes me how little the apartment looks lived in. The place is virtually spotless, something I never would have expected from the equivalent of college freshmen in their first time away from home. The only sign I see of someone having moved in at all is a Kindle plugged into a charger by the wall outlet, a little current converter awkwardly bulging from the end. By now, I'd expect to see clothes strewn about haphazardly, boxes of leftovers about the tables, and maybe a few wine bottles in the garbage, but the place looks impeccably tidy.

I take a few more strides around the room, inspecting the place for any signs of what might have happened. It's clear that they've at least entered the apartment, but for such tidy people to have abandoned the first day of class makes me even more suspicious as to what might have happened. With no further hesitation, I take a few steps into the girls' shared room.

Here, it's almost as bare as the living room, but there are more signs of life. The beds are newly made, and the suitcases are hardly unpacked. I glance between the two beds and raise an eyebrow with a soft smile. One of the beds surrounded with suitcases, each one laden with clothes to the point of bursting, and I can spot designer outfits in the open suitcase, along with a number of other personal affects that betray wealth. The other bed bears a lone suitcase with a few store-brand outfits stuffed neatly inside. Having recruited the girls personally, it's plain as day as to which belonged to whom.

I can't help but feel a little sympathy for Liv. Her frugal belongings remind me of my own upbringing back in Russia. It was harsh, harsher than anything I'd ever wish on the likes of any of the girls here, and far more frugal. I was never given the kind of opportunity I'm able to give the girls now. But for people like Liv, I can only imagine how overwhelming and inspiring this kind of chance must be. I almost chuckle to think back on the harsh winters of my homeland, my one good friend and I getting an offer to be whisked away from the frigid and desolate Siberian tundras to the city of lights and magic that is Paris — to get a university education, of all things. We probably would have turned it down, knowing us. We were too concerned with scrounging for food and not freezing to death each week to bother thinking about the kinds of luxuries France enjoys.

I can't help but see something of myself in Liv. Her little American hometown with probably fewer citizens than this university has gymnastics students didn't know wealth of any sort. It might not have been the crushing poverty I knew, but it was not a life of ease by any measure. I want to see her succeed. And I know talent when I see it.

And that makes me all the more sure something is amiss here.

I spot a laptop open on Liv's bed, and I turn it towards me, brushing my fingers over the touchpad to wake it up. The screen lights up, and I narrow my eyes to look at the email notification in the corner, pulling up the newest one that's already been read.

It takes me a moment to realize what I'm looking at, but realization dawns shortly, and my eyes widen.

"A party," I mutter out loud, my brow furrowing. The email I read doesn't sit well with me in the least. So the girls did indeed go out for a night on the town last night. Ordinarily, that would simply mean that they might be sleeping off a hangover this morning, and that they'd stumble into the gym later on, but as I straighten up and look around the apartment once more, the events piece together.

*The girls get to the apartment, they set their things down, start to unpack, and then this email comes in around the time they'd be getting settled. A couple of young foreigners might be easily enticed by the idea of a party with some Parisians...but who's this inviting her? What kind of man digs up a young woman's email address from a roster like that?*

Then again, I think to myself, what kind of man breaks into his students' apartment on a hunch? But my motives have some purpose behind them. She doesn't seem to know the sender of the email well, though.

I start to run a hand through my hair, thinking twice about my actions. Perhaps I truly am overreacting. It's perfectly natural and fairly frequent for young people, particularly these college types, to flirt and hook up with one another right off the plane, as it were. Liv probably met this man and decided to really start enjoying herself for her first night in Paris. Can I really blame her for that?

Of course not, but some things simply don't fit here. Suppose Liv really is waking up beside her new French lover in his cramped apartment — why is her roommate not around either? They must have been watching each other, so why would they have not helped each other home? And the email I see before me suggests that Will was the one making the advances when they met, and he was apologizing. He stepped over the boundaries and Olivia seemed to have rejected his advances. So unless something changed at the bar, what are the odds that she'd have gone home with him after turning down his kiss?

But all I have to go by is this email address and the name of the bar, I realize as I curse under my breath. There's nothing definitive here. But the evidence is deeply concerning: however I rationalize it, two young American girls went to a party their first night in Paris and did not come back home. I think back to my past, to everything I saw back in Russia. Even what I saw when I headed west. I grimace. Even in the best cases, that doesn't look good.

Then my heart sinks. I feel a burning drive to dig deeper into this matter, but as I glance back at the little email address on Liv's computer, I realize that I don't have the expertise to follow the rabbit hole further. On my own, the trail stops here, my lack of technical know-how finally catching up to me.

Anger swells within me. Two young women go missing, and what can I do? Sit in their apartment and strut around furiously while the trail gets colder because I don't know how to maneuver the back-doors of internet and computer systems. I've never taken kindly to my rustic background holding me back, an icy chain digging into my flesh no matter how hard I fight against it.

Perhaps that's overly dramatic; in truth, I *really* don't want to reach out to the one man who I know could open those encrypted doors for me.

I pull out my phone as I walk back into the living room, grimacing at the screen as I flick through my contacts to the name I have on my mind. A few times, I think again, putting the phone away and going back to the laptop myself, trying to trace it through a few simple searches and going through the university's database. Nothing.

A low groan escapes me, and I want to punch a wall as I draw the phone out yet again, staring at the contact on the screen before taking a deep breath.

One push of a button later, I put the phone to my ear and listen to it ring.

We cling together in the darkness, barely daring to breathe. I can feel Maggie's fingernails digging into my arms, her thin body trembling with fear. A lump forms in my throat but I can't bear to even swallow, I feel so frozen with terror. A beam of sickly light floods through the open doorway, blocked in part by the hulking mass of a man. He looks like a shadow creature, some kind of monstrous Minotaur come to feast on us, the unwilling sacrifices. My mind runs wild with horrifying scenarios of what he might do to us.

He's too big and bulky to be Will, and I don't remember anyone from the party at the bar looking like this guy. In fact, once he takes a few steps closer and turns his face slightly to one side, I have to stifle a gasp of horror.

His face is deformed, or perhaps just badly scarred. He looks like he might be a burn victim — and a bad one at that. Maggie whimpers, shaking in my arms. The man turns back to face us, and even in the darkness I can feel his eyes boring into me. I tighten my hold on Maggie, pulling her closer, as the scarred man begins his slow walk toward us in the dark. His footsteps are heavy and lumbering, slightly uneven as to indicate a limp. I wonder what could have happened to him to make him look this way. Who hurt him?

And is he going to hurt us?

I almost wish he would say something, anything at all, to break the cold silence over the room. In the faint light trickling in from the doorway, I can finally make out where we are, to some extent. Through the open door I can see a set of steep, moldy-looking stairs leading up, hinting that we are underground here, as I suspected. The room we're in is fairly large, but it's partitioned off into several sections with floor-to-ceiling chain link fencing. The floor is made of filthy concrete, and my stomach churns at the sight of more than a few large stains that look like they might just be made of blood. What happened here? What's going to happen to us?

The scarred man stops short in front of the fence separating our particular enclosure, his two meaty hands coming up to rattle the metal links, causing a horrible racket. Maggie yelps and begins to sob as the man's disfigured face cracks into a wide, malicious grin. He reaches up. There's a clicking sound as he pulls a string hanging from the ceiling and a single lightbulb illuminates the room. Maggie closes her eyes tightly and burrows into my arms.

I immediately survey the whole room, blinking in the sudden painful light. Yes, I conclude darkly, those stains across the floor are a blackish-red in hue. Definitely blood. And the man in front of us looks even more terrifying in the light, with his rippled, cracked skin, black eyes, and devilish grin. He had to have walked through fire to land a face like that. Some part of me wonders if he encountered that fire in hell.

Flameface walks along the length of the fence, shaking it violently, sometimes punching it, all the while smirking at us with his crooked, yellowed teeth. Then he stops suddenly, staring at us, standing totally still. He waits a long moment, and then reels back and slams his fist into the fence, making the whole enclosure shake and rattle. Maggie lets out a startled shriek and Flameface bursts into cruel laughter, cackling like a madman.

"Ooh, didn't mean to scare you," he growls in a heavy accent. "*Ozornoy devushki!* Are you ready for your *nakazaniye?*"

"P-please leave us alone," I stammer, struggling to make my voice sound clear and strong in spite of my overwhelming fear. I don't want him to see how frightened I am. I don't want to let him win so easily. If I'm going to die here, I'm going to die with dignity.

He chuckles and tilts his head to the side. "Oh, she speaks! How are you feeling, *malyutka*? Did you sleep well? We gave you our best milk and honey to help you rest."

"Please don't hurt us," Maggie sniffles, her voice barely audible with her face buried in my arms. Flameface clucks his tongue in mock pity.

"Hurt you? Nooo! Well, perhaps a little. But not to worry. I know how to twist and bend a little stick without breaking her for the next man. I'll only loosen you up, make you limber. You *are* gymnasts, after all, no? Just think of me as your *uchitel* — your coach," he sneers, shrugging as though it's the most innocuous statement in the world. Maggie's sobs wrack her entire body and I bite the inside of my cheek to keep my own tears in check.

I refuse to let this beast of a man see me cry.

"What do you want from us?" I ask, holding my head high.

Flameface lets out a long, low hiss of pleasure at my question.

"What do you have to offer?" he propositions, leaning against the fence. He leers at me through the links, his pitch-black eyes sizing me up.

"For you, nothing," I reply scathingly, surprised at my own bravery.

He turns quickly and grasps the fence, his thick fingers poking through the links as he gives me an angry, threatening glare. He bares his teeth like a wild animal, like a rabid dog.

"You've got a nasty tongue on you, *malyshka*," he snarls. "But I can temper your tongue along with the rest of you. And I need no offer in place to take what I desire."

My throat goes dry at this threat. I've never been in a situation like this before. I've never been so close to true danger. But I cannot let myself simply melt and fall to pieces like Maggie has — one of us has to stay strong. If I can only keep him distracted for as long as possible…

I've got to play his filthy game to stay alive.

"What would you do to tame me?" I ask, playing off his sadistic dirty talk. I feel disgusting for even engaging with him at all, but I can tell that provoking and angering him will only make him crueler toward us. If it were just me, I might try to deny him until the last possible moment, but with Maggie here I need to stay as close to his good side as I can. Even if it means resorting to flirtation with this hideous cretin.

Flameface has stopped in his tracks, reviewing me with a new, interested gaze. He's surprised by my words, obviously, not accustomed to anyone playing along. I assume he's used to more unwilling participants, and my upfront statement has put him off his usual game.

"Well, well, well. I did not expect such filthy talk from such a pure specimen. You dare to ask me what I would do to you? I wonder if you can even imagine," he hisses, his hand reaching down to squeeze his crotch. I try not to grimace.

"T-tell me," I continue. "I — I want to know."

Flameface grins, his jagged teeth glistening in the low light. "I'm not much for pretty words, *malyshka*, but I will gladly show you what I have to offer."

He steps forward and starts to fumble with the combination lock hanging on the gate. My heart races as I realize that I've probably only made things worse. My plan backfired. Instead of stalling his advances with talk, I've only stoked his filthy fire. I grab hold of Maggie and the two of us scoot backward, as far away from the fence as possible, until we're backed against a slimy, cold wall. Flameface opens the gate and strolls into our enclosure, his brutish frame blocking the exit as he reaches into the front of his stained pants.

He walks closer to us and gestures for me to get up, but I shake my head and press myself more firmly against the back wall. Maggie cowers beside me, not even daring to look up.

"Stand up, *shlyukha*," he orders, snapping his fingers.

"No," I murmur, shaking my head vigorously and

clinging to Maggie. My stomach turns in painful knots as I anticipate the blow to come.

"Ah, that's not how it works. You see, I make the orders, and you carry them out. You don't get to say no to me, little *suka*," Flameface barks. As he comes closer I can see every ridge of his disfigured face, every shining streak of barely-healed flesh. "Now, get up!"

I stagger to my feet, standing in front of Maggie in a protective stance, my arms outstretched. Flameface gives me a quizzical glare, then a devilish look comes across his ugly features as a different idea occurs to him.

"You're too easy, aren't you?" he says to me, standing with his hands on his hips.

"Please, just don't hurt my friend," I implore. Maggie is weeping inconsolably on the floor behind me, totally dissociated from the world around her.

Flameface cackles. "You know, I'm pretty hungry. I think I'm in the mood for something a little bigger than you. Your *sestra* here looks to be a little taller, isn't she?"

"No! Leave her alone!" I shout, shielding Maggie with my body as Flameface strides over to us. "Take me! Don't touch her!"

The scarred man gives me an almost pitying look. "Don't worry, *malyshka*. I'll save plenty of room for you next. There's enough of me to go around.

Besides, I think your friend needs a little loosening up, don't you agree?"

"No, please!" I cry out, but Flameface shoves right past me, flinging me out of the way so that I slam into the chain-link fence, hard. I slump to the concrete floor in a sickening daze, unable to get up in time to stop Flameface from yanking Maggie up by her arm. She screams in fear and hangs almost limply from his grasp, tears coursing down her splotchy cheeks.

"*Da*, this is what I was looking for," Flameface croons.

Suddenly, there are footsteps approaching, not as heavy as the first set, but faster. A slightly shorter and much more slender frame appears in the doorway, and Will steps through into the dank room. "Drop her, Boris!" he commands.

Flameface spins around and glares at Will, then gives him a plaintive expression. "I wasn't going to damage the merchandise, *nachalnik*. Just having a little fun."

"Back off," Will says, emphasizing each word intensely. With a sigh, Flameface lets go of Maggie's arm and swivels around to await his next order. Maggie collapses to the floor in a sobbing heap. I want to run to Will and scratch his eyes out, pummel him until he's black and blue, funnel my rage and betrayal into a savage attack against the evil, handsome man who trapped us here.

"*Bonjour*, Olivia," Will greets me, mockingly. "Good to see you. You overslept a little, though. Looks like you're going to miss your first lesson."

Flameface chuckles grimly, folding his arms over his chest.

"Why are you doing this to me?" I demand, my voice catching ever so slightly. Will notices the weakness.

"Oh, what a pity. You trusted me, didn't you? You know, I thought I'd lost you forever when you denied me that kiss. But then, lo and behold, you gave me another chance. Everybody deserves a second chance, don't they? Even me," he says, beaming at me.

"What did I do to you?" I ask shrilly, getting back to my feet. "Why me?"

"Well, there are a lot of reasons for that! First of all, you're very cute. And bendy. A gymnast? My clients will love that. *Deuxièmement*, you were very convenient, weren't you? Just sat down right next to me on that plane! Why, fate nearly landed you right in my lap. I couldn't have asked for an easier catch," he concludes with a shrug.

"What do you want with Maggie, then? Let her go. You can take me instead," I bargain.

Will and Boris both laugh. "That's very noble of you," Will begins, "but I wouldn't dare turn down a two-for-one deal. Not when I've already got a prospective buyer for your friend here. Innocent little rich girl? She was a fast sell, *bien sûr*."

"A… a buyer?" I repeat, feeling my veins run cold. What kind of business is this?

"Oh, yes. But don't feel left out. I'm sure we'll have a client interested in you before long. Especially once we, ah, tone you down a little bit. You've got just enough fire in you to make for a lousy product," he explains matter-of-factly.

"I am not a product, and neither is Maggie. We're human beings. Let us go!" I protest.

Will just rolls his beautiful blue eyes. "You can drop the martyr act anytime now, Olivia. If you haven't caught on yet, I'll assure you there's no escape. You belong to me now, until we find a suitable match for you."

He looks at Boris and gives him a quick nod. "Take the bigger one."

"No!" I shout, flinging myself in front of Maggie. But Boris easily peels me off of her and tosses me aside again, my knees skidding painfully across the rough floor as I fall. "Maggie! Maggie! It's okay, be strong! I won't give up on you! I promise everything will be okay!" I call out after her as Boris throws her over his shoulder and carries her off. She's weeping and reaching for me in vain, too frightened and in shock to even utter a word. The pair of them disappear through the doorway as Boris carries her up the stairs and away from me.

Leaving me alone in this holding cell with Will.

My terror twists and darkens into rage, and without even thinking about it I run full-force toward the gate of the enclosure, where he stands. I let out a frustrated scream as he calmly clicks the lock shut again, closing me off.

"You're a feisty one, aren't you, *petite fille?*" he whispers, leaning close so that his ice-blue eyes and pointed nose are mere centimeters from my face on the other side of the chain-link fence. "I'll break you of that."

I spit directly into his face. He blinks once, then wipes his face with a smirk.

"*Oui*, I've got special plans for you, Olivia," he growls. Then he turns on his heel and strides out of the room, turning off the light as he goes.

I sink to the floor, clinging to the cold metal gate, utterly alone.

Navigating the congested streets of Paris in the middle of the day is hard enough on the best of days. The grating voice of the man to my right makes it even less bearable than usual.

"Did they really not teach you any of this kind of tracking in Russia? Or whatever Russia-school you went to? This kind of stuff is, like, freshman-level kind of tracking," my tech-savvy friend says with a laugh as he scrolls through the blinking map that's pulled up on his laptop.

Felix Meunier is a name I wish I would never have to call upon again when it came to matters related to work, but he's one of the most talented computer specialists in the university, and more importantly, he's never been afraid to get his hands dirty. *Most* importantly, he owes me a favor.

If only it weren't for his insufferable personality.

I met Felix when he came to me shortly after getting my post at the university. Just like he is now, he was working then as one of the IT staff members who ensured the sprawling enclave of bureaucracy that was the University of Paris kept running smoothly. But apparently, Felix had been involved in some shady dealings with the criminal underworld of Paris. He was the kind of white-collar criminal who thought he could skim money from the university while playing the same game with some of the offshore accounts the local mob who had ties to the university.

Inevitably, he got himself into hot water, both the French police and the mobsters he'd managed to offend breathing hard down his neck from all angles. He came to me looking for help.

To this day, I don't know why he reached out to me specifically, but I suspect he did some digging into my background and thought I'd be the kind of person he'd want to have his back in a situation like his. The assumption was correct, but I only agreed to help him reluctantly, covering his trail and burning old bridges that might have tied him to his crimes. He was beyond grateful.

And despite my best efforts, I haven't been able to shake the little man since, so I suppose we could be called 'friends.'

"They did not teach us...'your expertise' in Spetsnaz training," I answer, trying desperately not to say *"they didn't teach us how to be nerds."*

"Right, right," he muses, his fingers flicking the screen back to his voluminous spreadsheets through which he's been inputting data that's been assembling the GPS signal we're tracking now, "have to keep all the training on killing enemy spies, climbing up sheer cliffs, wrestling bears with your bare hands, that kind of thing, right?"

"We were taught to track," I say, no smile on my face, "but we needed no such technology to hound our targets down like animals." He stares at me a moment before giving his head a light shake and turning back to his computer. I smile quietly to myself; it was helpful to recount the details of my past to keep the fear of god in men like Felix.

"Anyway, like I was saying: the email address you have was sent from a computer that was hooked up to the internet, just like any email, so that means it's got a server associated with it."

I've already stopped paying attention, but I nod.

"So I can trace that server and bounce a signal off it and figure out where it's coming from, kind of like echolocation, but with internet signals. Does that make sense?"

"Of course," I lie absently.

"It doesn't look like this person was using any sophisticated technique," he adds with a scoff, "even the most basically tech-savvy users who do so much as illegally download a movie will use something that masks your IP address at least, or maybe a program that can bounce signals around to confuse people like me who might want to track 'em, but it looks like your guy was just sending an email from a building, plain as day. I could pull up the email here if I wanted."

"Mmhmm," I say with a nod, pretending to be following along.

"Basically, I mean he's not trying to pull any tricks in keeping me from being able to figure out where your Liv's cell phone is, from what I can tell," he goes on. "Between triangulating the location of her phone, provided it's still on, and figuring out where this Will guy is sending his emails from, this is child's play. You sure this guy is doing something shady? Take a left at this light."

"Not everyone is as skilled as you, Felix," I say candidly, and Felix rolls his eyes as we take yet another turn down the winding streets. What I meant was that plenty of criminals did just fine without the help of technology, and even so, some-times a light touch did the trick just fine. That, and his question made me uncomfortable — because no, I was not sure.

"Anyway, I triangulated the signal, and I've just about —*voila*! Got an address for you."

"No dramatic pauses," I say with an arched brow.

"56 Rue Alfred de Vigny in the Parc Monceau

area," he says, and I feel my mouth grow cold at the name of the address. It's a respectable area of Paris, to be sure, but that makes the significance of that address no less familiar and dangerous.

"Uh...Max?" he asks, tilting his head and pushing his thick-rimmed glasses up his nose. "You alright? You look a little tense," he says as he eyes my tightening knuckles on the steering wheel.

"No, Felix," I say slowly, taking a breath and resisting the urge to carve a path of destruction through traffic to reach our destination faster. "I'm afraid this little excursion of ours is about to get complicated."

We speed towards the Parc Monceau, tires screeching as I take sharp turns, and Felix grips the safety handle of the car, trying to keep his computer steady. "What's the big deal? You've got your missing students, they're probably doing drugs with some locals in a fancy apartment or something."

"I recognize that address," I say, my voice tense with the anger I'm holding back. "Felix, you did some digging on my past, didn't you?"

The question throws him off, and he stammers a few syllables before I cut him off.

"You know some of my background, I have no doubt. You'll also know a thing or two about the Russian mob's activity in Paris, I'm certain. What you may not know is that this address is where the

Bratva established a base of operations to run their human trafficking ring here in France."

Felix paled as we turned onto Rue Alfred de Vigny, and he licked his lips nervously. "B-but that's impossible," he stammers, "the Russian mob hasn't had a sex slave ring in Paris for years — I mean, I keep an ear out for this kind of thing, just for safety's sake and all." He looks uneasy, but I don't bother casting him a glare. I know I'm not the only person Felix has been helping from among the Parisian underworld's denizens. He's a pencil-neck and a coward, but he's not a particularly predictable man, and he knows his skills are valuable to those willing to pay the right price. Despite his close calls with death in the past.

"Police databases have some kind of files on every ring that's active in Paris, and they've got agents deep undercover, but there's nothing on a Bratva slave ring based out of Paris. I'm sure they've been inactive here for ages." He pulls up a few more spreadsheets, scrolling through them while chewing his lip. "Right, see here, it says there was some kind of internal coup that ended the trafficking activity from within a few years ago. The slave ring's ended, Max."

"You're right," I say as we pull up at that old, familiar building, and I gaze up at the faded stone. "Because I'm the one who ended it."

I turn off the car and step out, Felix fumbling to

put his laptop away as he unbuckles his seatbelt and staggers out of the car, now casting nervous glances up at the building before us. The sky is overcast, gray clouds rolling overhead very quickly as wind blows above us. Felix follows me to the back of the car, where I pop the trunk.

"Well," Felix says, wringing his hands, "okay, so if we know she's here, and you think...well, what you think, then shouldn't we call the police and have them investi-"

"No," I snap, whirling around to look the man in the eye, my expression stony. "Felix, these girls are my responsibility — *mine*. It was me who took them from the comfort of their hometowns to come train in Paris. It was me who offered them everything when they never thought they'd get the chance to glimpse this thorny flower of a city. It was me in whom they put all their trust to guide them as they tried to make their homes here for the next few years. And it was me who saw the unbridled potential in them to be something *more* than they or their parents or their old teachers ever could have begun to imagine," I say, and I mean every word of it.

Felix looks hesitant, but nods slowly as he watches the determination burn bright in my eyes. "You must have a lot of respect for these girls."

"Far more than they know," I say, looking at the ominous doors of the apartment building. "I was harsh on them. I had to be. But there's something special about them that I want to see realized." *About Liv*, I want to add especially, but every one of them has untapped passion. "But that's not the only reason this is my battle to fight," I say as I reach into the trunk and move a panel aside, revealing a false bottom.

"I thought I'd put a permanent end to the Bratva's human trafficking days."

Felix's eyes widen as I pull a couple of silenced pistols out of the trunk's false bottom, followed by a set of knives I start strapping to my legs. "I thought that part of my life was gone entirely. If I was mistaken..."

I take out some ammunition and load up the pistols, strapping a pair of spares to my waist under my jacket as Felix looks around the empty street nervously.

"Then things are going to get ugly," I finish, loading my pistols. "These Russians are Bratva. They're ruthless, they're dedicated, and they have no qualms delving into the deepest depravities imaginable to man. If the girls are in their possession, they won't give them up without a fight, and they're every bit as vicious as the next mobster. These are men from my past, Felix," I say in a low tone, looking him dead in the eye.

"You can't be serious, Max," he breathes. I give him a silent look that tells him that I am every bit as serious as the weapons on my person are deadly. He swallows.

"Take the car back to my place, Felix," I say, "then get a cab. I'll pay you back. You've done me a service today. I won't forget this."

"No way," he says, stepping forward, "Max, this is too much. Okay, so yeah, I looked up the whole story on you. The orphanage in Yakutsk, the stint in the Russian Special Forces, the covert operations you did, the retirement to the Bratva here in France, I know it all. I know you've been involved with these guys before."

"Then you know that I know my enemy," I say calmly.

"I know that for all you know, the guys in there are a whole different breed of killers. They're slavers, Max, and if they're starting up again after you shut them down last time, they'll be expecting a visit from you. I don't need my spreadsheets and statistics to tell me that, but you sure sound like you need to hear the statistics on your chances of survival if you're thinking of going in there guns blazing with no plan!"

"The men in there are the reason I divorced myself from the Bratva," I say. "For them to start up again is a mockery of everything I did to earn my retirement... Do you think I made my career on helping white-collar criminals dodge the law?"

I smile a cold smile that sends a visible chill down

Felix's spine. I was more than just a killer. I was a hitman. One of the most feared hitmen in all of Paris. And to let the monstrous wretches in that building live would be an insult to everything I stood for.

Felix keeps an eye on me for some time before asking, "So there's no convincing you. What if I don't hear back from you?"

"If you think that's a possibility," I say over my shoulder as I make my way up the steps toward the apartment front doors, "then you don't know me very well, my friend."

I hear Felix starting the car behind me as I ready the pistol in my hand, put the other hand on the door handle, and push.

LIV

*I* don't know how long I've been sitting here in the dark. It could have been minutes… or hours. It feels like months. I have no idea what time it is or where my grisly prison is located. In my head, without any physical distractions to stimulate my thoughts, I start to go a little crazy. My theories range from the relatively benign to the outlandishly catastrophic.

Maybe this is all an elaborate prank! I'm just in the basement of some building on campus, not far from home. It's just part of a hazing ritual performed by the members of the gymnastics program or something. Any minute now, one of my coaches will pop out and tell me it's all over — I passed.

Or then again… I don't know how much time passed while I was knocked out. I could be halfway across the continent, in some Bulgarian holding cell.

Will talked about somebody buying Maggie. What if this really is a sex trafficking ring or something? I watched a documentary once, curled up in my blankets at home in Toast. It had seemed like something that couldn't possibly happen in my world. It was a far-away thing that happened to far-away people, not me.

But maybe, just maybe, that nightmarish world is colliding with mine.

And I'm caught in the intersection of two very different dimensions: the safe, cocoon-like shelter of my past, and the shadowy film noir of my imminent future. And where am I now? In limbo? The static place in between?

At this point, the loneliness of my predicament is digging in at me, tugging at the strings of my already-strained sense of sanity. There's not a single sound, hinting to me that I'm either so far underground that sound can't travel down here or that my little prison is sound-proof. Either way, I'm dying for any hint of humanity out there, even if it's sinister in nature. Although I hate him with every fiber of my being, I wish Will would return, if only to remind me that other human beings still exist out there somewhere. Because down here in the dark, it really feels like I could be all alone in the world and I would never know the difference.

A shiver runs down my spine and I pull my legs up to my chest, wrapping my arms around my calves and resting my chin on my knees. There are goose-bumps prickling up and down my limbs. It's so cold down here, especially now that I'm alone. I didn't realize how comforting it was to have Maggie curled up with me until she was gone. Now I long for any kind of human contact to make me feel alive again. I'm so lonely and lost and afraid.

Almost like a cruel answer to my wish, the door creaks open again and Flameface — Boris — hobbles into the room, a shaft of dull light following to cast his shadow long and tall on the concrete floor. I can't decide whether it would be better to run back and press myself against the opposing wall, as far away from him as possible, or to go to the gate in the dim hope of obtaining some human contact.

Instead, I simply stay put, curled up in my little ball.

"Feeling lonely, *malyshka*?" Boris sneers, his voice dripping with faux sympathy.

I don't respond, not even moving. He strolls to the gate and pokes his fat fingers through the links again, staring down at me with a hungry gaze. At this point, I hardly care what he says or does to me. I feel so empty and exhausted. It doesn't matter anymore.

"Oh, come. Don't be impolite. I know you've got to be dying for a friend by now. Isn't that right, *suka*?" he goes on, tapping his fingertips on the metal gate. I begrudgingly tilt my head ever so slightly upward to look at him and he grins.

"You know… I could be your friend," he growls lecherously. "We still have time before the team arrives to stand guard here. I could make you feel things you've never even imagined. The man who buys you won't know the difference if I punch the card first. And besides, if Will won't use up his finder's fee… I won't let it go to waste. They don't pay me enough. What's a man to do? Got to get my fair *stoimost* somehow — whether in money or flesh."

"Leave me alone," I murmur weakly, but at this point I hardly care anymore. Some man is going to buy me and run me into the ground. I get it now. This is exactly like the documentary I watched. Only I'm no longer the detached spectator; I'm the victim.

Boris chuckles and starts to pick up the combination lock to undo it. "No? I like when they fight, anyway. Adds just the right amount of spice, *vy znayete.*"

"Please," I mumble, trying to scoot back away. But my body is so tired from trembling and sitting still in the cold. It's as though the despair my mind is feeling has transferred to my body and now it's given up on me. Boris pops the combination lock open and reaches to pull the gate, but before he can finish, there is the sound of several sets of heavy footsteps approaching. He swears under his breath and quickly shuts and locks the gate again.

"Another time, then," he hisses to me as he turns around to stand up straight and face the team of burly men walking in. They all wear identical grave, empty expressions and plain black clothing. There are four of them, all staring straight ahead. One of them steps forward and nods to Boris.

"Egor, Bogdan, go up to guard the entrance," he barks in a heavy Russian accent. "Boris and Josef, you will stay in this room with me. *Nachalnik* has concerns over this one."

It takes me a second to realize I'm the "one" he's talking about.

"Special plans, *da*," Boris agrees, and there's a gruff indignation in his tone.

The speaker of the guard team nods and commands, "Assume positions."

Two of the men, presumably Bogdan and Egor, walk out and march up the stairs. Boris and Josef station themselves directly in front of the gate to my enclosure and the guard leader stands by the door.

"*Svet*," he says gruffly. Boris reaches up and pulls the light cord and the leader shuts the door, leaving the four of us in the dim cell.

"What's going to happen to me?" I can't help but ask.

Boris chuckles and the other two don't respond in any way.

"Please, just tell me," I beg, feeling the tears threatening to break free.

"*Tishina*," the leader hisses.

"Good things come to those who wait," laughs Boris darkly.

"What did I do wrong? Why is this happening to me? Where is Maggie?" I ask, all my questions bubbling forth in a fount of uncontrollable emotion. It's hitting me just how desperate my situation is. This isn't a hazing ritual. This isn't a joke. These guys are serious, and I can't take it quietly anymore. I'm unraveling.

"*Bud spokoyen!*" shouts the leader. "I have no patience for the buzzing of little flies in my ear. Now is not the time for questions."

"Please, just let me go. I'm sorry," I mumble, tears spilling down my cheeks.

"She is not very obedient," remarks Josef.

"I offered to break her in," Boris replies, shrugging.

"The *suka* could definitely use some discipline," Josef continues, turning to glare at me over his broad shoulder. "Maybe a team effort would suffice."

Boris straightened his shoulders and puffed out his chest in a show of indignation. "*Chert*, Josef, I am not a team player. I prefer solo acts."

"Everyone, shut up!" the leader growls, and the other two fall into sullen silence.

For a while, I sit there just quietly crying, and none of them even give me so much as a glance. I wonder how many times they've done this: imprisoned a girl and held her captive underground in this wretched cell. How many tears have stained this cold, filthy floor? And where are they now? What is the life expectancy of a girl in my predicament? Something tells me it's not a very long sentence to carry out. And in a very dark, morbid way, I think that might be a godsend.

Distantly, we hear a soft thud and all three of my guards tense up. They exchange mildly concerned expressions. I strain my ears to listen for more signs of activity elsewhere, outside of this dank little box. I don't know whether to anticipate something better or worse approaching, but either way, none of the guards seem particularly concerned.

But then suddenly the door bursts open with a loud bang — as though it were kicked down. I scream and bolt to the back of my enclosure, cowering against the back wall in terror. The guards all jump into action, running toward the door. At first, there's so much harried movement and shouting in the low light that I can't even begin to make heads or tails of what's happening out there. Then I see him — a stranger.

No... not a stranger.

A face I vaguely recognize.

The man slashes through the doorway and thrusts a large knife into the guard leader's throat, blood spurting in a grisly, almost surreal scarlet spray. I immediately feel lightheaded at the sight of so much blood, my mind swimming faintly. Boris and Josef go barreling at the attacker just as he turns to run toward the gate to my cell. He's definitely here for me — but whether his intentions are noble or dark I cannot tell. Maybe he's my savior. Or maybe he's my murderer.

"You!" howls Josef as he lunges for the strange man. But in one swift movement, the guy takes out something small and glinting in the light: a gun. He jabs the barrel into Josef's gut and pulls the trigger, a deafening crack splitting the air. Another spray of bright red blood splashed against the wall behind Josef and he sinks to the ground in a convulsing heap.

A panicked, horrified shriek escapes my lips and I have to hold back the urge to vomit. The strange man with the familiar face looks up and locks eyes with me.

I know him now.

It's Maksim Pavlenko.

MAX

Old reserves of adrenaline that have long lain dormant are pumping through my body as I watch the life eek out from the two men I've just dropped. My vision is focused on the men who could end my life just as quickly if I make a single wrong move.

The well-to-do visage of the apartment building outside had been a front. I had made my way inside, expecting to find armed men ready to take me on the moment I stepped through the doors, but there was no such welcoming party. In every way, the place had looked as honest as an actual apartment complex, and if I didn't know better, that's precisely what I might have assumed.

But the lack of security just told me they weren't expecting me. So I made my way to the one place I know they wouldn't care to tidy up for public

137

appearances — the door to the old superintendent's residence. And that's where I found the filth lying just below the surface. I had burst through the door, this time finding not an old and grouchy French super, but a room with a couple of Chechens smoking and watching television. Their hands went to their weapons the moment they'd seen me, and that was when I started to leave a trail of corpses.

I had been wrong. These weren't the same men who I'd slain all those years ago in this very building. The Chechen mafia was a different breed altogether I realize as I now lay eyes on the burned man in the room, whose eyes are wide at the familiar sight of me.

My gaze falls momentarily on Olivia, and my heart skips a beat at the sight of her unharmed and alive. We exchange a look of recognition, and I can see every bit as much relief in her eyes as there is in mine, mingled with terror from the firefight around her.

The scarred Russian in the room draws his gun and points it at me just as I whip around to train mine on him. I know the man, and I know he's smarter than the rest of him, and twice as vile.

"Max," the man, Boris, coos tauntingly, grinning a toothy grin as we hold our weapons to each other, muscles tense. "Can't you see you've come at a bad time? I was just trying to get to know this young lady a little better."

"What have you done to her?" I growl back in the Russian he speaks, about ready to pull the trigger despite the danger looking me in the eye down the barrel of a gun.

He tsks, narrowing his eyes. "Suddenly so sensitive, Max. That's not the man I remember barging into a penthouse and giving me this little makeover. It's a lot harder to get some action like this, you know," he adds with a grimace. Neither one of us is willing to move a muscle, and my heart is pounding — we won't be alone forever, and one of us will be forced to act. "But don't worry, I don't let that stop me. Those French girls you think you rescued? I caught up with them, after you thought you'd killed me." He licks his lips. "So many things they say about French women is true, you know," he croaks.

Before I have the chance to respond, the door is kicked open behind me, and I take the briefest flash of a distraction to dive out of the way just before Boris's gun fires, catching one of the two men bursting in in the leg as I hit the ground and roll.

Still on the ground as shouts in Russian and gunfire goes off all around me, I aim my pistol at the wounded man and put two bullets in his head, blood splattering on the man behind him as I roll out of the way and get to my feet.

I let the weapon fall out of my hand. It's out of bullets.

Before Boris can ready his pistol at me again, I

rise to my feet and dive for him, drawing a knife from my side as I hear Liv's shriek of alarm from my right. My body collides with his full-force, but I've caught him off-guard, and the two of us fall to the ground, struggling to grapple with each other.

Boris is strong, but I am stronger. I may have been out of the killing business these past years, but I never let myself grow weak. And nothing lets a man like me forget his killer instinct. His hands struggle to get a firm hold on my wrist as my knife wrenches around him, trying to find a suitable opening to sink into. I feel him wrapping his arm around my neck as he works his way behind me, and instinctively, I raise my knife defensively and slice his forearm.

I hear a scream of pain from him, and as we thrash, I catch a glimpse of the other mobster in the room, training his gun on us, trying to get in a good shot at me. My heart jumps in fear, not for myself, but out of fear that he might think to turn the weapon on Liv.

I know they won't do that without damn good reason. But I haven't given them cause to think I value her, and while these monsters might not see her as a living, thinking human being, they do see her as a walking paycheck, and they aren't willing to risk that without a damn good reason.

Boris's grip slackens after I slice him, but I don't let him get away from me. The moment I leave myself exposed is the moment I sign my own death warrant. Instead, I twist with him on the ground, and I feel the cold metal of his gun brush against my arm. It's still in his hand.

In an instant, I move my knife around and draw it across his hand, making him recoil and drop the firearm. When it hits the ground, to my horror, a round discharges, sending a bullet ricocheting around the room, and I catch a glimpse of Liv ducking for cover out of the corner of my eye.

Wrenching my knee free, I kick the pistol across the room and push Boris off me, using the moment of distraction to charge at the mobster in the doorway. He starts to point his gun at me as I close the distance, but I'm too fast for him. My free hand closes around his wrist with a sickening crunch, and he screams as he drops the gun to the ground, but there's no discharge this time.

Wasting no time, my knife hand plunges the blade into his throat in two quick stabs, one after the other. My hands are crimson with the blood flowing from his throat as he croaks his last, and I shove him back to choke on his own lifeblood in the stairway.

"Enough games, Max," I hear a chilling growl in accented English come from behind me, and I turn to see Boris's burned face pressed up against Liv's, his own long, wicked knife pressed against her throat as he holds her still, her eyes wide with fear.

"Boris," I say slowly, holding my knife at the

ready, "what kind of new low is this? Settle your score with me and me alone."

The scarred man tut-tuts mockingly, malevolent delight in his eyes as he toys with the blade at Liv's neck, and I see her take in a sharp breath as he puts a hand around her arm, securing her. "Those are the words of a dead man, Maxie. You've gone soft, *izmennik*." He practically spits the last word. "You've caused a bit of trouble here, but I don't think you know who you're dealing with. We're going to rebuild an empire in this city out of the ashes you left behind, and I think you'll make a fitting addition to the fertilizer. Unless you want a little American blood mingled with everything else on your hands," he says, pressing his face even closer against Liv's and letting his breath wash over her neck. "You're going to turn slowly with me, and I'm going to take her somewhere she'll be useful. You must have tracked her this far, so don't pretend you don't care about her."

My jaw clenches briefly. Boris is indeed sharper than most of the men here. "Your boss will gut you like a fish if you lay a finger on her. And even if she were worthless, I won't let you hurt my student."

"Student!" Boris laughs. "My my, a teacher? You've taken quite a career shift, my old friend. But I can't blame you," he adds, his tone getting low and raspy, "if your students are as lovely as this one."

My gaze is steely on him as Liv's body almost

visibly tenses, Boris's grip tightening just a bit on her arm and sliding up and down it. He presses his hips forward, and Liv's eyes widen at what she must be feeling from behind. My blood is boiling hot in my veins, and my muscles poise, ready to move at the slightest indication of weakness.

"This student must mean quite a lot to you for you to go through all this trouble," he says. "I wonder what the two of you get up to after class?"

My nostrils flare, but I won't dignify him with a response. At my silence, Boris tilts his head to Liv, directing his wretched, sensual mockery to her.

"Does he hold you like this at night, *dorogoy*? Maybe you even like the knife play, you little American slut. Does your teacher toy with you before he fucks you raw? Maybe if he makes it out of here alive, he'll buy you for himself, and then you'll be at his mercy all the time. You've seen what he can do to fully grown men. Just imagine what he would do to a tight little American cunt like yours...but I'm afraid I'll have to break you in before that," he says, and I see his hand start to slide around her arm down to her stomach, and I hear a sharp whimper from Liv as his fingers move down to reach into the front of her skirt.

There's a shriek from her a moment later as I fling my knife forward, sending it flying directly at the pair with deadly precision, and I watch Boris's attention snap back up to me for half an instant before my knife strikes true, sinking deep into his eye socket. Right to the hilt.

His muscles tighten for just a moment, Liv paralyzed with fear as she looks at me, and finally, Boris slumps to the ground on his back, a trail of blood and fluid streaming from where the blade had sank into his head.

The next instant, I run forward to catch Liv as she nearly crumples to the ground, sobbing, her whole body shaking in fear as I bring her into a tight hug.

"It's over," I whisper as calmly as I can bring my husky voice to pronounce clearly, "Olivia, he's dead. You're with me now."

"Oh my god," she breathes, "oh my god, they..." her eyes are fixed on the dead bodies in the room, and I realize grimly that she's never before been exposed to such violence.

"Liv, look at me," I say urgently, bringing her attention back to my eyes, trying to keep her from going into shock from everything she's seen. "Liv, are you hurt?"

"N-no," she manages, swallowing hard. "No, I'm okay. What are you doing here? How did you find me?"

The question is strange to me at first, but I remember that while she and Maggie have consumed my thoughts for the past few hours, I've surely been the farthest thing from her mind for all this time. "I'll explain later. We need to get out of here, now. Where is Maggie, is she still in the building?"

Liv thinks for a moment, trying to gather her thoughts amidst the storm of emotions she must be feeling, and she finally shakes her head. "I don't think so, no. Will, the man who led me here, he...he took her away." She clenches her eyes for just a moment, and I can tell how painful it must be to talk about this. "He said something about her already having a 'buyer.' M-Monsieur Pavlenko, is this...?"

I give her a look that gravely confirms her fears, but before I can speak to her again, the sounds of footsteps above us tells me we need to move quickly. "More coming," I say, taking out one of the spare pistols at my side and holding it up. I gently touch Liv's face, covering her eyes for a second as I aim the pistol at Boris' corpse. This time, I'm not taking a chance with him, and I put a bullet into his brain, the carnage gruesome at the close range.

"Let's move, *now*," I say, and without another moment's hesitation, I take Liv by the hand and head up the stairs, pistol at the ready. Once we're up in the main room, I rush her to one of the windows, sliding it up, my instincts kicking in to get us out of here as quickly as possible.

I can hear the Chechen backup approaching the doorway, and I glance at it briefly, considering how easy it would be to end all of their lives...but I cannot risk Liv's life again, not when we're so close to escape.

Before I can move to help her out, Liv vaults out the window into the alley behind the building. I smile, remembering that she is indeed a gymnast, after all. Just as I hear shouts from behind me, I vault out myself, and the two of us sprint down the alleyway as I stow my weapon.

"How far will they chase us?" Liv gasps as she keeps up with me while we turn another corner and I guide her through a narrow space between buildings, a few rats scurrying out of our path as we take routes I haven't had to use in years.

"Just stay close to me," I say sharply to her as I start to take her around the twisting alleyways near the building I'm all too familiar with, "and whatever you do, don't look back."

We've been walking for a while now, traipsing down the alleyways and narrow cobblestone streets of Le Marais. Historic buildings and elaborate architecture loom overhead, like aristocratic faces casting condescending glares down upon me. This place, this city, is too beautiful to house such evil. Pavlenko's large palm is pressed supportively against my back, gently steering me along and keeping me upright. I don't know how long we've been traveling, scurrying away in the soft, waning light of late afternoon. Something tells me that we're not making a straight beeline for our destination — that he's guiding us on a serpentine path intentionally to throw off any potential spies or followers. I try to put this thought far from my mind. I simply can't compute that right now, not when I'm already so overwhelmed. I'm still trying to come to terms with what happened last night and today. Trying not to think about Maggie and what horrible fate has caught up with her.

To Paris's credit, nobody even seems to notice or care how out of place we look. Granted, Pavlenko does look more the part than I do, navigating the streets with familiarity, dressed more appropriately. But I'm surprised that no one has stared at me yet — I know I must look dreadful after my night in hell. Especially since I'm wearing white, and it must show every bit of dirt on me.

Happy tourists shove past us, their children carrying fuzzy backpacks shaped like animals. Local Parisians are less enthusiastic about the surrounding scenery, as it forms the familiar backdrop to their everyday lives, and the tourists only clog up the sidewalks for the natives trying to get things done.

But we are neither tourists nor natives. For although we are headed toward what I assume is Pavlenko's apartment, I get the distinct sense that this city is not his true home. He does not belong here anymore than I do, even if his French is nearly perfect and he's found a career here. I can tell that these picturesque streets filled with laughter and light are contrary to his own nature.

There's something darker about him, something dangerous. The guns certainly lend credence to this impression. And the fact that Boris knew him. It sent a shiver down my spine. Should I even be trusting my rescuer at all?

My feet are aching by the time we reach a tall, white architectural masterpiece that looks like it could effortlessly house a king or queen. I guess it's his apartment building. Pavlenko nods to the doorman, who wordlessly lets us in. The man gratefully doesn't allow his eyes to linger on my disheveled appearance. I wonder if he knows more than he lets on, and if his training includes being discreet in the face of strange encounters. He's probably opened these doors for hundreds, maybe thousands, of people. Some of them had to have looked at least as odd as me.

We head directly to the elevator — a welcome sight, especially compared to my sixth floor walk-up. Once the sleek metal doors are shut, Pavlenko presses the button to take us to the very top floor of the building. He looks down at me with a grim, worried expression, as though he's just waiting for me to wither away right before his eyes. I hate when people think I'm fragile, but in this case… it's not an inaccurate assumption.

There's a ding and the doors slide silently open again.

"Come," he says, softly taking me by the arm to lead me down the hallway, which has glossy wood flooring and stark white walls. There are framed still life paintings and artfully sculpted sconces illuminating the hall with a friendly glow. We stop in front of an elaborately carved white door. Pavlenko unlocks it and leads me into his flat.

I am surprised to see that it doesn't vary all that sharply from my own little apartment, except that this one looks slightly more lived-in. The furnishings are simple, but upon a second glance, I can tell that the quality is much, much higher than what I have. I'm still too tired to really focus hard on my surroundings, but the black, velvety sofa Pavlenko situates me down on is soft and luxurious underneath my legs.

"You're injured," he comments, looking at my bloodied knees. I frown for a moment, not even sure how I got this way. Then I remember being flung across the room, my knees scraping on the dirty concrete floor. I'm used to slight injuries; they're a part of my life as a gymnast. Nothing to worry about. But I have to admit that my knees do look pretty grisly. Definitely worse than your garden-variety skinned knee. Still, I don't want Pavlenko to hover over me and treat me like some broken-down doll.

"It's nothing. I'm fine," I tell him, but he doesn't buy it.

"I'll get you cleaned up," he says. "Stay put."

I'm in no position to balk at any order he gives

me. After all, he did just save my life. And as soon as he walks away toward the kitchen, my stomach lurches. I realize with a jolt that I don't want to be alone. No — more than that — I cannot *bear* to be left alone right now.

"Please don't leave me," I whimper quietly, ashamed of my own weakness.

He instantly turns around, a soft and pitying look in his gray-green eyes. His jaw twitches, ever so slightly. I can tell he's struggling to contain some overbearing emotion, something pressing to overflow and take control. He comes back and kneels in front of me.

"I'll be just around the corner. You need to sit here and rest. I promise I will only take a moment," he assures me. There's not even the slightest hint of a sharp edge to his tone. Gone is the severe, uptight man who introduced himself to me at that gymnastics banquet back in North Carolina. And no longer is he the hardened killer that rescued me from a horrific fate I could scarcely imagine.

He doesn't belittle me for my weakness, nor infantilize my fear.

I nod reluctantly and swallow hard. Just the idea of sitting here alone for only a few minutes makes me feel nauseous, after those lonely hours in that dark cell. I never want to be alone again. But I can do it. He's not going anywhere, I remind myself.

"Good girl," he says, going to the kitchen. I sit

nervously, my eyes darting around the room, fearful that at any moment Will is going to slink out from behind a piece of furniture and capture me again. But Pavlenko comes back after only a minute or so, carrying a damp rag and a bottle of what looks like rubbing alcohol.

"This might sting a little," he says apologetically, crouching down. He dampens the rag with alcohol and gently dabs at my knees. I inhale sharply at the sudden pinch of pain. There's a lot more blood to clean off than I expected, and I start to feel slightly woozy. I've never been very good at dealing with blood. I've got a weak stomach, which I consider a huge embarrassment. It's such a cliché — the fragile young woman who faints at the sight of blood.

When he's finished, he stands up and surveys me with his hands on his hips.

"How do you feel?" he asks gravely.

I pause for a moment, biting my lip. There are so many things I want to say. I feel abused. I feel betrayed. I feel broken inside. Instead, I just say, "I feel like I need a bath."

"That place they kept you was filthy," he agrees. "I will run you a bath here, if you don't mind. I promise I'll give you as much privacy as you need."

He turns to leave and I instinctively reach out to grab his wrist. He looks down at my hand first, his eyes slowly raising to meet my gaze. I struggle to find the words I need.

"No… stay with me," I plead. "I want to take a bath but… I don't want to be alone."

Pavlenko looks like his mind is in turmoil over this. Finally, he concedes. "Okay. I will stay in the bathroom with you, but I won't look, *klyanus.*"

He gently helps me to my feet and leads me down a little hallway to his bedroom. He seats me on his smooth, simple gray bedspread while he goes into the adjoining bathroom to start a bath, leaving the door open so I can see that he's still there. I am astounded by his tenderness, his patience with me. I had him all wrong when I first met him, when I felt like I was so small and insignificant versus his tall, broody gorgeousness.

Now I feel like I've seen more of his true sides, the part that really is a hero. Boris had said that to Maksim, that they were rebuilding an empire that he'd eliminated… And that thing about the French woman… My heart breaks, thinking about Maksim saving a woman from those brutes, only for Boris to track her down. I wonder if it's weighing on Maksim's conscious as well…

I look around at his simplistic bedroom. Everything is neat and orderly, almost to a military standard. He has everything he needs, and not much more than that, but instead of looking shabby or empty, the room just looks neat. It reflects the fact that he works hard and doesn't expect much from his life outside of work. In a way, it makes me a little sad for him — while this place is comfortable enough, there isn't much personal touch.

He walks over, his sleeves rolled to his elbows, and helps me into the bathroom. He shifts his weight awkwardly when I stand looking at the claw foot tub filled with lightly scented water. Steam rises from its slightly pinkish surface. I wonder what kind of soap or oil he's put in the water. It almost makes me smile, the thought of this muscular, imposing man keeping frilly bath accoutrements on hand.

"I'll stand over here and face away," he says, a twinge of nerves in his voice.

"Okay. Thank you," I answer softly. He steps away and faces the doorway while I gingerly strip out of my white dress, panties, and bra. I glance back over my shoulder anxiously to make sure he's still not looking. He isn't. Of course.

I carefully climb into the hot bath, wincing when the scented water reaches my wounded knees. I see Pavlenko almost turn around at the sound of my pained gasp, but he catches himself in time. Sinking down into the warm water, I close my eyes and sigh. I lower myself completely until my hair is totally submerged, my face barely poking out of the water. I stare at the smooth white ceiling, the miniature chandelier dangling far above me. I'm so exhausted, so overwhelmed. All I want is to soak in this fragrant bath and let the water wash away all traces of my horrible experience. But I know better than to expect that. It will take more than a hot bath to scour those dark memories from my mind. My body, however, is relieved to finally get some physical comfort. Still, my stomach growls, and I realize that I haven't eaten since those crepes last night at the Champ de Mars.

With Maggie. My heart plummets and I feel tears burning in my eyes. Guilt floods my thoughts. I hate myself for being safe and sound here while my friend is out there enduring unspeakable horrors.

"Olivia," says Pavlenko, and I jump a little at his voice.

"Yes?"

"I'm going to order us some food. What would you like?"

I sit up and pull my knees up to my chest, biting my lip. "Oh, I don't know. I-I can't think of anything like that right now," I admit weakly. He nods, still facing away from me.

"I understand. I'll take care of it," he says, taking a cell phone out of his pocket. He dials a number and places an order entirely in rapid French while I simply stare at my own toes wrinkling in the water. For the next half hour we remain this way, Pavlenko standing guard at the door while I curl up in the tub. Finally, the food arrives and he goes to retrieve it, leaving me alone for the first time since he rescued me. But only after asking if I was okay.

"There's a robe hanging for you on the back of

the door," he instructs. "I'll set up our meal in the living room. Take your time. As long as you need. I will wait for you."

Once he's gone, I slowly rise out of the now-luke-warm water and wriggle into the gigantic, Pavlenko-sized white robe. The sleeves are comically long, falling several inches past my hands, and the bottom of the robe drags the floor. I feel like a kid playing dress-up, but I refuse to put on my white dress again. After the events that transpired while I was wearing it… I want nothing more than to burn it.

I trot out to the living room to see a full, impressive French meal arrayed on the coffee table, complete with croissants, jam, cream, cheese, fruit, olives, and a tray of thinly sliced meats. My stomach growls at the smell and sight of it, and without a single word I immediately sit down and start eating. Pavlenko watches me silently, sizing me up, like he's still worried I might totally break down and fall apart any second now.

I can't blame him for thinking it. I'm not totally positive I won't.

"How are you feeling now? Any better?" he questions.

I swallow the grape I just popped into my mouth. "Better. Thank you for saving me. Thank you… for everything."

"It's my duty," he replies simply.

"But what about Maggie?" I ask, the guilt that's been lurking in the back of my mind surging forward. "I don't know where they've taken her. I don't know if she's even alive."

His face darkens, his handsome features settling into the hard lines of a marble statue.

"I will find her. I promise you that," he says heavily.

"Don't make promises you can't keep," I answer, biting the inside of my cheek to keep from crying. The situation doesn't seem particularly hopeful. Who knows what kind of "buyer" Will had lined up for Maggie? She could be halfway across the world by now. Or worse.

He sets down his cup of tea and reaches across to take my hand firmly. His striking eyes blaze into mine when he says, "I swear to you, I will find her. I will bring her back."

"But how? How is any of this possible? How did you even find *me*?" I ask, leaning forward. For a split second, his eyes dart down to my chest and I realize that the oversized robe is hanging loosely, leaving my cleavage clearly visible. I immediately blush.

"I was not always the way you see me now. I walked a much different path many years ago, and sometimes my feet… they lead me in that old direction if I let them. I will find her, Liv. You can trust in me to do that," he affirms, his voice low and intense.

"Monsieur Pavlenko, I do trust you," I tell him earnestly, after a long pause.

He squeezes my hand gently and nods. "Call me Max."

As I clean up the remainder of takeout, I can feel Liv's eyes following me the whole time, watching me move about the kitchen remarkably calmly for the exchange that had just transpired between us.

I know what's on her mind. She wants to know more of what I've said about myself, and I know I've already said far too much. I should have just said I'm a well-connected man, or that I know the city very well. Neither of them would be complete lies, but I can read in those eyes of hers that half-truths would not escape her. She's clever, and even after what she's been through, she won't accept a lie. But how can she accept the truth?

I'm a hitman. A trained killer. What transpired in Liv's rescue came to me with ease. I've faced much greater odds with far less preparation and still come out with only a few scars. But that is not a life Liv needs to be exposed to. She is meant for so much more, and I will make sure she achieves it. I will protect her, and all the women the mafia thinks they can enslave for the sake of their greed. And I won't let her be stolen from me again.

But in my silence, I can't help but wonder how many of the blanks in my story she's filling in herself, and with what. I remind myself that I shouldn't be bothered by such things. I'm out to protect them and shut down the slave trade again, not worry about what my student thinks of me.

If things keep up the way they are, she may think far worse of me yet.

"I imagine you're about ready for bed," I say with a smile as I hear a long yawn come from the living room, and I hear her try to stifle it suddenly, embarrassed.

"It's been a day," she admits, weariness in her voice.

"I understand if your mind will be racing too much to get to sleep," I say, stepping back into the living room and leaning against the wall, my arms crossed. "I have some sleep aids that might put your mind at ease, if you like."

She shakes her head, a little bit of fright coming into her gaze, and I wonder if that's how they got her, was drugging her. I'd assumed it had all started off cordial enough, but maybe it wasn't. Maybe that asshole who sent her the email hadn't even bothered trying to charm her, and instead just knocked her out.

"I don't need it," she says, her voice a bit tight, her shoulders tensed.

"Good to hear it. You can take my bed for the night," I say, trying to keep things light as I gesture to the hallway. "It's the last door on the right, and the sheets are clean. I tend to wash them a little obsessively," I add, rubbing the back of my neck. "You grow up without a clean bed, and it makes you value fresh sheets."

That makes Liv smile, a heartwarming sight after the frightened gaze just a second ago, and she nods, but looks down for a moment, hesitating. "Thanks. But…"

I raise an eyebrow. "Is something the matter? You can take the couch, if you prefer."

"No that's alright, I just…I know this is going to sound dumb, but being alone and in the dark so much today has me kind of on edge. I don't know if I can — I mean, I'd feel better if—" she stammers, biting her lip before looking back up to me with those warm brown eyes, and my heart fills with pity, having forgotten what it's like to be so small and vulnerable. "Do you think you could sleep in the same room with me?" she finally asks with a sheepish smile. "I know it's childish, I just — I don't want to wake up and forget I'm somewhere safe."

I have to admit, she has a remarkable presence of mind for someone who's just gone through the hell she has. I give her a reassuring smile and nod, moving from the wall and stepping towards the hallway as she rises to her feet and follows me. "Of course, Liv. You don't need to feel ashamed about something like that. Come, I'll show you in."

I flick the lights on and illuminate the simple room I call my own. It's a modest place with few furnishings: a platform bed with light gray sheets and a black comforter over it, a small nightstand with a lamp and a Kindle on it, and a closet bearing the simple, tight-fitting clothes I wear on a daily basis.

"This is really nice," she says, and I give a laugh at the remark. "No, I mean it! I thought Maggie and I were tidy, and we'd only just moved in."

"A simple upbringing gives you simple tastes," I say, making my way over to the pillows and fluffing them a bit and smoothing the covers. I feel somewhat guilty for not being entirely honest with the room's presentation, however. There are some things I don't want even Liv to see. Not yet.

The room is not so much 'simple' as it is 'subtle.' Under the bed, there is a hidden compartment full of the weapons and other tools I used in my past life, the life that seems to be coming back to haunt me more with every passing hour. It weighs on me that I will be putting Liv to bed to sleep peacefully over a bed of the grisly weapons I used to take lives before even knowing her. But the poor girl has enough on her mind for now.

Briefly, I wonder if it would make her feel safer, or if it'd send her out on the streets, wondering what type of monster I really am. Then I have to wonder why I care so much. It's not even just about her being my student, or my seeing potential in her. There's something more, some way I'm drawn to her that I've never experienced before.

It's been years since I'd even done so much as gone on a date with a woman, so maybe that's why I don't recognize these feelings. The desire to help her isn't just motivated by pure intentions. There's something deeper at work.

"Where are you going to sleep?" she asks, moving over to the bed and testing the sheets out thoughtfully, pulling them out and testing the mattress.

"I have some thick spare sheets in the closet — I'll sleep on the floor beside you."

"What?!" she says, suddenly looking more guilty than I feel. "You can't-"

"Liv," I stop her gently, holding up a hand, "if you knew what I was used to, you'd know that even a slightly springy hardwood floor would be comfortable by my standards. And I'm not the one who's been through the trauma today. Take the bed," I say, and the firmness of my voice puts to rest any debate over the matter. She does respond remarkably well to commands, and that sends a little jolt of excitement through me. I add with a smile, "Just try not to trip over me if you get up in the night."

"Thanks, Monsieur Pavlenko." I turn my back as she climbs into bed, stripping off her socks and getting comfortable under the sheets with the kind of deep sigh only very tired limbs can afford you.

"Liv, please," I say as I pull the spare blankets from the closet, folding them into a makeshift bed on the floor, "call me Max. I think we're well over that threshold."

"That might take some getting used to," she says, but there's a lighthearted tone to her words, "but I think that suits you a little better. 'Night, Max."

"Sleep well, Liv," I say, clicking the lamp on to give us dim light for the night before I hit the main light and darken the room. Heading into the bathroom with a pair of sleeping pants, I strip my clothes off and replace them with the pants, heading back out. I cast a quick glance over to Liv, her slow breaths making her chest rise and fall as she already starts to doze peacefully into sleep. I feel a small smile forming on my lips before I turn and lie down onto my temporary bed, turning over into a cocoon in my covers and closing my eyes.

A SMALL YELP in the night wakes me up, and faster

than my mind can react, I throw the covers off and spring to my feet, eyes adjusted to the dark and looking around my room as my fists ball, looking for whatever caused the disturbance — were we followed? Did someone track us here? Have I slept through an abduction?

But after a moment of silence, my gaze falls on the only other person in the room, Liv, who's sitting up in bed with eyes wide open, recoiling from me in fear. Or rather, perhaps, recoiling from my reaction.

"Liv? Are you okay?" I ask, lowering my voice as I realize there's no threat in the room with us but me. "I'm sorry if I startled you. My reflexes are...a little overzealous, it seems."

"I'm sorry," she breathes, still half-asleep, "I'm sorry, I... no, everything's fine. I didn't mean to wake you." She takes a deep breath as she bunches up some of the blankets under her chin, laying her head down on the pillows again as she tries to calm her nerves. Frowning, I move over to the bed and sit beside her, putting a hand on her shoulder.

"You're safe here, Liv," I assure her, rubbing her arm slowly. "Trust me, I'm not a man to make such promises lightly."

Her eyes turn to me, the lamplight catching in them and making them sparkle even in their exhaustion. There's real trust in those eyes, even though we've only known each other for a short time, and I can feel her relaxing under my touch.

It's a funny thing about out of the ordinary experiences. Someone can date someone else for years, get married, have a family, and yet never feel the same connection as someone who's been through something as heinous as Liv and I were. Seeing someone at their worst, their absolute worst, and moving through it together is something not usually afforded to regular people, and for that I'm ever grateful.

But now, I know there's a thread between Liv and I, something that won't be easily broken.

"I'm sorry. I forgot you were here, and I felt so alone. God, I just keep thinking what they could be doing with Maggie. Max..." she says, and she seems hesitant to continue, closing her eyes before speaking more. "Would you... would you sleep in the bed with me?"

I'm taken aback by the question, but I don't let it show, my touch on her arm still slow and smooth. But even I can't deny that the request puts a warmth in my chest, a reassurance of how safe she feels with me. What's really getting me, though, is the jolt of excitement my body feels, and that's what makes me hesitate. She's my student, and I need to crush these inappropriate feelings, not tease them to new heights.

"It's okay if you don't think that's alright," she backpedals at my momentary silence, opening her eyes, "I know it — it wouldn't look appropriate. I just...I need to feel you close to me, Max," she confesses in a near whisper, her cheeks burning red, and I give her shoulder a light squeeze.

I should not do this. Liv is my student. She's 18. She's under my protection. She's put every ounce of her trust in me, and I've taken her out of the jaws of hell tonight, turning her heart inside out in the process.

And she needs me more than anything else right now. She needs to feel safe and protected, and what will make her feel safe and protected is to be held.

Without saying another word to worry her, I move around the side of the bed, slipping into the sheets and moving in close to Liv. I can feel the heat of her body radiating against mine, and she starts to move in closer to me instinctively, but she stops herself short, pulling the sheets tighter around herself and letting out a satisfied sigh.

"Thank you, Max," she breathes in a nearly inaudible whisper.

"Anything, Liv," my low intonation replies.

In a matter of minutes as we drift off into sleep together, I feel my mind start to descend into the twilight between waking and sleeping, but all that keeps me over the precipice is the thought of Liv beside me.

Were anyone to know of what I was doing here, we could both be dismissed from the university. But all that feels so far away from us now. This place feels like a sanctuary, a quiet pause amidst this storm suddenly brewing around our lives, and somehow, I realize why Liv wanted me to be near her, and I share the same desire.

Whether Liv is awake or not, I do not know, but I feel her body moving in closer to mine. First her shoulder touches my chest, and there's a pause, as if she or her body wonders whether she should stay or roll away. But a moment later, I feel her back press into me, her narrow, lithe frame curling against mine so naturally. She cuddles into my chest, and I hear a soft sigh from her, though her face is away from me.

Her body seems to pause there for some time. Perhaps she's feeling my heartbeat against her back, or maybe she's questioning herself again, wondering whether she deserves the comfort she's seeking.

I realize my heart is swelling for her. She deserves so much better than she allows herself, and I want her to feel that, but I feel the restraints of my relationship to her as an instructor chafing me as I think on her. There's so many reasons why I tried to erect that barrier between us, and now, in the twilight hours, her pure beauty is breaking them down.

She truly does deserve such human reassurance as she craves. She's not like me, not like the monster I keep housed in my heart and fists. She deserves only goodness and love. But can I be the one to give that to her?

Gently, I slip my arm around her, my thick forearm and bicep draping over her like a blanket in itself. As if acting on instinct, I feel her move back further, and she moves her rear back against me, not quite pressing into my pelvis, but melding into my body for warmth and comfort, all of her touching me. I stroke her arm with my hand as my heart pounds in my chest, and it only seems to encourage her as she snuggles in tighter to me until we're so very close to each other.

I know she can feel my breath on her neck now, and my mind starts to work faster, wondering what she thinks of the appropriateness of all this. Maybe she's truly asleep, and she will wake up with another shriek. Maybe she's in the same half-conscious state as I, acting on the merest impulse and drive for human closeness.

I hardly realize what I'm doing as I lean forward to close the inch between us, my lips brushing against her neck as I plant a gentle kiss there, holding her tighter against me in a brief hug. My concerns melt for a moment as I hear a soft sigh from her, her legs squirming around as she adjusts herself to get more comfortable against me, and I can almost see the smile on her lips from behind.

"You're a hero, Max," she whispers, and her words almost make me jump, not realizing she was every bit as wide-awake as me. "You said you weren't a good person, but I just want you to know that you are."

With that, she slips her hand into mine, giving it a light squeeze as she gets comfortable against me, and I feel her breath go steady and slow again as she's carried into a deep, comfortable sleep.

And now, I'm wide-awake, my mind racing in conflict as I fight to control the threateningly growing thing between my legs as she presses against me, my heartbeat quickening against what I realize is the first person in a very long time — probably ever — to see some good in the true side of who I am.

## LIV

*A* stream of pale morning sunlight pricks at my eyes until they open. My whole body aches with exhaustion, as though I recently ran a marathon. There are soft gray sheets cocooning me, and a cushy pillow under my cheek. Am I at home? More importantly, where is home? My bedroom back in Toast... or my shared bedroom at my flat with Maggie? My heart sinks at the thought of her. Wherever she is, I hope she's okay, at least alive. As I blink my eyes, the room around me comes into focus and it begins to dawn on me where exactly *I* am.

My mentor's bedroom.

My stomach twists into anxious knots and I flip over, dreading what I will find. I can't believe I'm doing this — sleeping in my instructor's bed! What would my parents think of me? What would my

171

friends back home say about me in their whispered conversations?

With mingled relief and disappointment I realize that the space beside me is empty. I'm all alone in the bed. I frown and start questioning what even happened last night. Maybe I did sleep here by myself all night. But then... I remember the faint sensation of Max's strong body curled around me protectively. I recall with a shiver the feeling of his feather-light kiss on my neck. No, he was definitely here last night. Where is he now?

A surge of terror passes through my body. What if he left me here? What if I'm alone?

Will and those other guys could come back for me. They could find me here. Suddenly, it becomes absolutely imperative that I find Max and stay close to him, no matter what. I can't stand to be alone right now. As I slip out of bed, I feel a twinge of self-loathing. I used to be so independent. I treasured my alone time. And now I'm proving everyone right — I *am* just as fragile as I look. I comb my fingers through my messy hair, wincing as I untangle the knots. I must have tossed and turned in my sleep a lot to make such a disaster of my hair. It was fine and soft, and usually didn't tangle easily. But with the experiences I've had since coming to Paris, I suppose it makes sense that I would have difficulty sleeping peacefully.

Will's cruel smirk flashes to the front of my mind

and I feel my knees buckle beneath me. I have to find Max. I can't be alone right now. I listen intently for any sounds — and notice the comforting pitter-patter of the shower running on the other side of the bathroom door. I stand in front of the door, conflicted.

We've already slept in the same bed together, and he's stood guard over me while I bathed. He rescued me from almost certain death — or a fate possibly worse — and nursed me patiently back to some semblance of sanity. How much worse can it be for me to walk in on him in the shower? Never mind the fact that I've never actually seen any man naked, much less my instructor. But I'll just go in but not look. I'll give him the same privacy he gave me, while feeling that protected calm that only his presence can afford me.

There's no one else I can trust in this city, no one else I know, and while that was isolating before, now it's next to unbearable. I feel vulnerable, and knowing how capable Max is gives me comfort.

And I admit, that sweet, momentary lapse between us... The kiss...

That was the only thing that soothed me enough to get a truly good night sleep. The memory of his hard, masculine body wrapped into mine and keeping me safe.

I cautiously turn the knob and walk into the bathroom. A thick coating of steam embraces me as I shut the door behind me. It's so warm, it's comforting. Against the opposite wall is the fogged-up shower stall, with Max standing under the stream of hot water, his eyes shut. I bite my lip nervously, afraid that I may have overstepped my boundaries. I certainly don't want to catch him off guard and freak him out. After all, even though we've skipped a lot of steps in our relationship with each other through the extenuating circumstances of the past couple of days, Max may not react very positively to my seeing him naked. Not that I can see him very clearly through the steamed-up glass panels of the shower stall, anyway.

I don't know if that's a godsend or a pity.

What I can make out through the fog are his enormous muscular arms, reaching up to shampoo his thick dark hair. My own body tingles at the remembrance of those arms around me last night in bed, holding me close, sheltering me from the bad dreams that haunted my thoughts. It surprises me just how natural it felt, how much it doesn't bother me. Of course, when I think about what other people would say, I feel ashamed. Weak. But if it were purely up to me and my own perception of the situation, it would be a different story.

Because as inappropriate as it may be, I can't help but feel at home with him in a way I never expected to. I'm sure a lot of that has to do with the fact that he's responsible for saving my life. That's a bond most people will never feel with another. But even before that, when I first met him and he caught me staring at him, I certainly felt something. A girlish crush, maybe, that was quickly snuffed out by how formal he was with me. But now I understand why he had to push me away, and why he needed to distance himself from others.

He's not who he says he is. More than that, I don't think he's who he believes he is either. I see the goodness in him, but when I told him that, I felt him tense, like he didn't agree.

As I'm standing here pondering the unusual depth of our dynamic, Max suddenly looks over and does a double-take at the sight of me. His green eyes flash brightly through the fog and I can see just the slightest hint of embarrassment cross his features. Instantly I feel guilty for walking in on him. I should have stayed put. But I just can't stand to be out of his sight. The feeling that I'm being stalked, being watched, is ever-present. And Max is my comfort, for better or for worse, and whatever it happens to mean for the both of us.

To his credit, he makes no attempt to shield his naked body from me. I don't think I could stand it if he did. But instead he simply goes on about washing himself as though I'm not here at all, which I'm thankful for. After all, I didn't sneak in here to gawk at him — although I can see now that there is a lot to gawk at. I recall something I heard years ago about people in Europe being more open about their bodies and sexualities. At the time I had just dismissed it as some stupid rumor Americans make up so foreigners sound more exotic, but now I'm wondering if that's part of why Max doesn't even seem bothered to have me as an audience.

His body is perfectly sculpted, his arm and leg muscles bulging just enough to hint at the immense strength he keeps tethered. My eyes follow the line of his broad shoulders and back, narrowing down to his waist and his taut ass. When he turns toward me, unabashedly, I see his flat stomach with his carved abdominal muscles and below that...

His cock.

I swallow hard, my eyes going wide at the sight of it. He's massive, even limp. I have to force my jaw not to drop. I've never seen a man's genitals before, but I had no idea they were this big. Or maybe it's just him. I feel my face growing flushed and I delicately hoist myself up to sit on the counter, feeling a little weak again. Somewhere in the back of my muddled mind, I wonder what it would feel like to touch it. To brush my fingertips along the head of his shaft, to feel it harden beneath my light machinations.

I inwardly shake myself of these thoughts. *Get yourself together, Liv!* Romantic hero-savior or not, he's still my teacher. And I am his student. There's got to be at least ten years' age difference between us. Though, looking at his body now, it's impossible to reason that he wouldn't be every bit as limber and powerful as a man my own age. Probably more so.

But I can't let myself think like that. Not now. What has gotten into me?

I convince myself it's just the trauma of what's happened to me which is clouding my judgement, but I'm lying to myself. I thought he was hot the second I set eyes on him, and was curious about him ever since, even as I tried to push it from my mind. Now that I'm alone with him, though, I'm greedy for more.

My eyes begin to catch other details of Max's physique — scars. I squint, straining to catalogue them as he rinses off his body. There are shiny, jagged lines marring his skin, some on his arms and legs, and one particularly nasty one on his upper chest, almost to his collarbone. I wonder what could have caused him such pain. What kind of life has he led? As a gymnast, I've had my own share of awful injuries, and there are battle scars I bear, as well. But nothing to this extent. Who hurt him? Who made him this way? One thing is for sure: he didn't get those scars as a mere gymnastics instructor in Paris.

The water cuts off and Max steps out of the shower stall. For a glorious split second I take in his full, glistening frame before he wraps a towel around his body. He shakes his head vigorously to loosen the excess water from his hair, almost like a fluffy dog.

The gesture is so cute and out of character it draws an unbidden smile to my face.

"How did you sleep?" he asks simply, roughly combing back the hair from his face with deft fingers. It takes me a moment to rip myself out of the trancelike state I'm in, intrigued by every movement this beautiful, mysterious man makes.

"Just fine," I lie. The truth is, I still dreamed of dark, dank places and cruelly handsome faces last night. But every time I awoke with a pained cry, I was lulled back to sleep by the comforting warmth of the man lying next to me.

"I apologize for the indecency," he remarks, but there's no hint of apology in his voice. I wonder if he's only saying this out of obligation, because he doesn't want to tread on my boundaries. But I'm relieved to hear his light, even tone. It means he's not upset at me for barging in at him and staring at him like a horny school girl. Which, in fairness, is kind of what I feel like, so I don't want his apologies. In my mind, there is nothing to apologize for. I needed a guardian to stay close. I asked him to come to bed with me.

He was only doing as I requested.

He was only protecting me. Again.

"It's nothing," I assure him, trying to strike a balance between dismissing his apology and not sounding too eager. In truth, I'd repeat my actions again, and even though he's my instructor, I think he did the perfectly decent thing.

The strangest thing, though, that I don't know how to deal with is my budding attraction to him. Or is it fully bloomed now? I've never really found myself attracted to anyone sexually before — not on this level. I've had silly, fleeting crushes in the past. I've even danced with boys at school formals. But nothing has ever stricken me so sharply as the proximity of Max's strong, powerful body to mine.

And I know what those captors wanted to do to me. I bet they'd have even fetched a higher price on my body if they knew I was a virgin. The documentary I watched said that untouched girls were always more highly prized, and that was precisely why I kept it to myself.

So maybe it's partly that fear bubbling over in me. I nearly had my virginity forced from me, and now I'm waking up to real, adult desires as a messed up way to deal with that. Or maybe it's just one of those near death things where suddenly I have a new appreciation for life and experiencing all the things I never got to yet.

And sex is definitely one of those experiences.

I find myself longing to be nearer to him, constantly. Even now, as I sit perched on the bathroom counter, it's difficult for me not to stare with desire. I can't believe the urges coming over me. I decide to just chalk it up to my recent trauma and leave the moral questioning for another time.

"I don't want to make you uncomfortable, Liv," Max continues, standing there with his towel wrapped around his waist. His chest and stomach muscles gleam with the fairest sheen of moisture, catching every sculpted line. Those smoldering green eyes watch me intently, waiting for a response. Like he's waiting for me to cry, to break down in front of him. It's almost as though he expects me to be afraid of him — like it would be easier if I did.

But I don't. I fear my confusing feelings toward him, but I don't fear Max in the least.

"You've done nothing to make me feel uncomfortable. You saved my life. I will never be able to thank you for what you've done for me," I explain to him, biting my lip.

Our eyes meet and I feel a tingling sensation travel down my spine. It's this powerful, unexplainable electric current, the same one I felt when I first sat down across from him at the banquet table in North Carolina. Something feels so primal, so natural about our meeting. Like we were always going to find ourselves here somehow.

But then he drags his eyes away from me, looking into the mirror as the steam begins to clear and reveal his handsome, conflicted face. He falls silent, and I wonder what kinds of thoughts are surging through his mind right now. I can feel that barrier coming up again, the same one he put between us the moment he offered me the position as his student.

"Your scars... how did you get them?" I ask suddenly, unable to stop myself, unwilling to let him recoil from me.

He doesn't look at me, keeping his gaze trained on his own reflection, and for a second, I wonder if I've instead pushed him away.

"I told you that I used to walk a darker path. I lived a very different life years ago. I ran with a crowd who would sneer at the way I live now, would call me a coward or a quitter. But I could not run alongside them forever. Olivia, I did terrible things, and terrible things happened to me, as well," he says slowly.

"That mark on your chest," I begin cautiously, "what is it?"

He sighs, staring down at his hands gripping the edge of the counter as though it physically pains him to look himself in the eye now. "You don't want to know."

"Please," I press, moving closer along the counter so that my bare legs, poking out of the bottom of the oversized T-shirt he gave me, are almost touching his arm.

Finally, he looks at me, and I feel that electric shock once again.

"It is the result of trying to burn away my past. It

was… it used to be a tattoo, marking me as a member of the brotherhood. The Bratva."

My blood runs cold.

The Bratva. I remember vaguely a voice saying those words coarsely in the backseat of the car while I was being kidnapped. I drifted in and out of consciousness, unable to move or find my bearings, but that word appears to me now out of the clearing mist.

Did the darker path he walk used to involve taking girls like me?

The horror I see in her gaze doesn't land on blind eyes. I can only imagine the terrible thoughts running through her mind, and it's inexpressibly painful to keep eye contact with her. I see her on the cusp of asking, was I once a part of the slavers who subjected her and Maggie to this fate? Have I done still more wretched things? Are the two of them just some form of penance for myself, a saved couple of girls among countless slaves I'd condemned?

I was never a slaver, but I wouldn't have been able to say 'no' to all of those questions written on her face.

"That life is far behind me, Liv," I say with some finality, but I can tell she doesn't fully believe me. "I burned that bridge when I burned the tattoo from my skin. What I do now has no ties to those men and the evil they conduct. I hope my actions speak for themselves."

The look on her face is pained, and I frown, letting my head hang a moment. "I understand if this is difficult for you. I don't expect you to believe me." I cross the room with a set of clothes and let my towel fall to the ground out of her sight, donning a tight and thin black t-shirt, jeans, and shoes. She needs time to digest what I just confessed to her, or else needs time to run from me.

I've been foolish, and let my guard down. For a few hours, there was a lingering question in the back of my mind if I could actually be worthy of a woman's love and respect. I'd written it off so long ago, accepted my fate as a life-long bachelor, until she came into my life.

Even then, I pushed those thoughts away, and was prepared to be professional with her, just like all my students. But fate had other plans for us. It gave me hope that there might be a future for me, outside of pain and death and work.

I had to be reminded that I am unredeemable, and that no one outside the Bratva will ever accept the true me. Especially not a woman so beautiful and delicate as Olivia.

When I return to the bathroom a few moments later, I'm earnestly surprised to see her still there. I almost thought she would have fled the room and my home, taking her chances away from anyone who's had any affiliation from the mafia.

I fear I'm her only hope in all this, and she knows this. Of course she won't run, if she thinks her friend's life is on the line.

But that's no basis for a relationship, so I turn back to the cold professional I should've been all along.

"For now, Liv, I must press on," I say, crossing the room and picking up my cellphone from the nightstand. For the first time since the revelation, I see her look up at me with a furrowed brow, as if watching me through a dream.

"What do you mean?"

"There are some things I must do on my own to help find Maggie," I explain, knowing she isn't going to like that explanation, but as she nods absently, I realize she's lost in thought over what she's learned about me.

Perhaps I should not have revealed my past so early to her. Hell, I never should've revealed anything to her. I was a fool to think that she'd accept me as I am. The things I've done...

But a hopeful voice within me reminds me that I would rather her be in shock now than lie to her and face my dishonesty later. I want her to trust me, even still.

"But don't worry," I say, a bit of reluctance in my voice as I thumb through my recent contacts on my phone. "The man I'm leaving you in care of is...capable, if nothing else. And a touch less frightening than me."

*And perhaps a little time away from me is precisely what she needs,* I think to myself with a heavier heart than I want to admit. I brace myself as I hear the phone ringing after I call my contact.

"FIRST OF ALL," says Felix, pacing around the room and running his fingers through his curly hair and pushing his thick-rimmed glasses up his nose, "thanks for letting me know you're *alive* after yesterday, asshole."

I roll my eyes, leaning against the back of the room with my arms crossed as I watch him, my eyes occasionally flitting back to Liv, who's sitting on the couch. She hasn't said much since I called Felix, and I'm becoming more concerned about her by the minute. Her being afraid of me at a time like this is potentially dangerous. If anything happens, I need her to know she can count on me.

But it may yet be helpful, if only to keep her out of danger. If she doesn't want to be around me, then I can pull off this rescue mission on Maggie without her interference, and that's safer for all of us.

"You would have known eventually, Felix," I say,

sounding bored. "We've had more than a few other things on our minds."

"Okay, sure, fine, but you can't go into an apartment building armed to the teeth with guns and knives and then expect me to be able to sleep at night, alright?"

I smile. "Here I thought you knew about my past."

"It's one thing to read about someone," says Felix in a fluster, "but to see him charging into a building like some kind of American cowboy, fuck! No offense," he adds offhandedly to Liv, who just raises her eyebrows a little.

"Anyway," I change the subject, "like I said on the phone, we have more tracking to do. As you can see," I say with a gesture to Liv, "we have one student somewhere safe, but we're missing one more. Her name is Maggie. I have her number here. Can you work your magic again?"

"Um duh?" he says, glancing to Liv as if asking if his use of the expression in English is correct. He speaks it heavily accented, but we converse in English to make sure she doesn't feel excluded. Particularly considering the circumstances. "Are we going on another car ride?"

"No," I say quickly, "I can't leave Liv alone. And I know she damn well doesn't want to be. If you can get me a location, I will take care of what needs to be done."

Felix gives me an incredulous look, and I know

what he's thinking: am I seriously leaving *him* on guard duty? But I shoot him a meaningful look back, meaning that yes, indeed, I am.

"This place is safe, Felix," I affirm. "We took no car here, and the mafia hasn't known about my location for years. This apartment is just another face in the crowd."

"Well then, yeah, I can uh, do that," he says, pushing his glasses up again before he moves over to his bag and takes his laptop out, taking it over to the little excuse for a dining table and plugging it in before opening it. "But you saw about how long it took me to get an exact location last time. So, y'know, give me a few minutes to let me 'work my magic.' You know, magic that you could learn in like twenty minutes if you cared to."

"Sure," I indulge him, "give me a tutorial on triangulating — I'm sure the slavers will put things on hold for us while we educate ourselves."

Felix rolls his eyes and starts typing on his computer after I slide my phone to him on the table with Maggie's number pulled up.

I spend a few minutes just pacing around the room while I wait on Felix, but before long, Liv gets up and heads into my room, flicking on the bathroom light and heading inside. I look after her a moment before Felix gets my attention with a click of his tongue.

He nods in her direction, raising an eyebrow at me. "She okay?" he says in a low tone.

I take a few long moments before responding. "She will be okay. She's... taken in quite a lot in the past day and a half." And though that much is true, what I'm really worried about is that I'm the one whose traumatized her most of all. Not long ago, just a few hours, she said I was a hero, and for that brief window of time, I felt something I never had before.

But now she knows the truth. I've never been a hero, and no matter what I do to atone for my past, it will never be enough. Not for her, and certainly not for me.

Frowning, Felix nods curtly and gets back to his work. As he does, I stand up and head into my room after Liv, waiting by my bed for her to get out.

The door opens, and she stops short as soon as she sees me, standing in the doorway to the bathroom and looking away from me, unsure what to do with herself as I turn my gaze up to her.

There are a few moments of awkward silence between us before either of us says anything, but something feels so...wrong about leaving her here without a word between us, without some closure.

"Liv, I..." I start, closing my mouth and frowning as words fail me momentarily. "I can't change anything about my past. I wish to god that I could, but..."

She isn't looking at me, just standing in the doorway with her gaze at the ground. I can feel the pain in her heart. She desperately wants to look back up at me, but after everything we shared last night, after everything she's been through, I can't blame her for her reticence.

"When I was growing up," I start slowly, "I had no parents. In America, such a start is incomparable. In my home city of Yakutsk, it is a near death sentence. The winters are harsher than anywhere else in the world, and the people can be just as cold to each other. I knew so little warmth in my life that I could never even begin to imagine what it might be like to share a bond with another person. In the orphanage where I spent my early boyhood, we were always in competition." I almost smile at the memory, though most of them feel so distant now, after I've come through so much.

"We fought against one another, we raced each other, we stole from the administrators and compared our loot with one another. It felt like that was expected of us. We had to compete to be the best, in hopes that we would one day be adopted by some kind soul. I had only one person who I could call 'friend' during that part of my life." I take a deep breath. I haven't spoken of this in a very long time. I can feel Liv's quiet gaze on me, but I keep my eyes on the wall.

"His name was Andrei. He was tall and sturdy,

not unlike myself. Through all the cutthroat competition of the boys' pecking order, we had each other's backs, no matter what. We fought together. We survived together. And when we passed into adolescence without a single prospect of adoption, we were ejected out into the cold Russian winters together." I pause, Andrei's face clear in my mind that day that we were discharged from the only home they'd ever known. "I felt so betrayed by the world by then. With so many families out there, not a single one would adopt us, give us the warmth every child should know? One more birthday rolled around, and I remember being so angry I wanted to flee the orphanage and starve to death out in the snow rather than face the icy shoulder of prospective parents." I pause, looking up and meeting Liv's gaze.

"That day, Andrei spoke to me. He said, 'Max, we humans, we find our greatest strengths in the bonds we forge with one another that we *can* choose, not in our families that we can't. We will do what we must to get by, you and I, because we know that we can work together to do what we have to." I squeeze my fists tight a moment, the memories quieting me despite myself. "That thought was in my mind when we left the orphanage together. And that was what kept me going when I started working for the Bratva to survive after my time in the military. None of us were truly free," I say, more fire in my voice than I had realized as I stand up, "but together, we *survived.*"

I step to the doorway and pause, looking back at her. "I understand if you don't wish to speak to me, and I won't blame you. No matter what. But I will keep you safe, and I will save Maggie. I promise."

With that, I move back into the main room and look to Felix, who's still at the computer, but the look on his face tells me he has something.

"Progress?" I ask him hopefully. I could use a distraction. I'm not a man who usually retreats into memory like that, and it puts me in a strange funk.

"Progress," Felix affirms with a smile, tapping something on his screen before turning the laptop around to face me. I see an address on the screen, as well as a map of the location the phone was traced to.

"That's quite a manor," I say, "on the outskirts of the city." I grimace, my fists flexing. "Liv said the bastards already have a buyer for Maggie. If they're at an estate like that..." I trail off, knowing that the answer may be that she's part of the entertainment for the night, and Felix looks concerned by my face.

"A manor is gonna have one hell of a security force, Max," Felix warns, but I'm not fazed as I cross the room and pick up the same weapons I used to storm the apartment the first time, strapping some to my legs and some into a leather jacket that I draw over my shoulders.

"Yes, but you forget, this is the Bratva," I say, rolling my shoulders. "I still have a few connections there — I only pissed off the ones tied to the slave trade, and most parties like this are mixed company. I am highly skilled, Felix," I say with a smile, glancing back at him to enjoy his perturbed expression. "More than a few high-ranking members will jump at the chance of having me back. Even if that means my crashing a party under friendly pretenses."

"So you're just gonna...waltz in there?"

"I'm more of a tango man myself, but yes," I reply candidly.

Felix opens his mouth a few times to protest, but sighs, taking a drink of the beer he's helped himself to from my fridge. "Well, shit. You know what? Okay. I'm not even gonna say anything. You go do your scary murderer thing, and I'll just uh, sit here with my spreadsheets and make sure your girlfriend doesn't go chasing after you."

"Student," I correct him, giving him a meaningful look, and he rolls his eyes.

"Alright, alright. Go on, get out of here. And Max?" he says as I'm halfway to the door. "Don't get shot — my hacking programs can't extract a bullet."

"No promises," I say, "just keep her safe." And without another word, I head out the door and down the stairs to walk into a manor full of the Russian mob.

We're awkwardly avoiding each other's eyes, both pretending to be totally engrossed in our own respective distractions. I'm fidgeting with my hands and looking down at a Kindle in my lap, even though I haven't turned the page in several minutes. It's open to some book about gymnastics training techniques, but the whole thing is written in French, so it's not like I can comprehend anything on the pages anyway. And Felix, my glorified babysitter, is fiddling with an iPad, clicking around on the screen and heaving dramatic sighs every now and then.

The near-silence is getting to me.

"So, how do you know Max again?" I ask suddenly, unable to stand the quiet tension any longer. The young man's bespectacled face quirks upward and he blinks at me, his dark eyes comically enlarged behind the frames of his glasses.

"Uh, well, we're good friends!" he begins. Then he quickly corrects himself: "Okay, more like okay friends. We go way back."

"Are you, like, a gymnast or something?" I question, doubting that would ever be possible. This guy doesn't look like he's ever done anything more strenuous in his life than post a Facebook status. But I'm determined to dig into the mysterious background of the man who saved me, the man whose hard body was pressed up against me in bed last night.

I want to know he isn't horrible.

I want to know that falling for him isn't the *second* biggest mistake since landing in France.

Felix snorts as though I've said the stupidest thing in the world.

"Oh, god no," he retorts, wrinkling his nose. Then, as it dawns on him that I might find this response a tad bit offensive, he backpedals. "I mean, I wish. It would be nice to be a jock. Might have better luck with the ladies, if you know what I mean…"

"Sure," I agree flatly. His smile fades away and he swallows hard. I can tell he's not used to spending time around women alone — or around women, period, for that matter. He's the kind of guy who's got a closer bond with his laptop than he's ever had with another human being. But I don't get the same sense of creepy desperation from him I would usually expect from such an awkward, mouthy, nerd type. He seems less threatening than that.

I don't suppose Max would have left me alone with him if he'd had any suspicion otherwise. Apparently, despite Max's heavy confession, I still trust his judgment. That comes as a bit of a surprise to me.

Anyway, I have a feeling I could probably take this shrimp down pretty easily, even if Max's judgment is off.

"Anyway, Max and I have known each other for a long time. I know, I know, we don't look like we run with the same kinda crowd, huh? Well, for your information I used to hang with some dangerous types back in my day," Felix says.

"Back in the day? You can't be much older than I am," I remark, frowning.

He sighs and sets down his iPad. "I'm twenty-two, alright? But let's just say I got an early start down the wrong track."

"What happened?" I press him, eager for any information he might have. While Max is gone, and I'm stuck with this guy who seems all too willing to talk my ear off if I let him, it seems like the best opportunity I'm ever going to have to find out what's actually going on. To make sense of what I'm actually feeling.

I mean, if Felix trusts Max and sees some of the

same things in him that I do, maybe I'm not so crazy after all for falling for him.

"Well, I came up through *famille d'accueil*, kept getting bounced around from one group home to the next. I've always been too smart to really get along with my fellow foster kids," he says, rolling his eyes. "It was never easy for me to make friends, I guess. Because I'm too smart, obviously. People just can't handle it."

"Mhmm," I agree reluctantly.

Felix looks a little giddy to have me agree with him on something. "So anyway, when I was eighteen I aged out of the system and luckily I got into college here in Paris. *Dieu merci.* Finally got me out of that slummy little town down south. But I was a scholarship kid, you know, and not one of the athletic rides like you. No offense, of course."

"Oh, none taken," I say rapidly, smiling. He looks genuinely taken aback to have received a smile from a member of the female gender. It's almost enough to make me pity him.

"So I was the poor kid, as usual. Once again, I didn't fit in with my peers. While everyone else was partying it up, I had to find myself a job to keep my ass housed and my expenses paid. Lucky for me, I've always been a whiz with computers, so I started working at the administrative offices, in billing. It was cool, having access to everybody's private information. I have the university to thank for sparking my interest in hacking," Felix says, his eyes glittering behind his spectacles, as though remembering an especially fond memory.

"How did you end up running into Max, though?" I push onward, my curiosity overwhelming me. He gives me a slightly annoyed look.

"I'm getting there. Well, I started looking into everybody's private school accounts... then their emails... and from there I figured out how to hack into people's bank accounts, too. That was the big breakthrough. But most of the students were too broke to be worth anything, anyway. The real jackpot was the donors. You wouldn't believe the kind of *le fric* these guys had. I'd never seen numbers like that! I started thinking, well, they had so much money they probably wouldn't even notice if I started skimming a little off the top," he explains, shrugging.

"Probably not the best idea," I comment, looking at him dubiously.

"I was desperate, alright? I was tired of being the shrimpy little poor kid!" he says defensively. "I just wanted to have money for the first time in my life."

"Alright, alright. Go on." I know what he was doing was wrong, but at the same time, I get it. There were a few poor kids in my classes growing up, and they always struggled. Grades, getting to class on time, bullies, everything was a struggle.

"Well, this went on for a while, no problem. I

finally had cash in my hand. It was awesome. But then one day I get this letter, pushed under my dorm room door. And it says they know who I am and what I'm doing, and if I don't pay them back every cent with interest by tomorrow, they're gonna flay me alive," he says, fidgeting.

"Geez!" I gasp, pulling my legs up into the armchair. "How did you get out of that?"

"Ah, that's where our hero Max comes in," Felix says triumphantly, brightening up. "You see, I found out everything about everyone who was affiliated with the university, and I remembered seeing something about a guy named Maksim. I remember thinking, hey that's a weird name. And so I researched him using some… less than legal methods… and found out he was running with the same kind of shady figures I was stealing from. Tracked him down, begged for his help. With dignity, obviously."

"Wait, if he was one of them then why did you reach out to him?" I ask suddenly, holding up my hand to slow him down. This isn't making any sense. And my heart is sinking to hear that Max was, in fact, one of the bad guys. I begin to feel antsy, unnerved by the fact that I just spent the night with a hardened criminal.

But god, he's also my savior, isn't he?

"I had found his name in some police databanks, that he gave up that life before he started working at the university. I knew I could use that against him if he refused to help me," Felix reasons.

"So you were going to just blackmail an ex-mobster to get his help against… other mobsters?" I clarify. Felix nods.

"Desperate times, desperate measures. Isn't that the phrase?" he says simply.

"Well, what did Max do?"

"He was pissed as all hell, first of all. Since I hacked into his private life and all, and brought up his past. He wanted to start fresh, and didn't want anyone to ever find out about any of that. But when I told him who was targeting me, he got all serious. Took care of it right away."

"How? And why did he ever leave that old life behind in the first place?" I ask, leaning forward anxiously. I feel like everything hinges on the answer to that question.

"Turns out he was only running with them at first because he got roped into it. He came from some shitty ice cube of a town back in Siberia and a life of crime was his ticket out. But once he found out about the human trafficking thing, he broke all ties with them, headed for the straight and narrow," Felix says.

I feel a little better, instantly. At least I know now that Max isn't one of them. He was telling me the truth.

"So what he did… he took me to this safe house

where I could hide out while he covered my tracks. Paid back all my debts, somehow. I had no idea he had that kind of money."

"And when he paid them off, they just let you off the hook? That easy?" I question, confused. Nothing about what limited knowledge I have of the mafia indicates to me that they would so easily give up a grudge. Especially against someone so insignificant as Felix. He had to have been just a blip on their radar. They could have easily disposed of him, or at least punished him. Couldn't they?

"Easy?" Felix repeats, raising his eyebrows. "*Pas moyen!* I had to stay in that safe house for months while Max took care of things. I couldn't go to class or work, couldn't even use the Internet for fear those thugs would track me that way. I had to virtually disappear. I had to drop out of university. Never did go back for my degree," he finishes bitterly.

"But you survived," I tell him. He nods slowly.

"That's true. And I got a lifelong friend out of it!" he says, beaming. I get the sense that Max doesn't quite see him the same way, but I won't be the one to tell him that.

"So he really did leave all that behind, right? He's not working for those guys anymore?" I press him. I want so badly for him to ease all my worries, for him to tell me that Max really is safe, and that my feelings for him aren't terrible. I wonder if Felix even knows, though. Max is a secretive guy with a dark, mysterious past. He doesn't seem like the kind who would easily trust others with his secrets — and especially not someone like Felix.

"Oh yeah. *Absolument.* I think he was already way over all that by the time he even met me, and after what he had to do to get me out of trouble with them... well, let's just say I don't think they were planning on inviting him to the reunion anymore," Felix explains. "Burned a lot of bridges back then, used up what little was left of his credit with them. But if you ask me, nobody ever really gets a clean break from an operation like that. You can't just retire and say goodbye to your old life without some... complications."

"Like what?" I ask, my stomach churning.

"Well, I'm not the best authority on the inner workings of the mafia, but I have a feeling they're still watching him. Just waiting for the right time to take their revenge."

My eyes go wide with fear. Felix notices this and winces a little, realizing that he's probably said far too much. "I'm sure they would've done something by now if they were really going to, though."

"How many are there out there?" I ask, my voice barely a whisper. I can feel the air leaving my lungs as it dawns on me just how big this whole ordeal really is. I wasn't just swept up in some small-time operation; I was a fly caught in the complex web of a very large and venomous spider.

"Mobsters?" Felix asks, cocking his head to one side thoughtfully. "Well, it's probably like trying to play that arcade game — Whack-a-Mole, I believe it's called? The second you crush one, another pops up. But to his credit, Max really took out a lot of them himself. The Russians didn't see him coming. After all, I think they still saw him as one of them, you know? But once he found out what all they were doing with the sex trade and whatnot, he really eliminated a lot of them. I mean, they're still out there, of course. But not here. He really cleaned up the Paris scene a lot more than anyone knows," he says proudly, as though he had any hand in the process.

Something confusing stands out in my mind, tugging at my thoughts. Something I remember from my time locked up down in that horrible cell. Even though most of my captors spoke Russian, I recall them discussing in hushed voices their hatred of the Russians. As though they were a separate entity entirely.

"But there's something I don't quite understand," I start off slowly, poring over my thoughts to try and make sense of them.

Felix looks positively overjoyed at the chance to potentially school me on something. He's definitely the kind of guy who gets off on being a know-it-all. It's actually kind of endearing, in an odd way.

"What don't you get? I explained everything. What do you wanna know?" he pipes up, a little too excitedly, but I'm caught up in trying to untangle the question in my head.

"Those guys… the ones who captured me and held me in that horrible place," I begin, "I-I don't think they were Russian."

"What do you mean?" Felix asks, squinting at me condescendingly, like he's talking to someone of severely diminished intellect.

"They spoke Russian sometimes, but they also talked about hating the Russians. Like they weren't part of the same thing. I don't know. It doesn't make sense, does it? Maybe I just misunderstood them," I say quietly. But Felix's already huge eyes are widening, his mouth falling open. He reaches up and drags a hand back through his curls, some kind of grim realization coming over him.

"Oh no," he breathes, standing up suddenly.

"Wh-what? What is it?" I ask, panic seizing me, too. He looks genuinely frightened, all traces of his old cockiness dissipated.

"I've got to call him — I've got to warn him —"

"Warn who? About what?" I demand.

"Max! If those guys he's going to meet aren't Russian… that means he's walking straight into the den of the enemy. Into a trap," Felix reveals, frantically dialing his cell phone.

"What?!" I burst, rushing to his side.

He silences me with a harried shush and presses the receiver to his ear, listening to it ring over and over… with no answer. "*Merde*," he swears under his breath.

"What do we do?" I ask, my voice shaking.

Felix meets my gaze, looking absolutely petrified. "I don't know what we *can* do."

I find myself enraged at his defeatist tone. He can't possibly be considering just leaving Max to the wolves while we sit here and twiddle our thumbs. "Get your things. We're going to find him and warn him before it's too late," I order him firmly.

He looks at me like I've lost my mind. "But what if it's already too late?"

"We don't know that for sure, and I'll be damned if I let something bad happen to him without even trying to help. He's saved your ass and mine, and now it's time to return the favor," I declare, scooping up my jacket and purse, suddenly very grateful that Max had Felix bring me a change of my own clothes from the flat.

Felix hesitates a moment, but seeing the fire in my eyes, he finally sighs and relents.

"Okay, fine. Let's go."

And I very well just might've signed our death certificates.

The manor I arrive at is more of a villa, arranged in Roman fashion complete with weathered, ivy-covered walls and wafting gardens that seem to sing in the midday Parisian sunlight. The only thing marring the sight as I pull up to the side of the road not far from the entrance is the legion of guards patrolling the estate.

Even through the tall trees that line the cobble-stone path to the manor, it's clear they haven't made much of an effort to conceal their security, even if the men I see aren't carrying weapons out in the open.

There are three guards standing watch at the entrance, at least six men strolling along the tops of the walls, and every balcony I can see from here has at least one person on it, and eyes are starting to turn to my black sedan. Locals know to avoid this place, but it isn't uncommon for tourists to mistakenly head this way and be turned back with a kind but firm word.

But the car I drive means something. My black sedan is one of my old vestiges of the Bratva, and to see one pull up means someone is here to do business.

But as my eyes scan the men that I see, none of them look familiar. This isn't so much of a surprise — I've been away from business for a very long time, and men in the rank and file come and go in the span of a year or less. Still it means I may have to do some fast talking. I grimace as some of the men at the gates eye my car. I'd much rather storm the place. Three quick shots would put those men down, and I could slip to cover before the rest even had a chance to react. Better yet, I could just wait until nightfall and scale the wall without any of the guards being the wiser.

Any such dramatics, however, would put Maggie's life at a terrible risk, especially if word of my actions rescuing Liv has gotten around.

I feel a sudden sinking of my stomach as I think of her again, and I grip the steering wheel while almost unconsciously watching the guards' patrol routes on the walls, keeping an eye out for weaknesses. What if Liv decides to abandon my protection and try to handle herself on her own? What if the fear of what I am drives her to do something foolish?

I was trying to keep her safe, but opening up to her was a mistake that could very well put her in danger.

I frown, shaking my head. She's a smarter person than that, I know. But fear can make someone act against their better judgement, despite everything they know. Fear is something I like to think I have conquered long ago, after all the horror I've seen and endured, and after all that I've done, but I know better than to let my guard down.

I step out of my car, and I can feel the eyes of everyone guarding the villa turning to me. From here on out, I'm a known man, however this goes down. I take out my phone to make sure it's still off, just in case any of my old contacts I may meet in here have my number and decide to track me in the same way I've been tracking Liv and Maggie. Seeing it safely off, I take a few steps down the road towards the compound, making eye contact with the guards.

But I haven't taken more than a few steps before the sound of a roaring engine reaches my ears, and I turn to look down the opposite end of the road to see a car barreling down the street.

Instinctively, my hand goes to my side where a gun is stored, and I step back to the car, my muscles poising as adrenaline starts to kick in. Did they get tipped off somehow? Are these friends of the men back at the apartment complex come to head me off?

I swear under my breath as I hear voices coming from the villa. The men on the walls are at full attention now, and the guards at the doors are getting twitchy, their own hands moving to where I know concealed weapons to be held.

Whatever is coming my way, it doesn't seem to be expected. My fingers wrap around the handle of my pistol when the car comes screeching to a halt just a few feet from mine…

…and Liv jumps out of the passenger's side, her eyes wide with alarm.

"Max!" she hisses, rushing toward me, and I see Felix looking at me from inside the car on the driver's side. I'm doubly surprised when she throws her arms around me briefly, and I stare at her, bewildered.

"What are you doing here?!" I hiss a whisper back, glancing at the manor. "What if they recognize you?"

"No time!" she snaps, gesturing wildly for me to get back into the driver's seat of my car, "we need to go, *now!*" She wastes no time in slipping past me and getting into the passenger's seat of my car, and I can only look between the cars, dumbfounded for a moment before nodding and moving over to the driver's side of my car.

I glance back at the villa and see a few of the

guards chattering into phones, looking at us with furrowed brows, and I turn to call to Felix, "Split up!"

He nods, and the moment I'm in my car, I turn the ignition and pull out of there, zipping down the road and turning right where Felix turns left at the earliest possible intersection as my eyes move to the rear-view mirror periodically.

"What the hell just happened, Liv?" I ask her, trying to sound composed in what very well might have just blown my entire cover.

"I just saved your life," she says simply, trying to get a hold of her own breathing as she buckles her seatbelt. "I didn't realize you didn't know—those men and the men you saved me from aren't Russian, Max. They're Chechen."

My eyes widen in realization as I grip the steering wheel as we take another turn. It isn't long before I notice a sedan with tinted windows on our tail, and I take another sharp turn into traffic, weaving in and out with expert ease.

"Chechens?" I repeat, and realization dawns on me. "Of course. The Bratva didn't reinitiate the slave trade after I drove them out, they must have known better than that. The Chechen just stepped in to fill the power vacuum when they had the chance."

"But I thought you knew that guy with the burn on his face?" Liv asked, her hands wringing her seatbelt idly.

"I did," I say gravely, "but he was a Chechen among the Russians when I knew him the first time. When the Chechens stepped in to take up the remains of the human trafficking ring, Boris must have been one of the key contacts they used to rebuild it. He must have known everything they'd want."

"And you would have been walking into your own execution the moment they recognized you at that manor," says Liv, retrospective anxiety mingled with the relief in her brown eyes as we drive. After some clever maneuvering and turns through tangled neighbourhoods, I notice the sedan that had been following us isn't there; we've shaken them.

Liv notices my glancing back periodically, and she furrows her brow. "Will Felix be okay?"

"If there's one thing Felix has excelled at besides his computer toys," I say, leaning back and relaxing a little in my seat, "it's running away. And I don't mean that in a condescending manner — lesser men would have been dead long ago. I trust him to save his own skin. That said…"

I pull out my phone and turn it on, calling Felix's number and putting the phone to my ear as it starts to ring.

"What are you doing?!" Liv exclaims, and I look around as though I'm about to run into a car.

"Huh? What's the matter?"

"You can't use the phone while you're driving

—*especially* not in European traffic, are you nuts?" Of all the things she could be concerned about today, safe driving is apparently top of her list.

I give her a flat look and roll my eyes, but as she holds her gaze steady on me, adorably, genuinely concerned, I hand it over, and she puts it on speaker, holding it up with a satisfied look on her face. I narrow my eyes at her, but I can't hide an affectionate smile as I do.

"Hello? Max?" I hear Felix's voice from the phone.

"Felix," I say, "thanks for the warning, I owe both of you my life."

"Yeah, sure, we'll get some *petit fours* to celebrate, but what do we do about the murderous, sex-trafficking Chechens first?"

"They've seen us and our cars," I say, taking a deep breath as I consider just how bad things look right now, "so they know our faces and our license plates—I assume you've already shaken whomever was tailing you."

"Left 'em in the dust five blocks ago, but they got a look at my tags, I'm sure."

"Right. It's only a matter of time before they track us. My home isn't safe anymore."

"*Merde.* Fine, I'll go pay my grandmother a visit, I guess. Keep me posted, though, she has a lovely kitchen that I'd rather not see get *shot up by the mafia!*"

I tilt my head away from his shouting and reply in a bored tone, "You'll be fine, Felix. But you can't go anywhere that's tied to you, or they'll worm their way there. We'll meet up with you when we know what the next step will be. For now, remember the safehouse I stashed you away at the first time you came to me?"

"That old place? Is it still secure?"

"Yes. Head there, and take a little comfort in the tremendous favor I owe you now."

"Don't think I'll forget," he drones, "but will you be joining me?"

"No," I say firmly, "we need to remain separate."

"What? Max, where are you going—" but I tap the button to hang the phone up, ending the call before Liv puts the phone in her lap as she chews on her lip thoughtfully.

"I'm guessing you don't have a French grand-mother we can go lie low with in the countryside, do you?" she asks carefully, and I smile a bit. After a pause, Liv tilts her head as if asking for more.

"So if we aren't going to your safe house," she starts, "then where exactly are we heading?"

# LIV

*I* glance over at Max, whose knuckles are tensed and white over the steering wheel, his green eyes staring straight ahead. He's right beside me physically, but mentally he's in another realm entirely. I wish I could read his mind, see the racing train of thoughts in his head. Even though his expression is relatively serene — probably the result of years of training himself to be calm under duress — I know he's in turmoil over what move to make next. There's no doubt that I'm in over my head with this one, and I have no way of knowing whether this is too much for Max to handle, too.

I get the impression that he's dealt with far worse situations, but then again, what do I really know about him anyway? I know he's a good man with good intentions. At least, I think he is. I hope. Everything he's shown me thus far indicates to me that he's not one of *them*.

Although, knowing that he was part of that same sort of group once upon a time definitely chips away at my confidence in him just a little. It's hard to comprehend how this beautiful, noble knight of a man could have ever walked along the dark side. And I know there are shades of gray here. Just how far into darkness did Max once dive? And for how long?

And why? Was it just desperation? Did he ever enjoy this depravity?

But now is not the time to ask such questions. I can see a tiny muscle twitching in Max's strong jaw, and I want so badly to reach over to stroke his face to calm him. To reassure him that I trust him. To tell him I'm with him, no matter what.

It surprises me just how strongly and assuredly I feel this way. After all, we barely know each other, at least by conventional standards. And we were never meant to fall into this kind of dynamic, were we? I was going to be his student and he my disciplined mentor. But now every little stepping stone of the life path I designed for myself is being overgrown with weeds, obscuring the destiny I once saw so clearly before.

I haven't talked to my parents in so long. I wonder if they worry about me. I'm sure they do.

My mother is always worrying, always fussing over me. And my father, the easy crier, is probably distraught. I wonder if they've already contacted Interpol. Or maybe, just maybe, they're just chalking up my reticence to a newfound independence and freedom as a college student. I can just hear my mother saying, "She's a college girl now. A jetsetter! She doesn't have time to text her mom and dad every five minutes. Let her live, Chuck!"

I smile to myself a little sadly. I love them, of course, but I hope they have no idea what's happening to me right now. I couldn't bear the thought of shattering their hopes and dreams for me and my future. They couldn't take it. I don't even know how to tell them what has happened, and I'm afraid that if I do, they'll take me back home, desperate for me to be away from this trauma.

And I don't want to go. I don't want to completely walk off the path, and more than that... I don't want to leave Max. He's seen me at my most vulnerable, and has protected me through the worst night's sleep I've ever had, and that might not seem like a lot, but it formed a fast connection between us.

Besides, there's a full-blown crisis blooming dangerously all around me, and I have enough to worry about in the here and now. First of all, where is Maggie? I still don't know if she's even alive or dead. With what little I know of these slaver assholes, it could go either way. It probably depends on whether things worked out with her "buyer." I shudder at the thought of my new friend being traded away like some luxury good. Like she's just a pretty thing to use and abuse until she drops dead.

And to think… that was very nearly my fate, too.

I can't allow myself to believe that Maggie is dead, even though I doubt her life is preferable at the moment. I desperately hope that whatever filthy man purchased her isn't abusing her too harshly. I feel sick at the thought of her being mistreated. Maggie is so sheltered and soft — how would she ever survive?

I wonder if her parents have any idea what's going on. I know they'd probably have the money and power to save her, if anyone did. But then again, I don't think these guys would so easily give her up just for the sake of money. I get the feeling that this goes beyond a simple pay-off, that there's something more sinister. Like they do this for the thrill. Or because they just flat-out hate women. And if they were so happy to torture me before, when I was just a vulnerable, helpless girl in their clutches, how much worse would it get now that they've seen me with Max? Now that they know I'm an accomplice? An active opponent?

"We're going away," Max says suddenly, shaking me from my thoughts.

"Where?" I ask quietly, peering over the console at the side of his smooth face. His expression still reveals nothing about his state of mind, and his even tone doesn't offer much either. I wish he would do something — anything — to indicate what he's feeling.

"A different safe house I have used in the past," he answers simply.

"For how long?" I question, feeling a little nauseous. I still don't have my phone or any of my stuff. And I remember what Felix said about his own time at a safe house years ago — no computer, no going out. No nothing.

"I can't answer that," Max says reluctantly. He glances over at me as the car turns round a corner. There's a soft pleading light to his gaze. "You have to trust me."

"I do," I reply quickly. And I know it to be true. I trust him, implicitly, with my life. He's earned that, at least. "Is Felix going to be okay?"

A smile twitches at Max's lips. "I think so. He's more resilient than his looks would have you think. He knows the drill. Don't worry about him."

"And what about us?" I press, biting my lip.

The hint of a smile dissipates instantly. "We're going to get through this. I won't let anything happen to you, Liv."

"I'm sorry I got you into this," I burst out

suddenly, the dam of emotions having broken open to allow a flood of pent-up guilt and shame. "If not for me, none of this would have happened. Maggie would be okay. We'd all just be at the university doing exactly what we were supposed to do."

Max's arm reaches over the console, his hand landing on my knee gently. I recoil at the soft touch, my jumpiness betraying how scared I really am. He gives me a pained, broken look.

"Do not blame yourself for this. It isn't your fault. The blame rests elsewhere — with me, with those Chechen thugs, but not with you. Liv. You have to understand: these men are veterans of the trade. They know exactly what to do. You never stood a chance," he explains.

I feel a lump forming in my throat. "If I had just stayed in that night... if I had listened to my instincts..."

"He would have only found another way to ensnare you," Max breaks in, shaking his head as he pulls the car onto a busy highway. I realize vaguely that we've been driving for quite some time, with Paris falling away behind us in the rear-view mirror.

"I just wish I had been smarter. I-I should have known better," I murmur.

"No, Liv. You are the victim here. You *and* Maggie. The guilt cannot be placed on the victim. You did not choose for this to happen to you," he says firmly, his hand finding mine and giving it a squeeze. I nod, gulping back the tears threatening to fall. I have to be strong now.

"Where are we going?" I ask, forcing myself to change the subject.

"A small house I own out in the countryside," he answers. "It's off the books, untraceable for now. We will stay there until I can determine our next move. It will be a few hours' drive, so if you want to rest, go ahead."

I feel an untameable tingle at his phrasing: *our* next move. Not his. Ours. As though he trusts me, considers me a worthy partner, despite all the trouble I've caused. I have to admit that the sentiment spurs my self-confidence.

"I don't know if I'll be able to sleep at the moment," I confess honestly. My nerves are still aflame and my whole body is tensed up. "There's a lot running through my mind right now."

"I understand. But try, if you can. You've been through quite a lot, *malyutka*," Max says gently, and I'm amazed at the tenderness in his voice. It still shocks me how sharply this version of Maksim Pavlenko contrasts with the stiff, intimidating man I met back in the States. It occurs to me that Boris called me the same word in Russian that Max just used, but with none of the sneering. It doesn't hurt when he says it. It's not an insult in his voice.

"What does that word mean? *Malyutka?*" I ask, sounding out the foreign word crudely.

"Ah, the closest in English is 'little one'," he says, seeming a little embarrassed by having to tell me, but I can't help but smile a little. It's a strange word, but the way he says it makes my heart pitter-patter.

He smiles in return, and for several moments, we sit in a calm sort of silence. It's not long before I can't tame my nagging thoughts, though.

"What's going to happen to Maggie?" I ask sadly, pulling my legs up into the seat and getting more comfortable. Max does his best to keep his expression neutral, but I can see the flicker of worry across his face.

"Nothing, provided I get to her soon enough. And I promise you I will. If what you heard them say is true and she's already been sold, then she's been moved to another facility to await the trade-off with her buyer. I won't lie to you, Liv, if they've taken her to that last stop… her current conditions may not be good," he relates to me, more openly than I expected.

"What do you mean? What will they do to her there?" I breathe, suddenly feeling terribly cold and depressed. I had hoped things would be better for her, not worse.

"Keep in mind that we do not know for sure if that's where they've taken her. It has been a long, long time since I ran with that pack of wolves. Their methods may have changed," Max says, clearly reluctant to share details. But I need to know, even if it hurts.

"Tell me what you know. Please," I beg him, folding both my hands over his. He looks over at me and sighs. I can tell he wants to lie to protect me, and there's a battle behind his beautiful eyes, but the truth wins out.

"Before a girl is handed off to her new master, she is taken to a place where she is kept separately from the others. Some of the brutes call it 'finishing school.' It is where she must be broken in, polished off and prepared for her new life," he explains darkly.

"Broken in... how?" I press.

"The methods vary. Sometimes they starve her, refuse to let her sleep. This weakens her and makes her more pliant for the master, who is almost always looking for a malleable, soft girl who will do as she's told. And if she retains any hint of spirit, any *iskra*, they will do whatever they deem necessary to break her. It is terrible, especially if the girl fights back," Max describes, his voice heavy. I can tell it hurts him deeply to discuss this.

"Well, then maybe it is better that Maggie is already so quiet and obedient," I assure the both us. "Besides, she's a smart girl. I'm sure she'll figure out their game and do whatever she has to do to survive."

What I don't say, what I'm really thinking, is that

it will be unnecessary to try and break her because she's already broken. She was inconsolable when we were trapped in that cell together, already falling apart beyond repair. Maggie was too afraid to even utter a coherent word, much less defy anything they asked of her.

"She will be alright," Max says assuredly. "I'm sure of it."

"Yeah," I say to myself softly, my eyes feeling heavy. I am exhausted, and before long I manage to drift off to a fitful sleep.

WHEN I WAKE, I'm being carried over the threshold into a little white Tudor-style cottage with brown trim and shutters. As my vision clears I realize that the sun is setting, and that we're in the middle of nowhere, surrounded by dense green forest. This looks like a picturesque fairy-tale illustration, like we stepped right out of reality and into a children's book. But it's real — from the Spartan furnishings to the unmistakable, ominous call of an owl somewhere in the woods.

It's terribly quiet here except for the sounds of birds and the trees bowing in the wind. There can't be another soul out here for miles. Just the two of us. Alone.

Max takes me into a tiny bedroom and lays me down softly on the small wooden bed. The sheets are clean, to my surprise, and I wonder who Max has been paying to come all the way out here to maintain this place. I'm sure some lucky maid is making a fortune from it.

Thinking I'm still asleep, Max heads back out into the main room to make a few calls. He speaks in hushed tones, one call in French, another in Russian. I can't make out a word of what's being said, only that the news he receives can't be good. He groans in frustration and I hear him lean against a wall heavily, defeated. I can't keep up my charade any longer. I have to go to him.

I slide off the bed, careful not to mess up the crisp white sheets, and walk into the other room cautiously. Max is standing with his eyes closed and his arms folded over his chest. He looks like a tragic hero, a romantic prince thwarted by the villain one too many times. I want nothing more than to rush to him and melt into his arms, reassure him. There's something about this place, so far from the bustling Parisian streets, like another world altogether. One inhabited by only two: Max and me.

"What happened?" I ask timidly. Max's eyes flutter open and he looks over at me.

"My connections are tied at the moment. We have to wait for more information before we move on. We'll have to stay here for at least the night," he admits grimly.

I'm a little disappointed, but I know that we won't save Maggie by rushing anything. We need to be cautious, even more so now, and I nod at him gently.

"It's okay. We'll take the time to do things right."

He runs a large hand back through his dark hair and sighs. "It isn't fair to you, Liv. I will stand guard tonight while you sleep."

"No, that's silly," I disagree, shaking my head. "You need to rest, too."

"I promise I will get some rest in here. On the floor."

"Why would you do that? There's a perfectly good bed in there," I tell him, confused as to why he's acting so cagey all of a sudden.

"That's where you will sleep," he replies.

"Right. And you, too."

Max stares at me, his expression conflicted. "We can't do that again, Liv," he says softly.

I take a step closer, frowning. "Why not?"

"As I said, it isn't fair. It isn't right."

"I'm not complaining," I tell him firmly. "Unless you… unless you just don't want to."

He looks physically pained by the assumption. "No," he responds quickly.

"Then why not, Max? We've shared a bed already. I've seen you — all of you. It doesn't matter anymore how we got here." My words aren't planned, they just tumble out, raw and unfinished, the unbridled truth. His blazing eyes search my face desperately, though I don't know what he's looking for. He turns to face me, reaching out hesitantly to take my hands.

"Why aren't you afraid of me?" he murmurs, almost more to himself than to me.

I cock my head to the side. "Because I know you. Felix told me everything, Max. I have no reason to fear you."

Max moves closer, the internal struggle evident on his face. "It was much easier for me when you did," he whispers.

"Too late now," I reply quietly, tilting my face upward as our lips meet in an inevitable, questioning kiss. His lips are so soft and sensuous against mine, cautious at first. And then his hands move to pull me closer and I gasp into his mouth as he kisses me more passionately. My whole body tingles with pent-up desire. I have known from the first moment his skin touched mine that this would happen. I knew we would end up here. It was only a matter of time.

We were always walking down this path. I just never saw it until now.

His one hand wraps itself in my hair, tugging gently, while the other slides down to cup my ass. I can feel his cock straining through his trousers, hard against my thigh. His arms wrap around me and in one shared, fluid movement, he supports me as I hoist myself up into his embrace, my legs folding around his waist. His lips trail down my jaw to nip at my neck, making me gasp and moan in pleasure. I've never been touched like this before — never even been kissed except for that one unnatural, unwanted kiss from Will.

But this... I want this more than anything, without a hint of doubt.

Being so close, his scent teases my nose, a rugged cologne that brings out his masculinity. I've never been so aware of how someone smells, how they touch, and certainly never how they tasted. His tongue presses in against mine and a thrill goes down my spine as my mouth opens to let him explore.

My eyes close, and for a moment, it's like the entire world stands still. All the tension of the day drains away as I'm held by him, as his mouth moves from mine down to my neck, and back again. He's ravenous for me, his body intent on exploring mine. It's a thrill I've never known, and my hips slowly start grinding against his waist, needy for more.

Max carries me easily into the bedroom and presses me down into the bed, crawling over me and kneeling to take off his jacket and shirt, revealing his strong, broad chest and muscular arms. I look again over his scarred chest, over all the marks of his storied past, and this time I don't recoil. This time I just accept them, like I accept him. My fingertips go to the burn mark, lightly touching it, as if in apology for all the pain it has caused him. It was a symbol of who he was, and now it's gone, but never forgotten.

He bends down to kiss me again, his fingers trailing down to tug my leggings down, tossing them aside, then doing the same with my flowy tank top. I feel so vulnerable, but at the same time... that feels good. Because I can trust him. The way he looks at me, over my partially nude body, makes my breathing hitch in my throat. I wonder what he's thinking about when he's looking at me.

I don't have to wonder long, though, because quickly his mouth drops to my collarbones, and he's licking and suckling my skin, his hands working up and down my legs.

"You're so beautiful," he says, his voice huskier with passion. "From the first moment I saw you, I knew I'd have to watch myself with you."

His words send a jolt through my nerves, and he lifts me up against him, grazing his teeth along the hollow behind my ear as he unhooks my bra and drops it over the side of the bed. Gently laying me back down, he hovers over me a moment, his enigmatic green eyes surveying my bare breasts. I always feared that I would feel uncertain in this moment, but instead I just feel liberated.

I feel wanted.

"I tried to resist you," he says, his fingers running

over my flesh, along my rib cage, exploring me with his fingertips. "I know I should, even now. But I've never felt like this for a woman, and I don't know if I'll ever have this chance again."

His honesty startles me, and I have to bite my lip just to keep from gasping. I had no idea I meant that much to him. I had no idea I could mean that much to anyone. My fingers go to his dark, tousled hair, and they run through it, guiding his mouth back to mine.

"I want you to be my first, Max," I say, and that makes him pause. That battle again goes on behind his eyes, the knowledge that we shouldn't be doing this. I'm his student, someone he's supposed to be looking out for, but I think he's done that better for me than anyone ever could.

And I know our connection, what we feel, won't go away. Our attraction was always meant to bubble over like this, and I don't want to fight it.

"Don't fight it," I say, and my mouth meets his once more. I've never learned how to kiss, but my tongue probes his lightly, like he'd done to mine, and within a few seconds, I feel him press back in before pulling back.

"I won't take advantage of you, after all you've been through," he says, and for a second I think that means he's going to leave, but instead his mouth encompasses my left breast, taking my nipple in between his teeth. The little spark of pain makes me moan.

"Ah, that feels good," I whimper, and he bites down a little bit harder, holding the pressure there until I'm squirming beneath him, my entire body feeling like it's filled with electricity.

Max's other hand cups my right breast, his thumbs sliding over my sensitive nipples so that I inhale sharply, my eyes rolling back in my head. I never knew I could feel this good, this blissful. But when he pinches the other nipple, I can't help but gyrate my hips a little with excitement.

"Oh god, Max," I whimper, and his green eyes look up at me, and seeing him there, sucking on my breast is the most erotic thing I've ever seen in my life. He lets my breast fall from his mouth as he grins at me, as if he's just figured me out.

"You like a little bit of pain, *malyutka?*" he asks, and it sends another shiver down my spine. I don't answer, and his fingers reach down between my legs, feeling out the source of my heat. "You do like it," he confirms, rubbing me gently, with only my panties separating us.

My body certainly does, and I try not to think about what that says about me. As he rubs me, he kisses my neck, my collarbone, my exposed breasts, with every touch feeling so new and different. Some are rougher, and then gentler, and the contrast is driving me mad.

He lets go of my nipple, all stiff and tingling with sensation, and lets his other hand roam down my body, feeling out along my hip.

"You're the most beautiful girl I've ever met, Olivia," he says, his fingers grazing over my athletic body. I've always been a bit self-conscious about my looks, but there's such earnestness in his voice that I can't dare question him.

His fingers pull away from my pussy, and for a second, I think he's going to leave me. Instead, his fingers work into the waistband of my panties, tugging them down so slowly I think I'm going to die. No one has ever seen me like this, and the way he's unveiling me, like a Christmas present, is at once scary and mind numbingly hot.

I watch as he does, as he inhales the scent of my pussy, and the rumble in his chest as he does so.

"Like a sweet peach," he says before grinning up at me. "I'm going to take a taste."

Before I can say another word, his face is buried between my thighs, and the most sensational pleasure ever is shooting through me. I can't help but cry out, and it's so intense, I try to squirm away. His large hands, though, clasp down on my thighs, and with his brute strength, he holds me still and makes me feel the explosive pleasure that I've never known.

"Oh god," I whimper, my fingers tangling in his hair.

It's so intense, especially as he slowly slides one

finger inside of me, my pussy clenching tightly around it. I've never had anyone inside of me before, in any way. Max drags his tongue in a tantalizing circle around my tight little bundle of nerves while his finger slides in and out, stroking against a part of me I never knew existed.

It brings a perfect silence to my mind, and everything else drifts away, leaving me to fully experience him and his body as it presses against mine. When I twitch and flinch away he firmly holds me in place, his eyes meeting with mine.

It's unlike any other sight in the world. This big, strong Russian man between my slender thighs, his mouth moving over my most private of parts. It looks so sexy that I can't hold back anymore, and the flood dams open, and I yelp — my first ever orgasm crashes over my body.

"*Khoroshaya devochka*," Max mumbles, his voice thick with need.

He's slow to move away, though, making sure every jolt of pleasure has passed through me before he finally sits up, wiping his mouth with the back of his hand as he looks down on me. There's a fire behind his eyes, and excitement that wasn't there before, as if he's just now come alive. I like it, and more than that, I like the fact that I made him look so blissful with just my own pleasure.

His large hands drop to the front of his trousers, his hand hanging there for a second as he studies my face. I'm not sure what he's looking for, but he seems to have found it in my post-orgasm expression, because his fingers then work his way out of his pants, letting his massive cock spring free.

I can't help but stare once more, and this time there's no shame of spying on him when I wasn't invited. This time, I can truly appreciate him in his full maleness. It's so much bigger than when he was in the shower, and it stands erect, bouncing every few moments as his eyes study my body.

"I'll go gentle for your first time," he says, and I nod as I reach out to touch him. It's so curious, so heated and hard, yet his skin is so soft and ribbed with pulsing veins. His cock jumps at my touch, and I recoil my hand, looking up at him.

He laughs, not cruelly, and reaches out for my hand once more, guiding it back to him. He wraps my fingers around him, and he must see that being taught what to do eases my tensions, because he begins teaching me how to stroke him.

Our eyes meet as our hands move up and down his cock, and I can't help but give him a small, excited smile.

"Get on your back again," he says, and I obey, laying my head back on the pillows. "Spread your legs."

Again, I obey, and this pleases him. He looks down on my wet, spread pussy, and it sends an illicit thrill through my body.

"You have the prettiest little pussy," he says, his voice heavy with lust, and he reaches down, drawing some of my juices up to my clit again. "There's no going back from this. If you give this to me, we'll forever be bonded," he says, and I love the way he says that.

And I love the idea that we'll always have a link to one another, something far happier and more fulfilling than him saving me from slavers. This is something I want, something I'm choosing.

Something I can give him that he desires.

He grabs hold of his cock as he leans over me, holding himself up on his right arm as he looks me in the eyes. And that's when I feel it. The head of his cock touches against my virginal opening, and I gasp. He pauses, and I wonder if he's concerned that I've changed my mind. I wrap my arms around his neck, though, and that assuages him enough to begin to sink his full, powerful length within me.

It feels like so long, yet so short of a time before he's rested into my depths. I was always warned it would hurt, but it's just a dull ache, a strange sensation that's not altogether unpleasant, and when he stills, it quickly fades into a distant memory.

He groans before his mouth finds mine, my scent still on his lips, filling my nostrils with its strange sweetness. My tongue lashes against his, and with that he pulls back, letting his hips fall back to mine once more, filling me over and over again.

"Max," I gasp, my head tilted back into the pillow, my fingers digging into his shoulders. "Oh, you feel so good," I manage between panted breaths.

With my encouragement, his pace quickens, his thrusts coming a bit harder, a bit faster, and I gasp, but hold on tighter. I don't want him to stop.

He bites my lip, and that little bit of pain excites me, sends me closer to that edge. Already I'm so sensitive from my earlier orgasm that each thrust seems to bring me closer and closer to the precipice. But when he lifts my right leg with his arm, pinning me back and fucking me even deeper, that's when I start screaming in pleasure.

I am fit and in shape, but there's nothing like the power in his thickly coiled muscles, not in me, not in anyone I've ever known. He's all power, and all that strength is put towards him pistoning into me, driving me into a delirious pleasure-fever as my body heats, my cries grow louder.

Just as my second orgasm bursts, Max shouts my name and buries himself inside me, holding perfectly still as a stream of his hot seed fills my pussy. It's so reckless, so dangerous, and so blissful all at once. It makes me feel more alive than I ever have, in all my years. Nothing, absolutely nothing, can compare to this moment.

We stay this way, panting breathlessly, for several minutes as we slowly come back to reality, and the realization of what line we've crossed comes back to us.

His eyes bore into mine, reflecting the same question back to me...

*Where do we go from here?*

MAX

As I put my clothing from earlier today back on, I can feel Liv's eyes watching me from the bed, the sheets half-off her naked body, and I know the question is going to come before she can even form it in her mind.

"You're planning on leaving me behind, aren't you?" Her voice is plaintive, but I don't fail to hear the defiance at the tail end of her words.

"I need to go back to the manor, Liv," I say, slipping on a pair of black gloves and making sure my jacket has everything I need in it. "Chechens or no, Felix traced Maggie's cell phone to that location, and that's precisely where I need to be. They're already on high alert after everything that happened during our visit, so I'll need to be extremely careful." I look her in the eye even as she starts to stand up. "That means I need to act alone tonight, Liv."

"You *cannot* expect me to sit back and let you walk into whatever you're walking into without me," she says incredulously as she pulls her pants and shirt back on, still only half-clothed as she follows after me while I head back into the living room and get the last of my things.

"*You* cannot expect me to let you follow me into this deathtrap," I fire back. "This place is quiet and safe — nobody will be able to find you here, and you can lie low as long as you need to. I've put Felix's number in your phone in case you need to contact him. Do so if you don't hear back from me by tomorrow morning."

"Max—" she starts, but I cut her off.

"These are men who are past the point of trying to take you back, Liv. If either of us were caught, we'd be killed." I start towards the door, but she follows at my heels, unrelenting.

"Exactly! And that's why I'm not letting you go alone. Max, you're unlike anyone I've ever met before, but you can't take on a manor full of mobsters alone."

I turn and raise an eyebrow at her as I'm halfway out the door, the cool night breeze flowing into the little homestead as the moon shines down on the countryside behind me, my form outlined as if on the precipice of heading out into an inky black dreamscape.

"And you want to do what, come with me into

that dark life, Liv? Pick up a gun and start shooting as if you were born doing it? I can't let you go down that road with me." Our eyes meet for a painfully long moment before I say, "I care for you far too much for that."

She clenches her jaw, unconvinced. "I don't want to kill anyone, but that doesn't mean I can't still help you keep yourself out of trouble!" Before I can respond, she ducks under my arm and zips out the door faster than I realized she could move, dashing for the car in long, bounding strides while I'm left dumbfounded on the doorstep.

"Liv!" I hiss, walking out after her even as she opens the passenger's door and clambers in, buckling her seatbelt defiantly and crossing her arms with a smug look on her face that reaches me by the time I arrive at the door.

"I'm going with you, Max," she says again, the look in her eyes downright daring me to try and stop her.

And so I do.

With a sigh, I reach into the car and unbuckle her seatbelt, trying to get a hold of her. "Hey! What the hell are you doing?!" she exclaims as she wriggles away from me. I manage to get a hold on her hips, but she inexplicably twists away and breaks my grip on her. The same happens when I take her by the wrists, and she puts her feet on the dashboard, squirming out of the way with frustrating ease.

"I'm not going to — ungh! — let you get killed, Liv!" I say while wrapping my arms around her midsection and pulling her out of the car entirely, but seemingly defying physics, she slithers down and out of my grip as though she were made of rubber, trying to hop back into the passenger's seat, and by the time I try wrapping my arms around hers and pin them behind her back, I have to slide myself in between her and the door to keep her from getting in, but she still manages to slip a leg around me.

I'm amazed that she's able to evade me for so long—I've been able to hold onto some of the most muscular men in the Bratva with no problem, and I've tussled with hardened killers, but this short girl is keeping away from my grasp as easily as if we were playing a game. Then I remember that she is a world-class gymnast, and I feel a smile tugging at my face while she wrestles with me. I'm trying to keep a grip on living water.

"Stop that! Hey!" she says in protest as she realizes I'm laughing, and I only catch myself doing so when she points it out. We're half tangled up in each other against the car door, and I relinquish myself into an embrace with her as we find ourselves locked against each other, and Liv slaps me on the chest plaintively even as we break down into laughter at each other. Finally, I step back, and she looks up at me, defiance mingled with the affection that makes her whole expression light up in the starlight.

"Alright," I say at least with a heavy breath, realizing that her tenacity is perhaps a force to be reckoned with, "get in. I'll need to brief you on a few things on the way over there." Her expression brightens up like a fireworks display, and we climb into the car, pulling out mere moments later into the evening roads.

I'm not thrilled with the arrangement, but I've just been given an idea about how she can help.

I BRING the car to a stop several blocks away from the manor, and we step out silently, beginning our trek to the estate like a pair of shadows among the French architecture. I have to glance over my shoulder a few times as we walk to make sure Liv is still behind me, and each time, I see her shining eyes looking back up at me, never deviating from her pace, even if my trained ears can't hear her.

She's good at keeping quiet. Whether she's as skilled at maneuvering through the compound once we arrive is another matter entirely.

"The space behind the manor is somewhat wooded," I explain as we approach, "that's why we're moving around the edge of the grounds. Any other route, and they'll spot us from a mile away. We're only here to scope the place out tonight."

"We aren't rescuing Maggie?" she whispers, incredulous.

"If we go in blind, we'll be killed within minutes," I say. "I spent days, sometimes weeks learning the patterns of my targets and their guards when I carried out my work for the Bratva. I consider this a rush job."

"And if they spot us?" she whispers back after a tense pause.

"Keep moving, don't worry about me. If your legs can carry you as fast as I saw earlier, you won't have trouble outmaneuvering them. Disappear into the city and take a cab to drive around for a while, then head to your old university dorm once you're sure nobody is tailing you. I'll wait for you there."

"If we get caught," she clarifies.

"If we get caught," I affirm.

Once we're up to the wooded area and moving up on the manor walls, Liv moves up ahead of me quickly and silently, making less sound than a fox sneaking around a guard dog. I watch her nimbly make her way a short distance up a tree nearby, squinting up at the walls of the villa while I crouch nearby. Her brow furrows, and she slithers back down to my side.

"No guards on the walls," she reports, and I blink in surprise, looking up there myself to confirm her statement. I don't have as good a view as she did, but it looks like she's right. I nod for us to proceed, and we sneak up to the base of the walls, where the ivy wafts above us in the breeze, moonlight catching on their broad leaves, but not a sound of footsteps can be heard up on the walls, nor the chatter of men on guard duty beyond.

Frowning, Liv glances at a tree that sways just next to the walls, and before I can stop her, she starts shimmying up the branches as if she were born in the trees. I look on in no little wonder at her body.

Despite being so small and fragile, she's remarkably nimble and dexterous, even for gymnastics students of her caliber. I give a smile, proud of her for being so quick to adapt her natural talents and hard-earned skill to a new environment so quickly. And as she moves, I admire her lithe legs all the way up to her ass, and I feel the lust for her I felt just a couple of hours ago back at our hideout. My mind starts to swim with the wrongness of it all — I slept with my student, a girl already in a new country and a desperate situation.

She put her life into my hands, and I made her mine.

And when she looks down and smiles at the look I'm giving her from below, I know we both crave more. For right or for wrong, there's no going back, and there's not an ounce of me that wants to. Hearing her sweet moans, seeing her body writhe against mine... it was the sweetest pleasure my life has ever known.

Then my heart nearly stops as I watch her push off the tree and catch herself on the edge of the wall, no fear in her eyes. She peeks up over the edge and looks around, but I hear no sounds of shouting, no gunshots, and no frenzy for Liv to scramble back down. Instead, she turns and hisses a whisper back down to me.

"Empty!"

I pause, staring up at her. "...empty?"

"Completely," she says, "nobody on the walls or the courtyard, not even the balconies."

My first thought is of ambush. But how could they anticipate our arrival, and what kind of ambush would entail all of them leaving the grounds like this? Something sits very sourly with me, and I gesture for Liv to get down.

She climbs her way back to the ground with ease, and we slip around the side of the building cautiously, peeking around each corner as if expecting a gunman behind each one, but there isn't a sign of life to be found.

Finally, we reach the guard post at the front entrance, and my suspicion is confirmed — there's nobody here. I draw my pistol, moving close to the booth, and I stand up over it and push the gun through the open window.

Nothing.

I look around at the courtyard and see only a lone squirrel bound away from us near a decorative tree. A fountain towards the center is turned off, and it's deathly silent all around. We head in, keeping close to the walls and moving around the side of the building.

My eyes are on the windows, waiting for a curtain to move or for me to see a pair of eyes watching us or a rifle scope trained on us, but there's simply nothing. Something starts to nag at me, and I start to take out my phone to call Felix when I catch Liv out of the corner of my eye, climbing up the side of the wall towards one of the balconies.

"Liv!" I hiss, alarmed and stepping forward towards the building.

But she's already up at a balcony, and to my astonishment, she just peeks into the window doors as if she were breaking into her own home. "Nothing," she mouths down to me.

I climb up after her, my old instincts kicking in like riding a bike after a long time, and I land beside her, moving forward to pick the lock to the place. The lock clicks after a moment, giving me pause. I'd have expected unlocked doors and windows if they were expecting to ambush us.

Before I can stop her, Liv slips inside, and I follow after her, pistol out and to the ready.

"Oh my god..." she breathes as she looks out on what she sees, and I frown deeply.

We're on the second floor of the building, standing on a walkway. The floor ends about five feet into the building, and an ornate metal railing lines the edge that opens out to a full view of the ground floor, which is a stunning sight. There are Italian busts and statues lining the walls, remarkably expensive plants garnishing each one at the base. What seems to be a marble fountain sits in the middle of the room, and I see rose petals scattered throughout the whole place.

"It's beautiful," Liv says.

"If you could see what takes place in lavish manors like these," I say grimly, "you'd change your tone."

We start to make our way inside, and it doesn't take long to realize the place seems as empty as the exterior was. There isn't a sound to be heard nor a light on. We make our way down the stairs, and the sight before us starts to become a little clearer.

There's a grand piano on display, and I can see empty champagne glasses sitting on it and the edge of the fountain, a bottle left here and there. As I move up to inspect them, I notice that some have red lipstick still on the rim. The black of the piano reveals a fine white powder in very trace amounts near some of the glasses, and to my disgust, I notice a used condom shoved behind the leg of the instrument.

"Hell of a party," Liv says, but her tone is more

somber now, and I know she's thinking of the same thing I am: where was Maggie for all this?

Further inspection of the room reveals more of the same. There seems to have been some kind of wild, hedonistic revelry here in the recent past, but everyone seems to have cleared out very quickly. The entire time Liv and I look the place over, my pistol is out, and my eyes spend half their time focusing on the doors to other rooms, just waiting for the mob to burst in.

No such thing happens.

I move over to the front door and find it locked. "Whoever left the house really abandoned this place," I say, unlocking the door for our convenience before moving back to the center of the room with Liv, who's sitting on the edge of the fountain and gazing down into the waters thoughtfully. "I don't think Maggie is here any longer, Liv."

"I want to check the basements and the guest rooms," she says, looking at me, but her eyes tell me she doesn't quite have confidence in her own claims.

"We will," I say, putting a hand on her shoulder as I sit down beside her, and the next moment, she throws her arms around me, pressing her face into my chest and suppressing a sob.

"They could have done anything to her here, Max," she says, fists clenching in my clothes. "How can people be so evil? She doesn't know *anyone* in this country but me. If it weren't for you, I might have been here too!" She looks up at me, tears in her eyes, and I put my hand against her cheek, leaning forward and kissing her on the lips.

"These men are hardly human," I say as I break the kiss, looking at her with a stony gaze. "They gave up their right to live when they began this ring under my watch. I said what I meant when I told you I'll find her. *We*'ll find her, Liv." I smile and return her hug, holding her tightly and comfortingly. "You're a remarkable woman with remarkable talents. Maggie couldn't ask for a better friend."

Liv looks up to me, some small reassurance in her eyes now, and she opens her mouth to talk when a sounds snaps our attention to the front door.

It swings open forcefully, and I stand up, my hands gripping my pistol with trained expertise as it moves up to point straight at the figure who bursts into the manor before our eyes.

*I* shrink back behind Max instinctively, my heart pounding violently in my ribcage. My eyes follow the length of his muscular arms to his fingers wrapped confidently around a gun. I can feel my blood running cold at the sight of the man I adore holding such a horrible weapon. People back home in North Carolina are obsessed with guns, but I've never been a fan, myself. Too many things can go wrong.

And I've never seen someone hold a gun like Max, never seen that expression in someone's eyes. It's the same expression I saw on him back in the basement when he saved me. Dark, cool. Prepared. There's no way he's going to mess this up.

There's a beat, though, and Max delays. I poke my head out from around him, curious as to what's happening, and I see Felix throw his arms up in a gesture of surrender, his eyes going even bigger behind his spectacles. His mouth falls open and he stops short, staring at Max's gun.

"Whoa! *Saint-merde!* I come with bad news, but don't shoot the messenger!" he squeaks, shaking his head vigorously.

Max lowers the gun and places it back in the holster at his hip, under his jacket. Somehow I hadn't even noticed it there, despite the fact that I've been with him almost every second for the past few days. I suppose that's why he's so good at this: years and years of experience have taught him how to be subtle. It would be terrifying if I was on the other end of it, but from where I'm standing, it's a godsend. Having Max on my side is encouraging in all kinds of ways. I know I don't have to be afraid when I'm with him. He can protect the both of us better than anyone else can.

Felix comes trudging over, shrugging off his former terror and adopting an air of casual detachment, as usual. Max asks, "You said you have bad news. Anything to do with the fact that this place is dead empty?"

The younger man nods, pushing his glasses back up the bridge of his nose. "Oh yeah. There's nobody here because the party has traded up venues. The signal's moved."

"To where?" Max questions, ready to jump into action. He reaches over to take my hand, preparing to run. It warms my heart to see just how naturally he reaches for me — like I'm second nature to him now, already. And it's true. Being with him, following him around, being at his side... it all feels right. Like I'm supposed to be here, and my whole life has just been one long waiting period, the calm before a beautiful, impossible storm.

And I know what I'm doing is dangerous, and he doesn't want me in the thick of it. Maybe being so close to death has made me more fearless, or maybe knowing that I need to save Maggie from an awful fate is what's pushing me forward.

Or maybe it's simply what I said to Max. I want to keep him safe, like he's been keeping me safe.

"Don't get too excited. I've got more bad news," Felix quips, holding up one finger. "The phone must be dead. The signal disappeared while I was tracking it, so I can only assume it ran out of juice or someone caught on and turned the damn thing off. I have no idea where they went, Max. I'm sorry."

For once, there's no note of derision or sarcasm in his voice. Felix knows what a blow this is, how truly screwed we are now. Max looks down, his dark brows furrowed. I squeeze his hand gently, watching his face. Finally, he looks back up, takes a deep breath, and shrugs.

"Well, *est' shto est'*. We can't stay here and wait on the off chance they'll come back. Our best bet right now is just to go somewhere safe and wait for more information," he says gravely.

"Where will we go? Back to the cottage in the country?" I ask, gazing up at Max.

He's deep in thought. Felix and I wait patiently for him to answer.

Finally, he says, "No. I don't want to go that far this time, just in case they're closer to the city. I want to be ready. Besides, it's late. We need to go somewhere to rest, and the cottage is a long drive from here. I'll get us hotel rooms. You, too, Felix."

"D'accord! We can spend the night strategizing! I've got an idea for —"

Max holds up his hand to stop him, shaking his head. There's a slightly bemused smile pulling at his lips. "No, you'll have your own room."

Felix looks back and forth between the two of us, realization dawning on his face. He looks a little put-out, but he plays it off like it's nothing. "Oh. Yeah, yeah. *Bien sûr,*" he quips, waving it off.

"How did you get here? Taxi?" Max asks, starting to head toward the exit. Felix and I stride after him, trying to keep up.

"Yeah."

"Good. You'll ride with us now to the hotel."

"What hotel?"

Max's face breaks into the first genuine, unabashed smile I've seen on his face for a while. He glances across at me, those bright green eyes flashing. "I think we've all had enough stress to warrant some, ah, more comfortable accommodations."

Felix lights up. "Free Wi-Fi, I assume?"

"*Bien sûr,*" Max says, winking at him. I don't think I've ever seen him wink before. He's trying to lighten the bleak mood that's overtaken us, and as crestfallen as I am, I appreciate the gesture.

I can't help but wonder where he's taking us as we load into the car and drive away from the manor. Felix is chattering away in the backseat, trying to make small talk. It's obvious that he's kind of a lonely guy. I get the feeling he's not used to having people around. I wonder what he does to pass the time these days, now that he's not working at the school anymore. I turn around in the front passenger seat to face him.

"Felix, what do you do nowadays? I mean, where do you work?" I ask. He blinks at me in complete surprise, then warms to the subject immediately. Next to me in the driver's seat Max is smiling, clearly pleased that I'm trying to make a connection with his friend. Felix may be weird and more than a little bit obnoxious, but I can tell he's got a good heart.

"Oh, mostly work-from-home hacker stuff. People hire me to... investigate things. Look into their cheating spouse's finances, check up on international business transactions, you know.

Sensitive stuff, but nothing too top-secret," he explains, trying to be nonchalant.

"That's impressive," I remark. "You're pretty much a private investigator."

The faintest blush colors his cheeks. "Yeah, basically. Gotta make a living somehow. Paris is not a cheap city to live in."

"You wouldn't change it for the world, though, would you?" I comment. Felix shakes his head incredulously.

"*Saperlotte*, no! This is the best city on the planet. Even if they raised my rent every single month, I would find a way to stay here," Felix replies passionately. "I never belonged back in that boring little town where I grew up. This is my home."

"And I guess now it's mine, too," I murmur, turning back around in my seat.

Max shoots me a slightly concerned glance at my shift in tone. I should know better than to try and hide anything from him. He picks up on my homesickness, the twinge of sorrow in my voice. I do love Paris — it's beautiful and historic, it feels like living in a fairy-tale setting. But it's still a foreign place to me. The streets don't feel welcoming and familiar like they do back home in the tiny, quiet town of Toast.

It probably hurt my first impression to be kidnapped my first night here.

"To be fair, you haven't really gotten the best

impression of Paris so far," Felix comments, reading my thoughts. It's true. So far, I've been drugged, kidnapped, threatened, and my roommate has been stolen to who knows where. My whole life has been turned upside down.

"I hope my parents are okay. I-I'm scared that they're worried about me," I say quietly.

Max reaches across the console to take my hand. "Don't be afraid. I've taken care of that," he says, a little mysteriously.

"What do you mean?" I ask, confused.

Felix pipes up, "Can I tell her?"

Max sighs and nods. "Go ahead."

"So, we knew your parents would want to hear from you so they wouldn't freak out and think something was wrong—"

"Because they would be right to think that," I interject.

"Yeah," Felix agrees, a little sheepishly. "So, basically, Max had me break into your phone to access your texts. I ran your outgoing messages through a style-simulation software I built and it basically learned how to emulate your way of speaking. Via text, of course."

"Wait, what?" I stop him, totally bewildered at this point, both by the confusing explanation and the apparent invasion of privacy I had no awareness of until now.

"Okay. Let me break it down for you," he says,

and I choose to ignore the hint of unintentional condescension in his tone. "Everyone has their own way of talking. Everyone sounds a little different. And your parents know you better than anyone, so if I were going to send them messages, I needed them to sound totally convincing. So what I did was take a sample of the texts you sent in the past, run them through my style-copy program on my computer, and it learned how to essentially mimic you. So I've been texting your parents *en secret*, keeping them updated on how things would be going at school… if you were actually going."

I sit in silence for a long moment, trying to work through how I should feel about this revelation. On the one hand, I'm a little miffed and offended at having my privacy so harshly intruded upon. After all, it kind of crosses a line to have Felix, a near stranger, impersonating me in conversations with my own parents whom he's never met. But on the other hand, it's nice to know that my parents have been kept totally out of the loop on this whole messy situation. The last thing I need is for them to worry about me. And knowing how overprotective my father is, he probably would have called the police, Interpol, and the President by now if he had even the slightest inclination to believe I'm in trouble. So really this is for the greater good. Even if it kind of sucks to have it happen this way.

"And you're sure they don't suspect a thing?" I ask slowly.

"They're convinced it's you talking to them. They're hanging on your every fake text. What's the phrase you Americans use? Hook, line, and sinker?" Felix says adamantly.

"Alright. Well, I can't say I'm particularly enthused about having your computer pretend to be me, but still, if it keeps my parents from having an aneurysm worrying about me, I guess it's okay," I admit reluctantly.

"We're here," Max comments, changing the subject. I look out the window into the midnight darkness. The streetlights cast a fuzzy, romantic glow over the cobblestone streets and I crane my neck to look up at the gorgeous, pale building beside us, numerous open windows decorating its smooth face. I squinted to make out the golden letters flanked on either side by French flags which read *Le Meurice*.

"*Merde*," Felix whispers, his eyes round and huge.

"I have a friend who works the concierge," Max remarks. "I've convinced him to book a junior suite for you, Felix."

"What about us?" I ask, turning to look at Max. He gives me a grin.

"We're on the seventh floor. The *Belle Etoile* Suite," he tells me. These words don't mean much to me until we enter the lobby of the building and my jaw drops instantly.

This place is beautiful, absolutely breathtaking. Felix heads off to his own suite, nearly floating away down the hall, he's so giddy. Max takes me by the hand and leads me up to the top floor, where our room is located.

"Max, this is amazing," I breathe, turning in a slow circle to take in the vaulted ceilings, white carved panel walls, luxurious fabrics, monstrously-huge bed, vintage furniture, and balcony. As I walk toward the double doors which open to the outside, I notice that it isn't just a balcony — it's a full terrace, with a full view of the cityscape in all directions.

I feel a strong hand on my shoulder, Max's thumb tracing a circle on the nape of my neck as we both step through the doors. Even though it's warm outside, this far up there's a lovely breeze that swirls around us, lifting my hair in playful tousles. We have a perfect view of the Eiffel Tower illuminated in the distance, the moon hanging like an antique lantern, casting a sepia glow over the sleeping city.

It's beautiful, and I can feel tears of over-whelming emotion rising in my eyes. Despite the terror of the past several days, the danger both past and future — I can't help but give in to the intense beauty of the moment. Everything is so still and quiet and calm up here, just the two of us pressed together under the starry sky.

And if I'd never been kidnapped, this never would've happened. I'd never have realized how much Max draws me in. I'd have been left with a stern instructor who was hiding so much inside, practicing every day and never experiencing this one, perfect moment.

"Thank you," I mumble, leaning into Max's side. His arm goes around me, pulling me closer as he bends to kiss the top of my head. I don't understand how this happened so quickly, so easily, but the two of us together just fit. I should have suspected it from the first moment our eyes met over the banquet table, the way my entire body just tingled like some magical electricity had crackled between our shared gaze. I should have known it would happen. I should have seen this coming from a mile away, despite the age difference, the ocean in between that separated us from ever meeting until that fateful night in the least assuming town in North Carolina. I never really looked for love, and I know without even having to ask that Max has spent all his years pretending not to need it.

But love has found us, along with chaos and pain. I just hope that when this clash of uncertainty and fear has ended, we will emerge from it together. Looking up to meet Max's expressive eyes, it occurs to me that despite the darkness we're fumbling through now, I'm confident that love will overwhelm every battle we encounter.

Wordlessly, I fold into his arms, tip my head upward, and stand on my tiptoes to kiss him.

There's such a silent beauty in the air, a sort of magic that I feel like Paris has been hiding for me since we arrived at that club that night. I feel like I'm getting myself back, finding that spark of excitement once more.

I'm finding what I've been missing in the arms of a killer.

I hold Liv tightly, my hands caressing her, memorizing her curves and the sensation of her soft skin. I've never touched someone with such tenderness. For so long, I thought of my hands as weapons of death, never of pleasure.

I never allowed myself to believe that I could find someone that would see through all the darkness that makes me who I am, and still want to feel my skin on hers.

She looks so beautiful by the sparkling light of the moon and stars above us, and I walk her backwards towards one of the luxurious lounging chairs. I know that falling for her is something I should have resisted, but I couldn't. Everything about her youth and vigor, the intelligence sparkling behind her eyes... It's what I've always wanted and never deserved. She's the person who can see the best in me, even at my worst, and when my teeth graze her throat, she moans for more.

I wonder if she always had this little desire for danger or if it's something that's changed in her since her life was nearly irreparably changed. I guess she doesn't know either, and I don't bother to ask. The silence overtakes us, and I don't want to talk. I just want to listen to the sweet pants of her breath into the quiet night, and make her break that quiet with an orgasmic scream.

The thought makes me grin and my fingers go to her pants, quickly working them down. She still smells faintly of sex, and it makes my nostrils flare with appreciation as my fingers move to her slick pussy.

She's so responsive, every touch making her sensitive body quiver, and when my mouth goes to her pussy, she bites down on her lower lip to keep from moaning. But I want her to moan. I want her completely unleashed on my tongue, and I reach up towards her jawline. My fingers trace it before going to her mouth, slowly guiding her lower lip from her teeth.

"This is a night for screaming," I say, my voice already husky with desire as my cock throbs in my pants. But I need to taste her before I take her, and my tongue works its way back to her slit, running the full length of her pussy before my lips wrap around her clit and I gently suck.

Her eyes go wide and she gasps, and I can tell it's almost too much for her. Almost, but not quite, so I pin her there and make her take that pleasure. It isn't until she's screaming and moaning, her hands batting at my face as her orgasm crashes over her and coats my jaw in her honey that I finally relinquish her.

And even then, she only gets a moment's reprieve before my fingers go back to her clit, pressing down on that throbbing bud, massaging it as she cries out and squirms.

With my free hand, I push up her top, revealing her bare tits, love bites having left their mark on her nipple where I sucked. I can't help but smile, and I bring my mouth back to that same place, my tongue flicking the nipple and making it stiffen instantly.

Her little pink areola swells with her arousal, and as I rub her clit, my mouth works against her tiny chest.

Liv cries out in pleasure, and her body twists away from me, so I remove my hand from her clit and give her a warning glance.

"You'll stay still if you want to be a good girl," I say with just a hint of teasing behind my dark words. I remember how she responded when I first met her, so eager to please, and the memory makes my cock jump as she quickly stills.

"I'll be good," she promises, her breathing so

heavy that her voice comes out as a tiny wisp on each breath. "Whatever you want."

I smile in reward and bring my hand back to her clit, massaging it in a circular motion as I look down on her, so vulnerable and beautiful in the midnight light.

"I want you to come on my hand. And then I want to know what your little lips feel like spread around my cock."

She doesn't shy away from the dirty words, and her eyes flash with excitement before I bring my lips back to her nipple, my teeth grabbing it and tugging upon it. I let it snap back to her chest before I repeat the motion, my fingers working their way into her pussy as my thumb keeps rubbing her pulsing bud.

With the stars sparkling overhead and all of Paris resting quietly seven stories below, I work her body with perfect harmony. I notice every time she jolts, every quick inhale of breath, and I memorize them, then repeat the motions that brought those dulcet sounds to her lips. It doesn't take long before I learn her perfect tempo, the one that brings her body crashing down around me, her pussy clenching my fingers so tightly as she screams into the night sky, breaking the serenity of the evening with an even more wonderful sound.

As she comes down from her high, I can see she's a bit embarrassed at having lost such control, but I push my mouth against hers and silence those fears.

After what she's been through, she deserves to lose control and really feel happy and good.

That's why, seconds later, I stand and straddle the lounge chair, and her on it, my throbbing cock bobbing just inches from her face. She stares at it, then me, skeptically and just when I think she's going to shyly back down, she instead reaches for me.

Still, she pauses. "I've never—".

"I know," I interrupt her, and bring my hand to the back of her head. "Just open your mouth, and let your tongue fall over your teeth." She's so obedient, and her eyes twinkle in the dim light, excitement and relief mingling there.

"Hold onto the base. Firmer than that. You won't hurt me," I promise, and my lip twitches with a smirk. "Now bring your mouth to me."

It's amateurish, but when her sweet little tongue darts out and runs along my head, collecting the precum there, it ignites something in me. I've never had a person so intent on pleasing me like her, and certainly never someone who knew what I was capable of.

And within a few minutes, and a few more simple instructions, her head is bobbing up and down my cock like a pro. I taught her just how I like it, and several times she nearly made me buckle over in pleasure, but I hold it back.

I still hunger for more, to be up within that tight

pussy of hers, yet the way she gazes up at me as she blows me...

I want to reward her diligent efforts, and I let myself come, coating her tongue in my seed. She's taken off guard and pulls back, and some of it lances across her mouth, to which she giggles happily before swallowing.

"There was more," she laughs nervously, and I nod as she wipes away my cream from her face. Her innocence and intelligence mingle, drawing me into her, and I can't help but lunge for her neck once more, biting her and sucking upon her skin. She tastes better than any food I've had, feels better than any pleasure I've tried.

How one person could make me feel so strongly for them in such a short time is a complete mystery to me, but I don't intend to question it.

I intend to mark her as mine. Again.

After just a few minutes of exploring her body with my hands and mouth, feeling over her slender curves and hearing her moans start rising once more, my cock is stiffer than ever. I grab her legs, spreading them, less gently than her first time. That time I wanted it to be all about her. This time, I want it to be all about us, exploring what really makes each other tick.

And when I thrust into her deep, she cries out with such a delicious moan, I know I've read her right. She wants to feel alive, and the perfect combination of pleasure and pain is what she seeks. I look down on her, keeping her gaze as my hips draw back, then push forward again.

With each thrust, her small breasts bounce, and I can still see that one is wet and glistening from my mouth. I push her ankle over my shoulder as my hand reaches down, tweaking that nipple again, feeling her pussy tighten in response.

"You like that," I say, more than ask, and she whimpers in response.

"Is this bad?"

I shake my head.

"No, *malyutka*. Nothing you do could ever be bad," I say, and I mean it. She relaxes into me, taking me deeper as her body writhes against mine, and before long, we're meeting one another at the peak of pleasure, her cries sending me over the brink. A hot fire travels down my spine, flooding my body as I flood her depths, holding her flexible body pinned against me.

We pant for breath as we slump into one another, and I slowly slip from her.

I smile a faded grin as I lift her limp body, her arms wrapping around my neck in a loose grip, exhaustion having taken her. I take her back into our room, and pull the blankets up over her. Already there's a look of serenity on her face. It's an expression I've never truly seen on a woman before, and it scares me how much it makes my heart pound with desire.

Everything about her — about our relationship — is dangerous, and she knows that as well as I do. But we can't help but collide into one another's bodies again and again, and her expression right now... That's what's going to keep me coming back for more.

She doesn't just want me for my body, or for what I can do to hers. She feels something far more deeply, far more pure than that.

I watch her as she sleeps, my fingers grazing over her jaw, over her shoulder, as I wonder if a killer like me even deserves something so pure and beautiful as love...

It isn't until the morning sun crests the sky, bathing my sleeping angel in a golden glow that I realize I missed something. I shift, reaching for my phone and heading out onto the terrace to make a quick call.

"Felix, meet us in the lobby. I know where we need to go next. It's... dangerous. I hoped we wouldn't have to go there, but it looks like it's our only choice."

* * *

MY CAR TEARS down the country road as I speed towards my destination, my knuckles white on the steering wheel, even if my black gloves conceal them. I might be too late already, if Maggie is where I suspect she is. And I wish I had reason to doubt my suspicions.

My route takes me far north of the city, far enough that the bright and sprawling metropolis of Paris is out of sight behind me, save for the glow over the horizon bright enough to be a beacon to everything around it.

For kilometers, there's nothing on this stretch of road to my left and right but farmlands and fields. The odd car I pass every few minutes is the only other source of company on this lonely stretch of road — so much so, that if I hadn't known where I was going, I would have missed my turn onto a narrow dirt road that leads a short distance to what to anyone else would look like some kind of garage for industrial shipping, a run-down, two-story building with few features and rusty corners, half-obscured by high, weathered walls and no gate.

The logo on the front of the walls belongs to a shipping company that has been out of business for many years. But none of the local authorities ever investigates this place, and no city official of the nearby towns and hamlets dare move to have it destroyed or repurposed.

Each and every one of them is bought, because my target used to be one of the most valuable junctions of the slave trade in France.

I stop just after my turn. My eyes are on those ruined walls as I silently slip out of my car and move around to the trunk, retrieving my equipment and strapping it on my person. As I strap guns to my chest and knives at my side, my eyes fall on a ski mask I've kept on hand for some time. I consider donning it but I reconsider and close the trunk.

Should anyone see me and live, I'm done hiding. I want them to know who's shutting down the slave ring again.

Crouching low, I make my way to the walls, pressing myself up against the side and listening for what's inside. I can hear little, but the occasional footsteps tell me there's at least one man outside the facility. Back in the old days, the Bratva usually ran things similarly, making it look like there was a lone employee in the parking lot.

I move up to where the walls part into an opening, just a few inches from the corner, and I slip my knife out. My other hand reaches into my pocket for my car keys. My lock has a relatively quiet horn, a light sound that won't carry beyond the exterior of the building. Taking a breath, I click the lock button twice.

My car gives a short beep as the lights flash once. I hear the footsteps in the courtyard pause, then start to come closer.

I breathe a sigh of relief. If he wasn't alone, he would have said something to his partner. A few moments later, I watch a man in a white tank top holding a cigarette in one hand and an Uzi in the other stride into view, craning his head to look for the source of the unscheduled arrival. He has time to catch sight of me and widen his eyes before I'm upon him like a tiger, wrapping a hand over his mouth and dragging him behind the wall before my knife slides between his ribs and silences him forever.

I lay his body down in the bushes beside the wall before I start searching him. Cigarette pack, spare pistol, wallet...and a cardkey on a lanyard. I free the cardkey and slip it into my jacket pocket, poking my head around the corner before advancing into the grounds.

The walls around me hold more than just sleazy men with more weaponry than they should ever be entrusted with. In the days of the Bratva's human trafficking ring, this place was a shipping facility of sorts.

Here, they prepared the women they enslaved to leave the country. This was the last stop for these women before they were sent to their new lives, if such slavery could be called living, and it was here that they would often break the more spirited women for all they could. Starvation, sleep deprivation, anything that would make them more pliable before their journeys to their buyers, whether they be in Europe or as far as Asia or, most commonly, North America.

Maggie is a tough person. I know her to be. I recruited her personally, just like all my other students, and I looked for a particular kind of mental resilience that could flourish in another country.

But nothing should have to prepare a human being for this. Nobody should be born to expect slavery.

I move to the side of the building, crouching behind a dumpster where a window is situated nearby. Faint light is visible from within, and I suspect there's someone home. But the window is shut, so I move up under it to try to listen inside.

"...wouldn't even listen when Vasili roughed her up a little, we had to take her away for most of the party," one of the men is saying in Russian.

"Fucking Americans," another man spits, "what are they teaching their girls over there? I bet he really gave it to her that night, eh?"

"No," says the first man, "boss said to keep hands off those parts of her, no wounds that show. The client has eh...high standards. Some rich fuck in the US or Canada, I don't know, I don't get to drive this one to the docks. They're gonna dress her up real nice though. Shipping her up to Calais in the morning to make her look good for her new husband."

"Well, what's stopping you from having some fun the boss won't notice?" the man says with a lewd lilt to his voice that makes my grip my knife tighter.

"Are you fucking serious? He's still fuming over the loss of that one bitch the Russian stole. So much as an extra stain on that filthy shirt of hers, and he'll have our balls."

I've heard enough, and I glance over at the dumpster. There's a rotting wood palette sitting beside it, and quietly as I can, I pick it up and toss it over the top of the dumpster, making it clatter in among the garbage with enough noise that a cat goes running out from behind the dumpster and into the fields.

"The fuck was that?" one of the men inside says after a pause.

"Fucking cats. I'll get it," he says, and I'm already crouching under the window when I hear it slide open.

"Psst! Fuck off, you overgrown rats!" he shouts, leaning out to brandish his beer bottle at the dumpster. In a swift motion, I reach up and yank him out the window, plunging my knife into the back of his neck the moment he hits the ground.

"Adrik?" the other man cries, rushing forward in time for me to rise to my feet as I whip my pistol out, pointing it directly at his wide-eyed face and pulling the trigger before he has time to get a word out.

Both bodies crumple to the ground within seconds of each other, I hop into the window and ready my gun. I'm on bought time now.

At the far end of the hall, I can see a set of stairs

leading down, and I have no time to waste; even if there are others in the building, I can't risk them getting away with Maggie, so I head swiftly down the hallway, weapon raised. I don't know how many people are lying in wait in this building. Back in the old days, there would have been far more, but I suspect this Chechen ring is just getting started. Otherwise, security would be much, much tighter. That, and there would be more girls here than I alone could rescue.

Besides, even though I'm out of this life, I'd have heard if the ring was in full operation. It's impossible to keep things quiet from the one person in the city who knows what to be looking for in the news reports.

I reach the steps, descending them quickly, rounding a final corner with my gun out before laying eyes on what looks like a heavy metal door, a security panel to the left of it. Drawing out the card-key, I watch the light flash green as the lock pops open and it opens with a loud creak. I wince, knowing that any element of surprise I have left is gone, but the whimper I hear from the other side of the door is doubly heart-wrenching.

The room I step into is a long and windowless hallway, all stained concrete. There are what look like cells lined up on both sides of the room, each one with a steel door on the front with nothing but a slat to push food and water through. I hurry down the hall, my eyes moving from cell to cell. Each one appears empty, save for one near the entrance. Nevertheless, I make a sweep of the room to make sure there are no other prisoners before I move to the one occupied cell and slide open the barred door.

Immediately, the young woman inside bursts into tears at the sight of me, and I step forward as Maggie buries her face in her hands.

I kneel down and speak softly to her. "Maggie. Maggie, look up, it's me — I'm here to get you out of here."

"Please, I-" she sobs before turning her tearstained face up to me, and as recognition dawns on her slowly, as if she's waking up from a nightmare, she bursts into tears all over again. I allow her to wrap her arms around my neck and cry into my shoulder. "M-m-monsieur P-"

"Breathe, Maggie," I assure her, stroking her back comfortingly, and my heart wells up with sorrow for the young woman in my arms. I dearly wish I could say this is the first time I've encountered a woman in her condition. And I dearly wish she'd be the last. But all I can do now is everything in my power to rescue her.

"We...we tried to go to a party and..." she gasps between sobs, trying to explain herself, but I shush her softly as I look around the room at her conditions.

"I know everything, Maggie. I'm here to end all

this." The light in the cell is out of reach, but still flickering noisily. The concrete here is rough, and it would be painful to the touch if I weren't wearing thick clothes. Maggie's torn and stained clothing is thin, though, a remnant of her night out. And there's no bed in here. All of it clearly amounts to means of sleep deprivation — torture.

"Liv," she gasps, looking panicked again, "Olivia, she was with me, have you-"

"She's safe," I say with a smile, helping Maggie to her feet as she puts her hands to her mouth in shock and gratitude.

"Oh my god, how?!" Maggie is in near disbelief, almost suspicious that this is happening, and not without good reason. "Are you some kind of officer?"

"I'm a few things," I say simply, sticking my head out into the hallway. "Let's save that for the car ride though, we're not out of hot water yet."

"What should I—" Maggie starts, but she's cut off as I take her by the hand and move down the hallway with my pistol raised.

"Keep my hand and move when I tell you to," I say, and without another word, I take off as fast as I can manage to get Maggie to run.

Up ahead, I can hear voices and footsteps down the stairs. I feel Maggie start to reflexively freeze up, and without another moment's thought, I guide her into a different cell just as two men arrive at the door with guns out.

As Maggie screams, I roll into the room with her as shots hit the wall behind us, and as soon as they're off, I reach around and blind-fire two shots before popping out of hiding and shooting one of the men dead as he dives for cover. The other man hits the ground, having been caught in the leg by my blind shot, and I sprint forward, but not fast enough that he can't let out a cry of pain that rings through the compound before I put a bullet in his head and finish the job.

Maggie peeks out of hiding, and I give her a nod to come catch up with me, and I take her hand to pull her along before she can let her gaze dwell on the bodies around her too long. There are mixed emotions in her eyes, and I can only imagine she feels some measure of satisfaction in seeing such vile men put down.

We move up the stairs, and I'm relieved to see nobody standing at the top of them waiting for us. But I know the men who saw the body on the way down will have called for backup, so we don't have much time.

I guide her down the hallway, and I'm about to round the corner towards the front door when a man lunges from the bathroom on my right, slashing across my face with a knife. I feel a sting on my cheekbone as it draws blood, and I stagger for a moment. I raise my gun as he curses and starts to lunge forward again, but the next instant, he falls to the ground with a scream as Maggie lurches forward and kicks his knee in, surprising even me with her strength. She staggers back, surprised at herself before I shoot the man in the back of the head as he holds his leg.

"Good work," I say to her with a nod, and she mouths something as I take her hand and bolt out the front door with her.

"We're still in France," she says as we cross the courtyard, and I realize she must have been blind-folded for most of the transfers. I wonder how badly these past few days have affected the passage of time for her.

"Just outside Paris," I say grimly, and I glance back to see her ashen face at the realization that all this horror, all this vile slavery has been taking place right in the heart of metropolitan civilization. It's a reality that shook me to the bone when I first learned of it. From Paris to London to New York City, it's often the epicenters of culture and civiliza-tion that hide the darkest vices.

We run towards the car, but from the building behind us, I hear shouts and the sounds of running feet. Reinforcements from the second floor must be on the way, and we need to be out of here already.

I hear the voices grow closer as we near the corner of the wall, not far from where my car is parked. Getting my keys out in one hand, I turn around to fire a few rounds with a new pistol at the door, and I see the four men who've come after us start to scatter as shots are exchanged.

We round the corner and start sprinting for the car, and I look down at the keys in my hand.

There's a trickle of red staining the shining metal of the keys, and as it starts to pool in my hand, my eyes move to my upper chest to see a small hole where the bullet hit me.

I'm sitting in our opulent terrace suite, chewing my lip anxiously, waiting for any updates from Max. It's nearly midnight and we still haven't heard back from him. All day, the three of us spent hours strategizing and trying to figure out the logistics of our next move. The two guys pored over an old map for a long time, Max showing Felix where he would be headed tonight just in case he needed to call for reinforcements or something. He assured me that it wouldn't be necessary anyway, that he had a solid plan. He knew the area well enough and he had enough experience dealing with creeps like these — he would be able to find Maggie and get back out without too much trouble.

But nothing he said could assuage my deep concerns. I have finally found the love I never knew I needed, and now I am poised to lose him if anything is to go wrong. I'm sending this most precious object of my affections into direct danger. And knowing his background, his extensive experience in dealing with the Chechen mafia in the past, does nothing to relieve my worry. Even though I've seen his skills in action, I know that it's been a long time since he last delved into such an intense situation. Until now, he's been living a totally different life, walking a tamer track. That's not to say he's out of shape or anything in the least — the way his muscles ripple under his clothing, the ease with which he can scoop me up and move my body… he's as strong and powerful as he ever was, I'm sure.

But he's softer now.

And I know that, in some small way at least, I am to blame. Even Felix, who is not particularly observant or tactful, noted this to me earlier tonight, about an hour after Max headed out. I was pacing back and forth nervously, my anxious tics in full drive as I twirled my hair, fidgeted with the hem of my shirt, and chewed my nails. Felix looked up at me from his laptop and shook his head.

"You and Max have gotten close so fast, haven't you?" he said.

I jumped at the sound of his voice, being shaken from my thoughts. "I-I guess so, yeah."

He scratched at his chin thoughtfully. "I've never seen him be so gentle with anyone before, you know. He's even nicer to me when you're around."

I had just shrugged off his words like they weighed nothing, but deep down I know he was right. I can feel it even when Max just looks at me, those vivid green eyes staring right down into the depths of my soul. I know time has changed him, and distance, too. He's spent some time away from the life and I worry he might be a little rusty. Felix assures me that he's well-trained enough that the coldness he was accustomed to will never totally thaw.

And that only breaks my heart a little bit.

I know that he needs that coldness to survive, at least for now. If he hesitates to take a guard down, if he's even a millimeter off his game, it could spell tragedy for him. Disaster. Even death. So I hope I haven't softened him up enough to weaken him. But now, curled up in the bed we shared not twenty-four hours ago, I make a silent vow to myself: if and when we survive this mess, I will make it my life's mission to work on softening him, melting the icy cage around his heart. I will bring him back to planet Earth, ground him with my love. I'll show him that light and happiness can be just as powerful a reservoir of strength as years of battle-tested darkness.

Suddenly, I'm ripped from my reverie as Felix's cell phone rings. I bound out of bed and rush to his side, staring anxiously at the phone as he slides it open and answers.

"Are you out? Max? What's going on? It's been hours —"

His words are cut off and his face goes pale. "What is it? What happened, Felix?" I ask quietly, tugging at his sleeve. He shakes his head, shushing me as he listens to Max for a moment, then hangs up.

"Get your stuff. We gotta go. Something's happened," Felix says worriedly.

I immediately feel a wave of nausea hit me. "What? Is he okay?"

"Come on, I'll tell you on the way," he replies quickly, urging me to follow him. We race out of the hotel down to the street, where Felix hails us a cab. After giving the driver specific instructions in rapid French, he rolls up the partition and explains to me in a hushed tone, "Max has been injured, but you've got to stay calm, okay?"

I'm surprised at how calm Felix is, considering his usual high-strung personality, but that only worries me more. If it's serious enough that even Felix is acting this way… it must be bad.

"What happened to him, Felix? Tell me," I demand.

"He… he was shot."

The world around me goes silent, my head spinning.

"Wh-what?" I murmur weakly, feeling bile rise in my throat.

"Shh, it's okay. He'll be alright. He didn't sound that bad on the phone —"

"It's not okay!" I cry, tears burning in my eyes. "Why are we driving so slowly? Come on, hurry up! Step on the gas!"

Felix takes my wrists and pushes them back down as I start to beat on the partition, working myself into a frenzy. "He can't hear you and he's going as fast as he can, Olivia. Just let the man drive. Listen to me: when we get there, I'm going to take Maggie and you're going to ride with Max to the hospital."

"Hospital?" I repeat breathlessly. "Wait — he found Maggie? He got her?"

"Yes, yes. Keep up, Liv, come on. Do you understand what's going to happen?"

"Oh — uh, sure. I got it. I'll get Max to the hospital," I say dutifully, even though I really don't know how I'm going to manage that. Max's car is a stick shift and I only vaguely know how to drive a manual vehicle, plus I don't know the way to a hospital. And then there's the added panic of the fact that the love of my life is gravely injured.

But I will figure it out. I have to, for Max's sake.

When we pull up, I jump out of the taxi before it's even completely stopped. Felix tells the cabbie to wait and runs after me, the two of us bolting around the corner toward Max's parked car. I race to the driver's side and throw the door open, kneeling by

Max, my heart hammering away in my chest. "You're hurt," I mumble, tears blurring my vision. There's so much blood, and it's streaming down from his shirt. He was shot in the upper chest.

"It looks worse than it is," Max replies, but his breathing is ragged, his voice rough. He doesn't sound good at all. I rip off my cardigan and tie it around his torso to stem the blood flow as much as I can.

"Maggie, come with me," Felix is saying, and I look up to meet my former roommate's terrified eyes. She looks like hell, which is only fitting considering the fact that she's just had a long, torturous walk through the inferno itself. We exchange knowing nods and she wordlessly goes with Felix, the two of them racing away to meet the cab.

"I'm going to drive you to get help," I explain to Max, forcing my voice not to tremble. "I'll need you to tell me the way, alright?"

"Do you even know how to drive a stick shift?" he asks, his eyelids fluttering. The color is draining from his gorgeous face, and I know this needs to happen fast.

"Kind of. I'll make it work," I insist, urging him gently to move into the passenger seat. With a painful lurch he lumbers out of the driver's side and walks around the front of the car, holding a hand to his chest with the other out to steady himself on the hood of the vehicle. He limps slowly around and into the seat, slumping back with an expression of intense agony on his face. I jump behind the wheel, murmuring to myself the tips my dad tried to instill in me in regards to driving a manual.

"Foot on the clutch," I whisper, reaching down to fling the car into first gear. To my infinite relief, the knowledge comes trickling back to me through the fog of panic in my brain. Max gives me mumbled directions as we make the jerky, awkward drive back into town toward the nearest hospital.

By the time we finally get there, Max is conked out entirely, his eyes having rolled back into his head. But I am in survival mode, my former frenzy sharpened into a needle-point focus. Mustering all my strength, I all but carry his enormous weight to the glass doors of the emergency room, the two of us collapsing to the tile floor. Overwhelmed and exhausted, I black out amidst the frantic muttering of French doctors and nurses.

ONE WEEK LATER, we're finally home from the hospital, both on the mend. Turns out, my lack of proper sleep coupled with extreme stress resulted in my having a physical breakdown of sorts. I was booked into a hospital room alongside Max, for exhaustion and overexertion. Next to Max's gunshot wound, I felt a little silly and weak, but the doctors assured me that I would be much better off repairing my body in the hospital. Besides, I think they caught onto the fact that I would probably be glued to Max's side. If I was going to spend every second in the hospital room anyway, I might as well be getting treatment, too.

But now we're both doing much better. I feel rejuvenated and relieved after our brush with near death. Max is up and mobile again, nearly back to his former strength already. Turns out, the bullet only grazed his left lung, too high up to fully puncture it or his heart. He is beyond lucky to have survived. Any further south and that bullet would have certainly killed him.

In the couple of days since leaving the hospital, Max has been fighting the desire to get up to his old ways again — not the hitman life, but the athletics. He wants to run and work out like he used to, but the doctors have urged me to keep him from doing anything too strenuous. To keep him busy and keep his mind off his current predicament, I've asked him to train me in self-defence so that he can live vicariously through me while he's on the mend.

Granted, it's not only self-defence he's been teaching me... Now that we're through the storm without any other distractions, we can explore each other's bodies like we couldn't before. And with his wound, I have been trying my best to give him all the TLC he deserves. Just because his body is weakened at the moment doesn't mean I have to tone down my own physical abilities. And I am a gymnast, after all.

We've also done some weapons training. Even though I dislike guns, I still feel as though it would be beneficial for me to learn how to use one properly, just in case the situation ever arises that I need it. And with Max's past still looming over us, it's entirely possible that such a situation may very well find us again. Especially right now, with Max vulnerable, I am more determined than ever to learn how to defend myself. And him.

Not that I'm allowing that dark cloud to rain on our little niche of paradise, though. One upside to Max's being on the mend is that we get a lot of quiet, soft time together, just the two of us. Tending to his wound and seeing a more exposed, tender side of him has been an eye-opening experience, a glimpse into how beautiful and complex his heart truly is. Underneath the layers of diamond-hard armor is an amazingly sweet man. We've spent many a night curled up in bed together, talking until the wee hours, baring our souls to each other. And during one of these late-night sessions, he let slip that he wanted to make this — us — official. It wasn't exactly a proposal; more like a natural development of our current bond. It is a question that doesn't need asking. Our union is inevitable.

So when he started talking about "when we're married..." it didn't come as a surprise to either of us. It's just as natural as the air we breathe. That's not to say he simply assumed it without my consent. Once he realized how assumptive his phrasing was, he stopped short and looked deeply into my eyes, then uttered the words I knew were coming.

"Will you marry me?"

Of course I gave the only answer there could be: yes! And sometime in between our training sessions, he managed to slip out and buy me the most beautiful, jaw-dropping ring I've ever seen. Rose-gold with a gigantic pink diamond. It's more than even a princess could ask for. And our wedding is going to be absolutely gorgeous. At first, we toyed with the idea of simply eloping, but now we're planning the big wedding of my dreams.

"I hope your parents will be pleased," Max says, worry etched across his face. I lean over the coffee table to kiss the concerns away.

"As soon as they see how happy I am, they'll understand," I assure him. "Besides, how could anyone not love you? Especially with everything you've done for me."

"I just don't want to be the source of any disputes or anything," he says. "I don't have much by way of family, and the last thing I want is to ruin things for you. I know how much your family means to you, Liv."

"Don't worry, okay? This is a good thing, and my parents will see it the same way, I swear," I tell him earnestly. At first, I was a little worried that my mom and dad would be put off by our age difference. But I'm old enough and mature enough to know what I want. They know how headstrong and intelligent I am. I wouldn't decide to do something like this on a whim — I've always been cautious in life and love, and I know without a single shred of doubt this is what I want: to be with Max forever.

*I just had no idea how short forever could be.*

## LIV

$\mathcal{I}$ stand in front of a floor-length silver mirror in the back alcove of a tiny historic chapel on the outskirts of Paris, surveying my own reflection in mingled astonishment and joy. I am nineteen years old as of one month ago, with my first semester abroad finally over. I take a deep, slow breath, blinking in disbelief at the way I look — so foreign to my own eyes.

Not much about my physical appearance has changed, of course. I still have the same long, wavy auburn hair and huge cinnamon-brown eyes. But right now my hair is parted down the center, the smooth waves decorated with a delicate crown of little white flowers. My eyes are wide and luminous, accented by expertly-applied smoky eye makeup and mascara, courtesy of my wonderful French makeup artist. There's a deep, raspberry-red stain to my full lips, and they part to reveal a glittering and white, yet slightly anxious, smile.

I look beautiful in a way I never could have predicted. And more importantly, I actually feel beautiful — truly and unabashedly. It's not the professional makeup job that's caused my transformation, however. It's the love which beats like a second heartbeat beside my own, filling me with light, making me glow.

It's an appropriate look for a woman about to walk down the aisle.

My body is adorned in a gorgeous, pearly-white lace gown designed by Lili Hod, with a silky, scalloped swath of fabric draped from my breasts to dangle over my abdomen, smoothing out to a floor-length rippling skirt. The dress is much more expensive than my plane ticket here was, more expensive than my rent back at the flat I would have shared with Maggie, had I gotten the chance.

I am proud of her, though. Despite everything that had happened to her over the course of the semester, she didn't cower in fear and shrink back into the smothering arms of her parents like I feared. Instead, she pulled a total one-eighty. After spending nearly a month in a hospital being treated for her extensive injuries both physical and psychological, she emerged standing tall and proud. The day before her release, she called me and asked for me to be the one who would pick her up, and not to tell her parents yet that the doctors were letting her out. She wanted to have a chance to breathe the free air and walk the streets of the city which had scarred her without her parents hovering around. So I obliged her happily, a little uncertain of what she would be like when she came walking out of the hospital.

To my relief and happiness, Maggie looked even better than she did when I first saw her on the campus green. She was still thinner than before, after the starvation under the thumb of the Chechens. Her cheeks were a little hollow, her hair slightly limp. But there is a sparkle in her eye now, a kindling of a powerful fire ignited by adversity. In fact, she is now bolder and more open than I am.

She leads a monthly therapy group for sexual assault and human trafficking survivors, in which she describes her trauma and helps others learn to cope with their own issues. On top of that, she also came back to school, like I did, and the two of us finished with new records in our category. She's refused to let her parents yank her out of university and keep her holed up in some foreign fortress far away. She's taken charge of her own life, realizing that if she could survive the experiences she'd had this year, she can probably do just about anything she sets her mind to.

We've become fast friends, and that's why I asked her to be my maid of honor today.

All morning, she's been by my side, chit-chatting

excitedly with my makeup artist, Helene, and my mom, who came all the way from North Carolina to be here today. Of course, my mother has also had to split her time between tending to my bridal concerns and tending to my father's nerves and emotions, as he is preparing to be the one walking me down the aisle.

Knowing how easily his emotional boat is rocked, I'm sure he's spent most of the day weeping happy tears. I smile at the thought. I can't wait to have him link arms with me and guide me down the flower-scattered aisle of this chapel, right into the arms of my prince.

I'm a little antsy because I haven't been allowed to see Max all day. I know it's only traditional for the bride to be hidden away from the groom until the ceremony, but I've gotten so attached to him that it feels odd not to be sharing every moment of this day with him by my side. Soon, though, we will be united in that most beautiful and sacred of ways, and I'll never have to walk alone again.

Tears burn in my eyes and I blink them back, not wanting to ruin the perfect makeup job Helene did for me. We've really pulled out all the stops for this wedding. It is a small congregation of only our closest friends and family — mostly mine, since Max doesn't have much by way of family... or friends. Except for one, whom I have invited unbeknownst to Max. I can't wait to see the look on his face when he sees the person I've asked to attend, someone he hasn't seen in a very long time.

I want so badly to sweep away the musty cobwebs in the dark corners of his life, throw open the windows, and let the sun warm him once again. I am determined to bring joy into his world, show him what it feels like to live freely and happily, away from the tragedy and pain of his past. I cannot go back in time and rid his memory of such terrible events. I don't have the power to eradicate the debts and strikes against him, and I know he will never truly forget the awful things he has seen and done. His past is his own, and I can't change it. But his future… that rests in my hands. I am so excited to start this next chapter of our lives together, seeking the same bliss we have found in one another.

Still, I have to admit that I am somewhat grateful for his past, in that it has given us both a newfound strength. Especially for me. I will continue to regard the world around me with wonder and love, but I know now to be cautious. I can embrace life with wide open arms, provided that I have my eyes wide open and watching, as well.

And that is why, underneath the frilly, fragile lace of my wedding dress, there is a little sheathed knife strapped to my garter. I know now how important it is to always be prepared. Sometimes, in the pursuit of beautiful things, ugliness can still follow.

Suddenly, the door behind me creaks open and I

don't immediately turn around, expecting that it's probably just my mom or Maggie coming back to fawn over my dress or give me an update on how the pre-ceremony is progressing. Maggie, for one, has been sneaking whispered tidbits back to me about how handsome and proud Max looks, how swimmingly he's getting along with my father. I had been a little concerned about that at first, seeing as my dad is a little bit protective over me, and Max was originally in my life to be an authority figure and therefore, off-limits romantically speaking. And while Max is calm and hard to read, my dad is effervescent, wearing his emotions on his sleeve. But to my relief, they seem to click. Like opposite magnets. I'm elated.

Just as I'm turning around to ask Maggie if it's almost time to get everybody into the pews for the ceremony, a hand clasps over my mouth, the words dying in my throat.

My eyes go wide as I glance around in horror, trying to figure out who is holding me. I know it can't be my mother or Maggie, as the person behind me is much taller and broader than either of them, nearly dwarfing me by comparison. I glance up to the mirror and let out a strangled scream of realization.

It's Will.

His lips are grinning, but there's a cold, cruel glint in his eyes. He is just as handsome as before, but now I know to associate his attractive features with undeniable evil. He is a wolf in a Prince Charming costume. A villain with a hero's face.

How the hell did he manage to slip in unnoticed? With so many people milling around, how in the world did he get to me? Especially with Max out there somewhere. But then I realize that apart from Maggie and Max, nobody here knows what he looks like. He's wearing a black designer suit with a pale pink tie, perfectly matching my wedding color scheme.

As though he's been watching me, planning this for months.

And I never even saw him coming.

Will leans down close to my ear, his breath tickling my neck and giving me goosebumps as I start to tremble, realizing just how dire this situation is. At any moment, Maggie or someone else could come in, putting them in danger along with me. And Maggie… if she sees him, there's no telling how she will react. Sure, she's stronger now than before, but I worry that even just seeing Will's face might make her relapse into her former near-catatonic state. And if he hurts my mother…

"Don't worry, *mon chou*, I don't have eyes for anyone but you today," he growls in my ear, sickly-sweet evil dripping with every cruel word, as if he can read my mind. "Now, I have arranged a getaway car for us. Consider it a chariot to take us away on a honeymoon, if you like."

He roves one hand down over my breasts, groping its way back around to my ass. Will sucks in a deep, lewd inhale, closing his eyes as though he's truly savoring the moment.

"I wonder... have you missed me as much as I have missed you?" he muses aloud, his raspy whisper sending shivers down my spine. "It's true what they say, you know, about the one who got away. Once you get a little taste, you really never can let it go. And you, *mon amour*? You are the one who got away. But we are reunited again, aren't we? Isn't it poetic? Romantic, even?"

Will presses himself into me, his cock hard against my ass. I want to scream, but his hand is completely blocking my airway. And besides, I don't doubt for one second that he has a gun on his person. If I scream, someone will come running. And finding us like this would surely end in that person's demise. I can't be responsible for anyone else being hurt on my account. No... the only thing I can do is obey. There's too much at stake.

I should have known that trouble would follow me... even to the altar.

"Here's how this is going to work," Will says slowly, grinding against me. "You and I are going to leave through that window over there, walk up the hill, and get into my car. You are not going to scream or make a single sound, or my men will rain bullets into that crowd of your most beloved friends and family, okay? And when we get back to headquarters, you and I will finally get the alone time we both so dearly deserve. You are precious merchandise, Olivia, but you've also been a very, very bad girl. I don't think our buyers will want you unless I get you properly broken in. Besides, I need to rid you of the stench that filthy Ruskie left on your skin."

He spits on the floor, and I feel tears prickling in my eyes. There is no way out. I have to do as I am told, even if it means losing everything that lies just beyond the door — the happy life, the beautiful future, the man of my dreams.

My past has caught up to me.

"Let's go. Move," he commands, dragging me away and pushing me out through the open window. He starts pulling me up the grassy hill overlooking the whole wedding party. I glance back in desperation, half-hoping and half-terrified that someone will see us. I want someone to save me, but I also know that there's little chance anyone could save me at this point. I don't think Max has his gun today, and I don't want to risk anyone getting hurt.

But still, despite my obedience and silence, I hear a deep voice ring out across the pastoral scene. It's Max.

"No!" he bellows, and I look back instinctively to see him at the window of the chapel, looking out. A split second later he disappears from view, obviously barreling through the crowded little church to get out and follow us.

People are starting to point and take notice of what's going on, but by now we are already getting into the car, Will shoving me into the backseat, almost exactly the same way he did months ago when he captured me the first time.

The bullet wound to my chest might have slowed me down, but I'll be damned if it lets the bastards steal my Olivia from me again. Pain ripples through my torso and down my limbs, but I ignore it as adrenaline kicks in, and I push past the few guests who haven't already started to panic.

Rain patters on my face as I tear out the old wooden doors of the chapel and down the wet stone steps. It's said that rain is a sign of good luck on a wedding day. I say a quick prayer as I pass out the doors of the church that my fortunes save themselves for our married life. Today, all I will need is my skill.

I catch a glimpse of Will as he enters his car, another mobster shoving Liv into the back with him, and the car peels out into the road with two others following after. There's a black sports car I arranged to be waiting for us at the bottom of the steps — it was going to be the chariot I whisked Liv away in after the ceremony, onto a better life. It still will be. The reception will just be a little more exciting, it seems.

Pushing more of the confused guests out of the way, I bound down the steps and vault into the vehicle, and a moment later, my car roars, smoke flaring up behind me to the sounds of gasps from the guests as I leave them in the dust on the trail of my bride.

Slavers never know when to stop. They never can. They cater to a beastly lust that seems bottomless in men, and putting this ring down for good will bring me nothing but the utmost satisfaction — not only because of what they are, but because of what they dare try to take from me.

The three cars are fast, and they're past the point of regarding caution in any capacity. I wonder how long it will be before the police are on our tail, but I suspect we'll be long gone before that's a concern. I see the last car taking a sharp turn down the lane, and mere seconds later, I'm right behind it.

"*Mudak,*" I mutter under my breath as I realize the rear vehicle is putting on the brakes as we careen down a narrow road, pedestrians crying out in terror and a man on a bicycle leaping off and onto the sidewalk. The rear of the car swerves in my path as I try to get around, the small vehicles lining the road blocking our path as bumpers. I realize that there's no way around him, and the two cars in the lead are quickly getting away.

I reach under my seat and pull out the gun I'd stowed there. There's an alley coming up on my right — narrow, but it will have to do. Even at my own wedding day, I can't seem to shake the old habits. I roll down the window, and the moment I reach the alley, I use the handbrake to screech to the side, aiming my gun and firing off two shots at the car in front of me before I blaze down the narrow alley. The pops I hear from the rear car's tires tell me my shots landed true, and I smile as I smash through a trashcan in the alleyway, a terrified cat leaping up into a window to watch me fly by.

My car exits the alley into oncoming traffic. All around me, petrified motorists honk and jerk their wheels away as I surge upstream, gathering speed rapidly, and to my left, I soon start to catch flashes of the other two cars the next street over. But I won't be trapped in the back again.

In a matter of seconds, the road curves into where the other two are heading, and my tires screech as I turn into traffic after them, driving parallel with the rear car. I have a clear shot at Will's car, but I can't risk hurting Liv. And damn it all, Will knows that.

But the next moment, I look over to my left as I realize the rear car is turning into me, and the side of the car collides with mine, sparks flying, and I lower my head as gunshots ring out a moment later from their passenger's side. I pop up and fire back, and I hear one of them curse as the gunman's blood gets on the driver, his face falling forward onto the dashboard. Both cars take a sharp turn, and my car zips by, just missing it. Once again, I tear around the block to see them heading for a road that leads out of the city, back into the country, towards the *Domaniale d'Armainvilliers* in the southeast.

Once we're out of the sea of buildings, the damage to the rear car is more obvious, and I make a mental note to see about getting a new car to replace this one. It's a shame. I'd looked forward to giving Liv this car, but scratch marks and bullet holes just won't do.

But the open road affords too much exposure for their comfort, and before I can get a shot in on the rear car's tires, they take a turn into a sleepy suburb between the city and the forest, and we find ourselves racing through a sea of upscale houses with ample fencing.

Dogs bark at our passing, and a few of the joggers start getting on cell phones and climbing house fences for safety as we approach. I see the two cars heading for a narrower road up ahead, but I'm not about to let that happen. Accelerating, I get up beside the rear car and waste no time in ramming into the side of it, feeling glass shards from their window pierce my arm.

"*Ruskie svin'ya!*" I hear the growl from the other car, and I steer the car sharply to the left, silencing the man as the car collides with a telephone pole, leaving it behind as I blaze past after the car driven by Will: the car bearing my bride.

In the rear-view mirror, I see the car in the back looking half-melted around the telephone pole, smoke rising from it, and I turn my attention back to the front, where I realize Will is taking the nearest road off into the forest, onto a dirt path leading through thick foliage.

My face sours into a grimace. This isn't an accident — I'm driving right into whatever they have planned, and I know it. But I'm going to press on.

I've taken a bullet for a student I hardly know. For Liv, I'd give my life.

For a moment, I see her in the back of the car, and my heart leaps into my throat. I want to blow out the brains of every man in that car with her, and I will. But one wrong shot, one slight movement at the wrong time could make the unthinkable happen, so I have to stay my weapon. My blood boils as I see the man holding her down bring his hand across her face, though, and I raise my weapon and let out a shot that takes off the left side-mirror. I can almost feel Will flinch, and it gives me a special pleasure.

Then the man in the back leans out the side window with an Uzi in hand, and I nearly have to drive off the road to avoid the spray of bullets that flies out. We drive towards a pair of thick trees, and I brace myself to go off-road when the man is suddenly jerked back into the car, and I realize Liv has got a hold of them, and they're grappling in the backseat.

My whole body tenses at the sight, fraught with concern for her. I've started to train her well, but if she angers the men too much, I wouldn't put it past them to do something drastic before reaching their destination. I'm so concerned with the sight that I don't fully notice his sudden acceleration, and it's too late when I notice the man by the side of the road rolling a small, round, metal object into the road in front of me.

I feel fire under me as the grenade goes off below the car, glass shattering all around and smoke and dirt billowing up in every direction as my ears are deafened to a harsh ringing. Bits and pieces of the car go flying, and the driver's side door is lost, leaving the smoke-filled air to fan the flames within the vehicle as I charge forward.

In truth, the pain hardly registers with me. I feel it like a thought in the back of my mind, but I'm so driven by adrenaline towards my goal. Up ahead, I have just enough time to see Will's car coming to a halt before another grenade goes off in front of me, sending up another wave of smoke and dirt, and the sound of metal clinking tells me bullets are peppering the vehicle like a thousand angry wasps, and there's a burning sensation under my feet.

## LIV

*I* hear the second explosion go off, but the brute on top of me has his knee on the back of mine, and he's pinning my arms behind my back, pressing my face into the seat, and I all I can do is feel my heart leap into my throat again.

"Much better," I hear Will's insufferably cruel voice say, and that pushes me over the edge. Feeling the slightest slack in the henchman's grip, I wrench my arms free the way Max taught me how, and in a flash, I push myself up, and an elbow shoots back to smack the man in the mouth, and I feel teeth crack under the blow as he howls and I turn my eyes to the rear window.

I wish I hadn't.

Out of the smoke, I watch Max's car roll forward, the once-splendid vehicle we'd planned to drive away to a new life inside, coasting across the French countryside away from all this terror. Instead, I watch it sputter forward, smoke billowing from every opening, and as we come to a stop, the men who'd been hiding in the forest on the sides of the road step out, guns blazing as they riddle the sides, the back, and the front with bullets.

I let out a scream, tears streaming down my eyes as I slam my fist into the rear window, not even caring that the ogre-like man beside me is pinning my arms again. I can't even feel the pain compared to the sight of Max's car, and visions of what he must look like inside flash in front of my mind's eye unbidden. I clench my eyes and look away, tears stinging terribly.

It isn't fair. This can't be real. This isn't real. Absurdly, I become vaguely aware that I'm still in my wedding dress, half-torn and filthy by now. This was supposed to be the best day of my life, a day I'd dreamed about since I was a little girl, even if I'd never imagined it taking place in such a place as this.

This whole time has been a kind of dream turned nightmare. And just when I think Max had woken me from the nightmare and brought me back into the real world, into my real life, I just slipped back into the depths, getting dragged down as I watch my last glimmer of hope get gunned to pieces on a dirt road in the woods.

My mind flits to everyone back at the wedding. Did the bastards take anyone else? Oh god, what about Maggie? She saw them all again, she saw Will, she relived the trauma. Was she okay? What if they took her? Could she stand the pain of being plunged into darkness all over again?

Then there's a third explosion, and as Will laughs, I realize one of the shots must have hit the car's gas tank, as I open my eyes and see the car hitting the ground with a metallic thud a moment later, upside-down.

There's a tug at my hair, then a sudden jerk as Will pulls me close to him, his hands forcing me to look at the burning remains of the car.

"Take a good look, *ma chérie*," he taunts me, "I don't want you getting the wrong impression. Maksim Pavlenko is somewhere in there — or at least, bits and pieces of him are."

I hate myself so much for having ever trusted Will, for having ever come close to letting myself feel attracted to this devil wearing human skin.

"What are you?" I say through choked sobs as Will strokes my hair. I want to kill him. I want so dearly to break that snide nose of his and toss him into the inferno along with the love of my life. I want so much, but I can do so little.

"Merely a man," says Will, purring the words into my ear as I try to pull away. He glances to the man with me in the back, and he nods to him out the door. "Take a hold of her and get out. Confirm the bastard's death."

I'm pulled out into the smoky air, the smell of the burning car and gunshots mingling toxically with the otherwise pleasant scents of the French countryside in autumn. This is the kind of place bikers come careening through, or lovers come walking. I might have come here with Max one day, walking hand in hand with him without the faintest care in the world. Never in my darkest nightmares would I have imagined knowing such a forest as a place of death.

I try to pull part of my dress back up over my shoulder to cover myself. My shoes are long gone, and my captor's sweaty hands have stained my ensemble. He yanks me with him as Will gets out and spreads his arms out wide, beaming. Men are stepping out of the woods now, guns pointed at the burning remains of the car as the shooting finally stops.

"I should say, Olivia," Will says as the men approach the car and he turns to face me, stepping forward with a smile, "I'm genuinely sorry you became so personally involved in this business." He reaches out and takes my chin in his hand the way Max used to, and I want to bite his fucking fingers off, but my face is swollen from crying and I can only stare into those heartless eyes.

"You know nothing about human caring," I spit at him.

"Me? I know more than anyone here," he practically hisses back at me, his eyes narrowing. "Do you think it's for the money that I work with all these Chechens? Well, partly, but I find in them a lot of empathy in their hatred of the Russians, particularly of these Russian assassins." Will flashes a quick smile to the man holding me, who nods back curtly. "But I must say, Liv," Will goes on with a sigh, looking me up and down with ravenous eyes, "you do look lovely in your wedding gown, so it would be a shame to let you go through the whole day without the comfort of a man. Maybe I will be your groom instead? You seemed to be keen on that when we first met," he says with a silky smile, and I want to burst with fury, my jaw clenched. "But I should introduce myself properly, first. My name is Guillaume Bouchard, and my brother Jean was murdered by a Russian pig, just like your late fiancé," he growls, clenching his fist as he shoots a glare back at my lover's fiery grave.

The men near the car, poking around different parts of it, and one of them holds up a burnt jacket —the tuxedo jacket Max was wearing. I'm unable to hold back another wave of tears, my head hanging.

"Fuck you," I sob, "fuck you, fuck you." I try to come up with something more biting, but I've had to be strong against these men so long that I feel utterly spent. Will — Guillaume — frowns, rolling his eyes at me.

"Stupid girl. You really are in love with him, aren't you? Well, maybe your love for the Russian has ruined you for me. It's a shame. I was looking forward to letting you live, but I see he's made you far too much of a liability. So before you go thinking this is something personal on your part, dear Olivia," he says, stroking my chin before taking his pistol out and pointing it at my head as my eyes focus on the barrel, my short life flashing before my eyes, "You can blame Mother Russia."

A gunshot splits the air, and for a second, I wonder if this is what death feels like. Silent and like all the air has been sucked out of the world.

But then Will spins around, eyes wide, as one of his men near the car falls to the ground, dead. Shouts in Russian ring out in the forest, and men start taking cover as a firefight breaks out by the ruins of the car, and Will swears, ducking. The man holding my arms back jerks me to the side as he takes cover, but my heart jumps as I see a glimpse of something in the forest beyond the smoke, a tall, dark-haired figure, clothes half-burnt off and smoke staining his face, his piercing eyes unmistakable.

"Max!" I cry out, my lungs unable to contain the joy welling up in me.

"Kill the bastard!" Will barks hoarsely, aiming his pistol and taking a few shots into the woods where my lover disappeared. "A half-mill to the man who lands the killing shot!"

Immediately, the men seem emboldened, and bullets spray the trees, but two more thuds signal the deaths of two more of the Mafiosi. The men are looking around wildly, not even sure where the shots are coming from now. Before they can react, I watch a man standing in front of a fallen log get yanked behind it with a shout, and there's another gunshot before Max leaps from cover, firing the dead man's Uzi into the crowd of shooters by the car. His tuxedo shirt is mostly burned off, but his face is unscathed, fury in his eyes as he guns the men down. Then his eyes meet mine.

A thousand words could have passed silently between us in that split second. I forgive him for letting me think he was dead before he could apologize for having to torment my heart so. He tells me how much he loved me and that I was unharmed. We tell each other how dearly we wanted to put these wretched men down, permanently. *All that in a look.*

The brute holding me pulls me close, holding his gun up in Max's direction, but before he can even aim the gun, Max draws another pistol from his side, the same weapon he used to save me from the apartment, and I hear the bullet whiz past my head as it lands true in the gunman's throat, and his grip on me slackens as I recoil and he hits the ground.

More gunshots as the remaining men react. I can hear the screams of the Chechens as Max dashes through the smoke of the car again, and for a moment I see him flash past the trees, taking on one of the men with his bare hands.

Gathering my bearings, I reach down to pick up the weapon of the dead man at my feet, and my hands nearly wrap around the handle of the gun when I feel a strong grip on the back of my dress that yanks me up, and before I can react, I feel cold steel on my temple as Will wraps his arm around my neck and stands me up, and his pistol cocks.

*"Pavlenko!"* he roars, and in an instant, the forest falls silent, save for the rustling of the leaves in a gentle breeze. The wind parts the smoke, and I see Max less than ten feet away, pistol raised to Will, all the rest of the Chechens dead on the forest floor all around us. "Put. The weapon. Down," Will growls. I don't need to look at him to feel his wide, wild eyes, truly on the edge of doing something drastic.

I can see Max recognizing that look. "Max," I whisper, but Will tightens his grip at my throat.

"Quiet, bitch," he hushes me, and Max tenses. "Alright, assassin, weapon on the ground now, or I'll decorate the woods with this cunt's brains."

Max looks ready to shoot, but Will's finger is on the trigger, his voice steady, his hands not shaking. But is he willing to take that chance?

"Now, Pavlenko!" Will barks, and finally, Max nods, taking his hand off the trigger and holding the gun out in front of him, slowly setting it on the forest floor. "Everything else," Will says, and Max turns around slowly, displaying the two more pistols he has strapped to his back. My heart sinking, I watch him do the same with those, then the knife on his leg, and the pistol on the other leg, and the smoke grenades in his pockets before he raises his hands and puts them on the back of his head.

"I'm yours, Will," Max says calmly, his voice as even as if he were chatting casually with me. "Release Liv, and I'll come with you. It's me you want more, after all, isn't it? I can think of a lot of people who have a high price on my head."

"I was going to kill you," Will says, "but perhaps you'll have better uses. Bitch," Will addresses me, giving me a squeeze, "I'm going to let you go and turn the gun on your Russian lover-boy. Then you're going to walk far away and get a cab to wherever the fuck you want. Call the police, they won't catch us."

Max nods significantly to me, and I take a deep breath before I nod my head a little, the metal of the gun barrel still pushing into my skin. "Okay, Will. Okay."

Next thing I know, Will shoves me to the ground roughly, and he starts to step forward to Max, pistol now turned on him. My hand tightens around the torn dress draped over my thigh. Then it slides the dress up, and my fingers wrap around the knife in my garter.

The motion is quick and fluid. I draw the blade, leaping to my feet and diving for Will, and before he can turn around, eyes wide, I drive the blade with all my strength into the side of his head, and as his reflexes fire the gun wildly into the forest, his balance gives out, and his weight carries him to the ground, the blade lodged in his head breaking off the knife as Guillaume Bouchard hits the dirt, dead.

I let the handle slip from my fingers as I turn to meet Max, who's rushing forward to catch me in his arms as we melt into one another, his strong muscles lifting me off my feet and swinging me around as he squeezes me tight into that strong, comforting grip.

"Oh my god," I sob into his chest, "oh my god, Max, I thought I'd lost you."

"Liv," he says back, his own voice choked with joy as he sets me back down and looks into my tear-stained eyes, "it's over, Liv, truly over. He's gone, my love."

"How did you-"

"I leaped from the car before the gunmen started firing," he said, "into the ditch, then dashed to the forest. I killed one of the men I landed near and started from there."

"Are you hurt?"

"Only that your wedding day was ruined, *lyubov moya.*"

A smile tugs at my face involuntarily, and I hug him back as hard as I can, meeting his lips for a kiss. "Alongside you, Max, no day can be ruined."

We look at each other a long time, our hearts

sailing together out of the darkest storm of our lives, and even in the smoke-filled forest, tattered and battered, for the first time in so, so long, we share in each other's peace. "Come on," he finally says, his voice low. "Let's get out of here."

I glance back at Will's car, by now a shot-up mess. "I'm not sure bullet holes are street legal in France."

"No," Max admits, glancing at the road behind us, then flashing me a coyly raised eyebrow, "but didn't you mention wanting to take a walk through the French woods some time?"

My smile broadens, and I burst into laughter, punching him playfully in the side of the arm before giving a yelp as he sweeps me off my feet, carrying me back down the road and through the autumn woods, leaving everything else behind us at last.

When I first came to Paris, it was something like a dream come true, some kind of wild fantasy I'd only imagined being thrust into. My outlook might have changed a lot since then, but that doesn't stop me from appreciating the surreal beauty of Monaco from the balcony of our hotel suite any less. Over the past few minutes, I've been losing myself as I gaze out onto the sunset that's casting a pink light over the Mediterranean, thinking about what a storm the last month was, and what a breath of fresh air these past few days have been.

The firefight in the forest is still burned bright in my memory. The first few nights afterwards, I woke up in a cold sweat next to Max, forgetting he was right there beside me just like that first night we spent together. Remembering that first night always dispelled the night terrors, though, as I recalled the feeling of him curling around me protectively. I smile, remembering how embarrassing that felt, asking him to sleep beside me. He was *my teacher*, for goodness' sake! My towering, muscular Russian teacher. That all seems so far away now.

"What are you smiling about, *lyubov moya?*" Max's voice is like silk behind me as he strides out of the open glass doors to the balcony, slipping his arms around me to give me a hug and stroke his hand over my stomach, feeling the baby that's yet to start showing visibly. I smile as I turn my head to kiss him, letting out a soft moan as he presses into my back and slides his hands to my shoulders to start massaging gently.

"Hm, just you," I say, turning my eyes back to the glittering water out there. I hear him chuckle as he rubs my back. That sound has been a pleasant new experience — a genuine, mirthful chuckle, free of all the worries that burdened him down back in Paris. Not that the city itself held too many bad memories to bear. Our little house on the outskirts of the city is a testament to that.

We even had the wedding in the city, both to enjoy the living spirit of the city that could at least for a little while be free of the pall it had cast over us and to send a message to onlookers that we would never be cowed by our enemies. And now, all of that is put to rest. The second ceremony was even more beautiful than the first one was going to be, and it was everything I could have hoped for. The light at the end of the darkest tunnel of my life is turning out to be the brightest, now.

Well, almost. I'm having to put a hold on my gymnastics career, largely thanks to the child I'll be carrying for the next eight months, but after everything that's happened, a break is more than welcome, and Max has taken steps to ensure that as soon as I'm ready to get back out there, I'll have a place at the university waiting for me.

Maggie, meanwhile, seems to be channeling her trauma into a kind of renewed energy in leaps and bounds — literally. Max says he sees something in her that supersedes even the potential he saw when he recruited her. She's excelling so quickly that she's already helping tutor some of the other students, and as a trauma survivor, getting out there and being physically active again has done wonders for her mental health. Of course, we're around each other nearly all the time she isn't at school — you don't go through something like that with someone and not feel a special kind of connection.

I know it will take a lot more than just gymnastics for her to heal entirely, just like it will take a lot more than my relationship with Max to heal me, mentally and emotionally, but keeping up our friendship has been invaluable. We never thought we'd be this close when we first walked off that plane, but here we are — and I couldn't ask for a better friend.

And she needs a friend now more than ever. When we talked before I left for this honeymoon trip, she told me her talks with her parents have been a little awkward. "It's not like they're upset," she'd said reluctantly, "it's just that what happened to me — to us — was never really part of their plan for my life, you know? So they don't really know what to do with me."

"Oh my god," I'd said, shocked. "I'm so sorry, Mag. They're your parents, I'd hope that they'd be there for you now more than ever."

"I'm not that sorry," she'd said unexpectedly, looking me in the eye with a small smile that was braver than I knew she was capable of. "I've been smothered my whole life, Liv. Maybe this is a good chance to grow into myself — healing has a lot of change involved already, right?"

She still has plenty of rough days, of course, and her parents are paying for her to have an apartment of her own, since the old dorm holds some rough associations, but it's a step-by-step process that's bringing her forward every day. I'm so proud of her, and Max is too.

"Well," Max says softly into my ear, "don't get too lost in thought. Don't forget the last thing we have planned for this evening."

"How could I forget?" I said, looking back at him,

unable to hold back the grin on my face. Despite all of Max's reticence in the past, he seems to be an endless stream of surprises now. Well, not that he wasn't exactly a surprising man before. "But we've already made a killing at the casinos, should we need to catch the next cab out of here before security decides we won too much?"

Max laughs, kissing me on the neck. "Ah, you've got a taste for danger now, what am I going to do with you? But no, we'll save that for tomorrow," he says, rubbing my hips. "Come on, let's get down to the docks — I hope you have an appetite."

HALF AN HOUR LATER, we're gliding across the waters on the deck of a large, spacious yacht that's headed out of the little port and out onto the glittering water that's painted in the sparkling white ink of the late autumn's full moon. Lights from the other boats out and about tonight sparkle in the bay like fireflies, and there's a small fireworks display being put on a little further out, setting the night's sky aglow with reds and purples and greens, and as I look over to Max as he sits beside me, a plate of fine food in his lap, I see the fire reflected in his eyes, and my heart grows warmer as I snuggle in beside him.

"Not the most quiet place to enjoy escargot," he

admits, and I giggle, taking a sip of the non-alcoholic wine in front of me.

"Are you kidding? This is the smoothest ride I've ever had. You need to come check out the boat rides in North Carolina with me sometime."

"Visit America? That might be something to look forward to, with you," he says, and we lean in for a quick kiss when a crackling sound behind us catches our attention. I glance back and notice the captain adjusting his radio until the news comes in clearly for a few moments, and I hear the sound of a newscaster speaking in accented English over an international news station.

"*. . . and the investigation into a major crime ring bust in Paris is underway in full swing thanks to a particularly tech-savvy anonymous source who has begun collaborating with Parisian and international authorities, identifying himself only as 'F.' Correspondents at INTERPOL have refused to comment on the specifics of F's activities and relation to law enforcement, save that they have been aware of his activities for some time and look forward to discussing a permanent position for F at the agency, citing the value of such independent investigative work. This development has sparked some heated conversation among officials regarding the place of vigilante justice in law enforcement, and . . .*"

The sound fades as the captain notices us paying attention, and he gives an embarrassed smile, turning the sound down quickly, but Max is quick to give a smile, letting him know it's quite alright before he turns to me.

"Sounds like Felix has been keeping busy," he whispers, and I smile.

"Let's hope the attention doesn't get to his head."

"If it does," Max admits reluctantly, "I think he's earned it. Honestly, I didn't expect him to stick around as long as he did. He's come a long way from the simpering techie who came to me for help at the university. If he thinks he can stomach working for something with as much red tape as INTERPOL, he might just have a successful career ahead of him. I wouldn't take a job like that," he's quick to add with a smile, "but that's just me."

I smile, biting my lip, and Max raises an eyebrow at me, knowing I'm holding something back. "What's that smile for?" he asks, leaning forward and touching my chin lightly.

"Well, you've been going all out with the surprises for me on this trip," I say, looking over to the captain and nodding at him. He nods back understandingly, saying something quietly into his collar microphone with a smile. "Felix has been busier than you thought — I convinced him to help me with one more thing: track down someone who's a hell of a lot harder to find than you'd think. A little surprise for you that I think you'll appreciate."

Max blinks, not understanding until the sound of heavy footsteps coming up the stairs to the deck turns his attention, and his eyes widen as a large man with a stony face and a small smile makes his way onto the deck.

"Andrei!" exclaims Max, standing up and crossing the deck.

"Maksim," the man greets in return, and I get a little choked up at the look on Max's face as the two old friends embrace in a tight, powerful hug. "Look at you," Andrei says, stepping back and looking Max up and down with a warm smile. "France has been good to you, *tovarishch.*"

"And what has America done to you?" Max says back, beaming. "You've got a light in your gaze I didn't think those dark eyes could harbor."

"Well, that's a long story," says Andrei with a smile, "one that I'd like to have in our mother tongue."

Before anything else, Max looks over to me and says, "I suppose this was your co-conspirator? Andrei, meet the love of my life, Olivia."

"A pleasure to meet you formally," Andrei says to me, and I give a little wave back, wondering if all the men in Russia are mountains of muscle. Max makes his way over to me, sweeping me up as I giggle, and we meet in a passionate, deep kiss. When it finally breaks, he holds my face, looking into my eyes.

"Liv," he says, "I can't tell you how much this means to me. How much all of this means to me."

"I want to tell you all about how much everything

you've done means to me," I breathe back, "but we'll have all the time in the world for that now. I love you, Max."

"I love you, Olivia," he says. And after one final kiss, I watch Max head off to the other side of the deck with Andrei to recount old stories and new as our little yacht carries us around the Monaco bay, around whatever new dreams and new life me and Max will be able to build with each other. Free at last.

THANK you so much for reading! I hope you enjoyed <3 If you have a moment, please leave a review. Other readers are dying to know what you thought.

I have plenty more bad boy romance for you, including the rest of the Hitman Series, so make sure you check out my other books on the next couple of pages, and sign up for my newsletter to be notified when I have a new release on the way!

*Owned by the Hitman*
*Ebook | Audiobook | Paperback*

*Sold to the Hitman*
*Ebook | Audiobook | Paperback*

*Saved by the Hitman*

*Ebook | Paperback*

*Captive of the Hitman*
*Ebook | Paperback*

*Stolen from the Hitman*
*Ebook | Paperback*

*Hostage of the Hitman*
*Ebook | Paperback*

*Taken by the Hitman*
*Ebook | Paperback*

# GLOSSARY

***FRENCH***

- *excusez-moi* : excuse me
- *en ce moment* : right now
- *bonjour* : good day
- *À bientôt* : see you soon
- *je suis désolé* : I'm sorry
- *pas de quoi* : it's nothing
- *merci beaucoup, bonne nuit* : thank you very much, good night
- *que recommandez-vous* : what do you recommend
- *je m'appelle Will, ça va* : my name is Will, what's up
- *d'accord* : okay
- *oui* : yes
- *deuxièmement* : secondly

- *bien sûr* : (colloquial) that's for sure / of course
- *petite fille* : little girl
- *merde* : shit
- *famille d'accueil* : foster care
- *Dieu merci* : thank god
- *le fric* : cash
- *pas moyen* : no way
- *absolument* : absolutely
- *saint-merde* : (colloquial) holy crap
- *saperlotte* : good heavens
- *ma chérie* : my darling
- *mon chou* : (colloquial) sweetie

* * *

## *RUSSIAN*

- *ozornoy devushki* : naughty girls
- *nakazaniye* : punishment
- *malyutka* : little one
- *uchitel* : teacher
- *malyshka* : little girl
- *suka* : bitch
- *da*: yes
- *nachalnik* : boss
- *izmennik* : traitor
- *dorogoy* : slut
- *stoimost* : pay/value

- *vy znayete* : you know
- *tishina* : silence
- *klyanus* : I swear
- *iskra* : spark
- *khoroshaya devochka* : good girl
- *est' shto est'* : it is what it is
- *mudak* : bastard
- *ruskie svin'ya* : Russian pig
- *lyubov moya* : my love
- *tovarishch* : comrade

Killing For Her

Abducted

**STEPBROTHERS:**

Ruthless

Criminal

**STANDALONES:**

Betting on Love

Hunter's Baby

I Hired A Hitman

Vegas Boss

Rock Hard Bodyguard

Innocence For Sale: Jane

Redeeming Viktor

**<u>Romance:</u>**

Falling for her Boss (Novella)

Most Wanted: Lilly (Novella)

Bound as the World Burns (SFF)

**<u>Erotic Thriller:</u>**

**THE DANGEROUS MEN SERIES:**

The Narrow Path

Strayed from the Path

Path to Ruin

# ABOUT THE AUTHOR

Alexis Abbott is a Wall Street Journal & USA Today bestselling author who writes about bad boys protecting their girls! Pick up her books today if you can't resist a bad boy who is a good man, and find yourself transported with super steamy sex, gritty suspense, and lots of romance.

She lives in beautiful St. John's, NL, Canada with her amazing husband.

facebook.com/abbottauthor

twitter.com/abbottauthor

instagram.com/alexisabbottauthor

bookbub.com/authors/alexis-abbott

pinterest.com/badboyromance

youtube.com/AlexisAbbott

Get an EXCLUSIVE book, **FREE** just as a thank you for signing up for my newsletter! Plus you'll never miss a new release, cover reveal, or promotion!

http://alexisabbott.com/newsletter

facebook.com/abbottauthor

twitter.com/abbottauthor

instagram.com/alexisabbottauthor

bookbub.com/authors/alexis-abbott

pinterest.com/badboyromance

ACKNOWLEDGMENTS

Thank you to my amazing Patrons. I'm constantly humbled and grateful for your support.

*Ramona Cabrera*
*Melissa Hedrick*
*Virginia Swanson*
*Dawn Daughenbaugh*
*Don Doss*
*Stacie Currie*

If you'd like to join them — and get my ebooks or paperbacks — you can find me here on Patreon.
https://www.patreon.com/alexisabbott